THE
GOSPEL
OF
WINTER

THE GOSPEL

OF

WINTER

A NOVEL BY

BRENDAN
KIELY

Margaret K. McElderry Books

New York   London   Toronto   Sydney   New Delhi

For Jessie, who said
what if

MARGARET K. McELDERRY BOOKS
An imprint of Simon & Schuster Children's Publishing Division
1230 Avenue of the Americas, New York, New York 10020
This book is a work of fiction. Any references to historical events, real people,
or real places are used fictitiously. Other names, characters, places, and events
are products of the author's imagination, and any resemblance to actual
events or places or persons, living or dead, is entirely coincidental.
Copyright © 2014 by Brendan Kiely
All rights reserved, including the right of reproduction in whole or in part in any form.
MARGARET K. McELDERRY BOOKS is a trademark of Simon & Schuster, Inc.
For information about special discounts for bulk purchases, please contact Simon & Schuster
Special Sales at 1-866-506-1949 or business@simonandschuster.com.
The Simon & Schuster Speakers Bureau can bring authors to your live event. For more
information or to book an event, contact the Simon & Schuster Speakers Bureau at
1-866-248-3049 or visit our website at www.simonspeakers.com.
The text for this book is set in Palatino LT.
Manufactured in the United States of America
2 4 6 8 10 9 7 5 3 1
CIP data has been applied for.
ISBN 978-1-4424-8489-4
ISBN 978-1-4424-8491-7 (eBook)

FIRST
EDITION

The question is not what am I to believe,
but what am I to do?

—SØREN KIERKEGAARD

CHAPTER 1

In order to tell you what really happened, what you don't know, what the journalists didn't report, I have to start at Mother's annual Christmas Eve party. Two nights before, as if the universe were the coproducer of her big show, a snowstorm whitewashed our little corner of Connecticut. Mother was thrilled. Electric candles in the windows, wreaths on the doors, picturesque drifts of snow snuggled up against the house—everything was "just wonderful," as her friends would say. Spirits would soar, or at least appear to. That was Mother—survival of the cheeriest— and everyone was ready to suck down her holiday cure-all. We were about to welcome more than a hundred and fifty guests into our home and ignore the fact that although the invitations had been mailed out in late October with my father's name next to hers in embossed script, Old Donovan was in Europe, where he'd spent most of the year and where he now planned to stay for good.

I'd never been allowed to go in Old Donovan's office, but precisely because he was no longer home, I'd recently made it mine, lurking among his books and curios from around the world, hoping to find some wisdom to fill this awful emptiness widening inside me. If not for the party, I'd have sat in the office all night reading *Frankenstein* for Mr. Weinstein's class, but there was the party and Mother was upstairs getting ready, so I said fuck it. If I was going to survive it, I needed a jump start.

I locked the door to the office and sat in the swivel chair behind his desk. Nothing but the necklaces of white lights hanging on the bushes outside the windows lit up the room. I sat in the semidarkness for a while, listening to the caterers scurry around elsewhere in the house, and then I turned on the small reading lamp, only to see what I was about to do. The day calendar hadn't been adjusted in weeks, and I left it that way as I dragged it across the desk pad and flipped it facedown. The metal surface glinted in the lamplight. I shook out a couple of pills of Adderall and placed them on the back of the calendar. Using one of Old Donovan's heavy pens, I ground them down, divided the pile into smaller piles, took the pen apart, and snorted a line up the empty tube.

A scattershot of thoughts and memories exploded in my mind, and I imagined an apparition of Old Donovan nosing out of the darkness—his pale, bald head; two eyes fixed in a scrutinizing glare. He leaned toward me and grumbled one of his usual disquisitions. *Boy, you can be one of two people: someone who makes reality for others or someone who has reality made for him.* Old Donovan was a man I read about in the paper, one of those men who gathered in Davos, Beijing, or Mumbai and shook hands in a way that affected the world economy. *Think globally, act locally,* I wanted to tell him, but he was never home to work on the local part. Besides, when did I ever tell him anything—when did he ask?

I banged another rail. The ghostly Old Donovan dropped into the armchair, and a memory materialized in the room. He was reading an issue of *Barron's.* His socks were stuffed into his shoes on the floor nearby, and his bare feet rested on the ottoman. They looked like translucent, white raisins, shriveled up and drying out in front of the fireplace. He sweated, and he scratched at the crown of stubble above his ears. On the table beside him, a pile of newspapers lay folded and stacked beneath a small ashtray with crushed stubs rising from the mound like tombstones. A glass rested on the wide arm of the chair. There was plenty left in it, but he pressed his big nose against the rim and drained it anyway. The usual gluey strand remained lodged in his throat however, and he tried to clear it. *Boy, you'll be lucky if you're a goddamn footnote in history. Most people live inconsequential and meaningless lives. I'm trying to help you.*

I concentrated until there was only one voice left in my head. I guess it sounded like me; at least it sounded familiar. "I'm in the room," I finally said into the emptiness around me.

"I'm right here." But it was just me and the silence around me, and in that nothingness, I was afraid. I was terrified of other people and of my own damn self, and my fears were overwhelming, closing in on me like something near and breathing. Without my chemical surges, I didn't know how I would stay focused and move beyond those fears. I hosed up the last of the Adderall, tidied the desk, slipped out of the office, and finally felt ready to face the night.

Fresh garlands had been wrapped around the banister of the grand staircase from the foyer to the balcony upstairs. In every room, the catering staff fussed with last-minute details. Two tuxedoed waiters fluffed the gauze of fake snow around the base of the tree in the sitting room. In the library, a bartender set up rows of glasses atop a makeshift bar he'd positioned in the doorway to the kitchen. The catering company never sent the same people twice to Mother's parties, but they all knew how to handle the production. Throughout the party, their silent ensemble would appear on cue and recede again into the scenery. As soon as guests arrived, I'd get my call to enter from the wings, but for now, nobody seemed to notice me.

In the kitchen, I found Elena speaking with a few of the caterers. She winced as she glanced over at the mess they were making, but when she saw me she came right over. She wore the same white-collared shirt she always wore when Mother threw a party. Her hair was fixed up, and when I stooped to hug her I thought I might crush the delicate ruffles cascading down the button line. "You're going to have fun tonight?" she asked me in Spanish.

"No, I won't."

She straightened my collar. "You need to take better care of yourself."

"But you're here," I said.

"Ah, *m'ijo*, please," she grumbled. She never called me that in front of my parents, of course, and we never spoke Spanish in front of them either. I practiced my Spanish with her when we were alone in the house and, by now, after all that time together, I was nearly fluent.

She kissed her fingers and reached them up to my face. Her cheeks made her eyes squint when she smiled. "Please. Be sensible."

"Look at me," I said, pointing to my coat and tie, the ones I knew Mother wanted me to wear. "I'm ready to play my part." She watched the caterers fiddle with the two wall ovens, and I took her hand. "Can't we just hide out in your apartment?" I asked. "She won't even notice we're gone. Look at all these people she's hired. She doesn't need us."

Elena stared at me. "Are you okay? What's the matter with your eyes?"

"Nothing."

I'm sure my eyes were red rimmed, but she only shook her head and, as usual, didn't ask anything else about it. She hugged me, then she stepped back and put her hands to my cheeks. "Please. You'll help too. For your mother. Do it for her." She kissed me and hugged me again, wrapping me up in those arms as she so often did.

I would have held on longer if a waiter didn't knock a bowl off the counter. It crashed, and the glass shattered on the kitchen floor. Elena turned around quickly. *"Ay, dios mio."* She glared at him. "They never care," she muttered as she went to the pantry for a broom.

With a sense of duty hanging over me, I went looking for Mother. I heard her voice call out from the living room. "No fumé blanc?" she asked. I couldn't help it: Sometimes when I heard her all twisted up like that, I thought of dolphins chirping. "No fumé blanc?" She spoke to a phantom only she could see. The cut of her deep-red evening gown revealed nearly all of her back. "Chardonnay and fumé blanc. *Y* fumé blanc, I told Elena. *Y, Y, Y.* This isn't a charity party we're hosting. It's a Christmas party. Choices are part of the elegance." Mother always found the loose stitch that could reduce a priceless carpet to a pile of threads. There was more wine than anyone could drink and, if it was like any of her other parties, even the caterers would be slugging down the open bottles, stumbling back into their vans at the end of the night.

"She ordered it," I said. "I saw the bartender chilling some."

"What are you doing skulking behind the furniture?" she asked. "I thought you were going to help me tonight."

"Who's skulking? I'm right here. I'm just saying, you don't always have to blame her."

"As usual. Her lawyer. Saint Elena."

She measured her breath through her nose, counting, or turtle breathing, as she called it when she was doing her yoga or tai chi or Pilates or soul stretching or whatever the hell was the regimen du jour. "Okay," she said in a bright new tone. "Let's get a smile on your face. It's a party. You'll be meeting people."

"I am smiling."

"Relax," she said. She put her hand on her hip. "Try to look a little like your father, not so morose. We're all friends here, Aidan." I couldn't remember Old Donovan grinning like a politician when he'd greeted the guests the year before.

"I'm not him," I said.

"No," she said softly. "But fake it, then." She looked out the windows to the backyard and sighed. "Please."

I wanted to. For her.

Candles flickered along the windowsills and on end tables. Logs crackled and sparked in the hearth. The ivory walls and furniture picked up an orange glow in the firelight. When she turned back to me, I gave her what she wanted.

"Merry Christmas," I said.

"See? That's better. That's who everybody wants to see."

"Let's party, then," I said.

She smiled triumphantly.

When the doorbell rang, Mother smoothed her evening dress around her waistline and blinked rapidly. It was time.

One of the hired staff adjusted his bow tie and opened the front door. My hands were in my pockets, and it occurred to me that I should pull them out. But it was only Cindy, one of Mother's closest friends, and Mother glided into the foyer as if she were back on stage at City Center and twenty years hadn't passed. They made their way to the bar immediately. Once they had their drinks, Cindy held hers high. "To another one of Gwen's incredible holiday parties," she said. "Jack and his Belgian slut be damned."

Although they'd both grown up in the city, they hadn't known each other until they were both enthroned in the high social courts of Connecticut. Cindy was even more petite than Mother, but she had an open-mouthed smile that stretched over her entire face. I occasionally saw Cindy's family at Most Precious Blood, and her son, James, was two years behind me at Country Day Academy. That was the only way to keep track of Mother's friends: to keep them penned in their various social circles. When the circles overlapped enough, I could begin to remember the faces, the necessary biographies, too, like the statistics on the back of a baseball card. Instead of ERA or RBI, the categories were Personal Wealth, Philanthropic Interests, or Number of Donovan Parties Attended—which in Cindy's case was "all."

Before long, the doorbell rang again. I answered, said hello, and began my drift from one quick greeting to the next. I blinked as often as I could to stop my eyes from feeling like two eggs frying on my face. The guests just flashed their neon smiles back at me and kept walking. "Hello," I said as another person arrived. "Hello." I directed guests, smiled grossly, and slowly tuned right out, slipping back into a dull void where I found myself thinking about that paperback edition of *Frankenstein* upstairs on the seat of my armchair—the creature waking, peering up from the table with his jaundiced eyes.

The party filled quickly, and moving from one spot to another often required bumping people as you passed them. Guests slugged down their drinks so as not to spill them. They pitched toward me, speaking in their *won-derful* voices. "Top marks," I'd scream back. "Oh, Yale, definitely Yale." To really pull off the part, I almost affected one of those weird accents some Americans adopt, where they sound vaguely British but they're really from the Upper East Side. Instead, I just careened from room to room, strategizing how to disappear amid the sweaty and aggressive laughter.

As I slid past a knot of people beside the piano, trying to make a break for the office, one of Old Donovan's former colleagues, Mike Kowolski, saw me and waved. He shuffled across the foyer, balancing the weight of his belly on his legs. Mark, his son, followed behind. If Mark hadn't had his father's strong, hammerhead jaw, it would've been hard to believe they were related. He strode around CDA with a cool, confident distance I always imagined was boredom. We met at the foot of the grand staircase, and Mike slapped down hard on my shoulder. "Look at you working the party like a solicitor. My God, Aidan, it's been a while. You're as tall as I am, and since when did your old man let you run around with hair like that? A man shouldn't hide his eyes." He wagged his finger between us. "You'll introduce Mark to a few men tonight, won't you? Can't have you grabbing all the internship opportunities before your friend here, right?"

"What's up, Donovan?" Mark said. We were both sophomores at CDA, but the last time he had said hello to me was at the mandatory swim test at the beginning of the year. To call us friends was a joke. He was already a cocaptain of the swim team, and he'd had to greet all of us, one by one, before we dove into the water and proved we could make it across the pool and back without drowning. Mostly, I thought of him as the Bronze Man because his skin was naturally amber all year round, and the tight curls against his head never seemed to grow or get trimmed. We'd been in Sunday school together, but by middle school the only time we really talked was when our fathers had made our families get together for dinner, and, of course, the last time had been years ago, before my father had left the firm to start his own.

"Mark's got to talk to some of the men," Mike said. "There's no way around it. This isn't a party, it's a job fair, right?" He nodded to his son.

"I know, Dad."

"It's all in the way you look at things, boys. Make it an opportunity." Mike poked me in the chest.

Mark glanced back and forth between his father and me. "Well, maybe Aidan should show me around, then."

Mike took Mark by the arm.

"*Carpe diem,*" Mark said. "Look, I got it. But I can just hang with Aidan right now. It's cool."

"I'll tour him around," I said, trying to sound as cool as possible.

Mark tried to pull out of his father's grip, but Mike wouldn't let go. He leaned toward us. "It's about focus, boys. It's not a game. Focus, focus, focus. When you see something you want, you've got to go after it and fucking nail it." He smiled at us and pulled me in close too, so we were locked tightly together. There was a whiff of shrimp in his breath. "Right?" he asked.

"You said it," I responded.

Mark gave me a *thanks-a-lot* smile, and Mike pushed his son toward a circle of men by the fireplace in the sitting room. Although they made space for them, Mark looked through the space between shoulders to me. His startlingly light blue eyes landed on me with only a glance, and stuck. *Get me the hell out of here,* he intimated. I wasn't used to anyone looking to me for help. Soon enough, though, Mark was doing the drill I was accustomed to doing at Mother's parties—rolling out the résumé—and he was beyond saving for the moment.

Go take your face off, I wanted to say to Mike. It's what I wanted to say to many of the kids at CDA too. Take off those big, plastic faces that bulldoze their way into rooms with their fucking grins. I hung out with kids occasionally—sometimes the debate club or the chess club would have dinner at someone's house, or I'd go sit in the stands with other kids to watch the field hockey team or the football team—but I'd sit there listening to everyone talk to one another as if confidence had come to them as a birthright. Nobody ever said *I don't know* or *I'm afraid*, and they acted like the masks they wore were their real faces and that they could sustain themselves forever on their own self-assurance—like they really believed they didn't need anybody else. What was that John Donne poem we'd read in Weinstein's class, "No Man Is An Island"? Not here. We were a goddamn social archipelago that called itself a community. Why did I feel like I was the only one who lived in a nightmare?

What was worse was that I knew people did have fears. I'd seen it briefly on the faces of everyone at CDA earlier that fall, when, on a bright, clear Tuesday morning, we all became afraid of airplanes and the word *jihad*. After that day, fear had become our way of life—kids, adults, it didn't matter. I'd heard the guidance counselors talking about it: "I don't know what to say to these kids. I'm afraid too!" So why did I feel like I was the only one looking for some kind of stability, some kind of normalcy, someone who could hold back the vast tide of bullshit and tell me *everything is going to be okay*?

I did a loop down the side hall to the library, leaving Mark to fend for himself, and I took a seat at the foot of the small staircase near the makeshift bar. *Take your face off,* I wanted to say to all of Mother's guests. They weren't any better than the kids at CDA. Mother had declared that this year's Christmas Eve party would be the biggest and most extravagant ever. *We need it,* she had said, *all of us,* and her guests seemed to agree. Like the movies I'd seen about Mexico's Day of the Dead or of Carnival, everyone at Mother's party had their faces painted with too much makeup or the flush of alcohol.

After a while, Mother found me. I was surprised she'd been able to locate me in the packed room, but she was determined. When she squeezed through a group of men in line for the bar, she pulled along two more of my classmates from CDA. It was obvious from the way she beamed as she brought them toward me that she had invited these two in particular. She just hadn't told me.

I fixed my posture immediately. Every idiot with a beating heart knew Josie Fenton and Sophie Harrington. So many of us at CDA thought of them as celebrities, as if life would be glamorous if you carried yourself the right way. For a brief stint that fall, Josie had dated a senior, but she had called it off after only a month. I was used to looking at Josie and talking to her with my eyes. She sat in front of me in Honors English 10. I imagined combing my hand through her long brown hair. She cocked her head while she wrote at her desk, making her hair fall to one side. It would expose the smooth, cool slope of her neck, the spot where there was no better place to kiss a girl, I thought. Sophie had a different reputation, which too many guys were too eager to brag about—and since guys were always looking at her, she had developed the confidence to stare back with her dark eyes and thin-lipped smirk that made her look older than the rest of us, or at least more cynical.

Mother was obviously delusional enough to think the girls talked to me at school because they were her friends' daughters, and she wore one of those smiles I wasn't supposed to let fall as she dragged them through the room toward me. "Be a good host now," she said as she withdrew herself. "You have guests tonight too."

Josie and Sophie stood beside me, peering through the crowd as if they were looking for someone. In their high heels and close-fitting skirts, they looked like the adults in the room. I got up and wiped my palms on my legs. "I didn't know you were coming tonight," I said, and knew I'd lost the only moment I had to offer up some wit or charm.

"Last-minute kind of thing, I guess," Sophie said. The lone freckle on her pale cheek rose up her face as she smiled.

"Hope it didn't ruin any other plans?"

"No. Whatever," Sophie said. Josie flashed a quick smile. She wore silver earrings with blue beads that matched her eyes.

"I hope they didn't bribe you to come here."

"Come on," Josie said, rolling her eyes. She sounded tired.

"Everyone knows your mother throws great parties. No one turns down an invitation, right?" She glanced toward the bar. "Look at all that alcohol."

Even if she didn't mean it, I appreciated it. "Can I offer you a drink?" I asked her.

She was still gazing at something back in the foyer and remained quiet. Sophie looked at her. "Maybe a couple of Diet Cokes?"

"No," I said. "I mean a real drink."

"What?" Josie asked quickly. "Really?"

"It's a party, right?"

"That'd be cool," Sophie said. "My mother will be smashed, anyway."

"Mine would probably encourage it," I said. "Especially if she saw me hanging out with the two of you all night." They shot tight-lipped glances at each other, and so I quickly, added, "And Mark's here."

"Mark Kowolski?" Josie asked.

"See if you can drag him away from his father. He's got Mark leashed to a pack of guys in the living room, last I saw."

"Oooh, a rescue," Sophie said. "We can handle that. Where do we meet you with the drinks?"

I gave them directions across the foyer to Old Donovan's study. They threaded their arms and moved away as one unit, squeezing through the crowd in the library. It looked like a dance and, probably because they were in my house, I thought maybe I could join them.

I convinced the bartender to give me a couple of unopened bottles of soda water and some wineglasses, and I marched through the party as quickly as I could. When I got to Old Donovan's study, they were all there. Josie and Sophie walked alongside one wall of books. They weren't scowling. They didn't hush up as I approached. In fact, I was surprised: They looked like they were having a good time. Mark stood by the giant sepia-toned globe that stood between two leather chairs.

"Your dad likes to read, huh?" Josie asked. "He has this office and the library out there?"

"What's a *dad*?" I said as I put the bottles on the desk. Sophie turned and gave me a sympathetic look. Josie nodded.

"The boss," Mark said. "*Results!* That's my dad. *Results, results, results.*"

"Maybe he'll have a breakdown," Josie said. "That's what happened to my dad. Now he's, like, Ayurveda-vinyasa Dad."

"Maybe," Mark said.

"Well, if Old Donovan were here, we couldn't use his room," I continued. "Check this out." I unlatched the lock on the globe in front of Mark, lifted its top half, and revealed the bar within it. "Vodka sodas?" I asked, lifting the bottle from its slot. "We can toast to our fathers, whether they're already gone or we wish they were."

"Seriously," Josie said.

"Dudes," Mark said. "Think about this clearly. We'll

get caught drinking. They'll smell it on us. Last time I got caught, my dad nearly strangled me. I was, like, chained up at the house for a month. Don't we have anything else?" Mark asked. He jabbed at me. "You got to have something else, man. Got any herb? We all *poke smot*. I never get caught when I'm *poking*."

I smiled at him; I was happy to dish out the pills, too. "Let's start with a drink, though. We won't get caught. I never do." They took seats beside the globe, and I set to work fixing the drinks. It was good to have a task, something to keep me in motion, because my heart raced as if I'd done another bump. I had no idea what to say to Josie, Sophie, or Mark. Conversation required spontaneity, and spontaneity made me nervous. I didn't want to say anything stupid, or anything I'd regret.

"Take a sip," I said as I handed them their glasses.

"Belvedere, right?" Josie asked after she tasted it. "Smooth."

"I thought you only liked Ketel One." Sophie laughed and then took a sip. "Remember that at Dustin's? Oh my God, we got so wasted."

I raised my glass the way I'd seen some of the adults do out in the party, holding it by the base and not the stem. "Cheers, I guess."

We clinked glasses and laughed about the rest of the party getting drunker. I tried not to smile too much, but I couldn't help it. I didn't like my smile. I liked what my face looked like when I listened, or when I smoked a cigarette—I'd looked in the mirror as I'd done both, and I could live with it—but when I smiled, I was someone severely deranged.

I was surprised every time I made them laugh, and I hoped I wouldn't run out of things to say. I was more than halfway through my drink when I realized they still had nearly full glasses. Especially Mark. He had put his down on Old Donovan's desk. There was a pause in the conversation. Sophie stared at her feet. Josie got up and walked to the window that looked across the yard to the hedgerow along the Fieldings' property.

"What are we doing at this old-person party?" Mark asked. Sophie rolled her eyes in agreement. "I mean, no offense, Donovan, but this would be cooler if we weren't ten feet away from our parents."

"Doesn't matter to me," I said. "Here's how I get through it." I pulled the bottle of Adderall out of my inside pocket and shook it. "I'm already zooming."

Sophie squinted. "You just pop these like vitamins or whatever?"

"No," Josie said. "You snort them, right?" She walked back toward me and smiled deviously. "Is that what you're doing every day?"

"Not every day." I grinned. She laughed. It wasn't exactly a lie. I'd done it at school before, when I hadn't slept all night and I was nodding off.

"Should we go for it?" I asked.

"That's not my thing, dudes," Mark said. "Not tonight. Man. I sound like a downer tonight. You know I'm not."

"Fine," Sophie said. "I'm game. I'm always game." She raised her glass. "Let's finish these first."

I raised my glass with her and took a big swallow, but I gulped too many ice cubes at once. One lodged in my throat, and the passage clamped shut. My mouth was full and airless. The soda burned into my nose. I seized up.

"Oh my God, are you okay?" Sophie asked, leaning forward.

I inhaled deeply through my nose but couldn't take anything in, or if I did, I couldn't feel it. I snorted violently after air. Soda fizzed in my mouth and nose, and my eyes burned. There was a belt going around my neck and chest, cinching one notch tighter at a time. Fear floated up from within me, because I could feel my head going light like it had when I'd tried that game where you make yourself black out for the hell of it and just before the darkness you wonder, *Shit, what if I've gone too far? What if I can't come back?*

"Jesus, you sound like you're hyperventilating," Josie said.

"He's choking," Sophie said. "Is he choking?"

I tried to shake my head and leaned forward to spit something back into my glass, but the whole frothing mouthful came rushing out, and I sprayed Sophie on her blouse and skirt.

"Holy shit!" she yelled.

My eyes were so full of tears, I could barely see. "I'm sorry," I managed. "I'm so sorry."

"Shut up!" Josie said. "Pull yourselves together. Don't make a scene or we *will* get caught."

"I'm sorry. I really am."

"Did he ruin my skirt?" Sophie demanded. "Look at my blouse? What the hell?"

"Shut up! Seriously."

Mark moved to the door and listened closely to the noises in the hall. I wiped my eyes. The burn still crackled in my throat, so instinctively I took another sip, then without good reason slurped down the rest of the drink, using my teeth as a dam against the ice. It chilled me to my toes, but it felt good, the fat syrup of vodka sliding beneath the soda. I put the glass down and grabbed tissues from a box on the desk. I handed them to Sophie, but they were useless. The music was loud in the other rooms, and people shouted over it and over one another. Nobody could hear us.

Josie pulled Sophie out of the chair, and they surveyed the dark spots scattered across the green skirt. "What am I going to tell my mother?" Sophie asked. "What's wrong with you?" she snapped in a hushed voice.

Josie grabbed my arm. "Do something! Get us to a bathroom a-sap."

With my face burning, I led the girls out into the hallway.

Mark followed behind them. A group of Mother's willowy friends huddling in the foyer saw us. "Barbara. Barbara. Here he is," one of the women sang. I was a step ahead of Josie and Sophie, but I could picture them scowling behind me as they heard the woman. I tried to ignore what she said, but that sinking feeling opened up within me again. I waved the girls on, and we went down the hall, away from the party and toward one of the spare bedrooms, the one Old Donovan had slept in for a few months, before he was finally gone.

I held open the door to the en suite bathroom. "This'll be private," I told them. Josie brushed past me, and I stepped out of the way so Sophie could follow her.

"Why don't we just meet you out in the party later?" Josie suggested. "I'll clean her up." She had carried the drinks with her, and she set them on the counter next to the sink.

"I'll make sure they're okay," Mark said. They shut the door, and I could hear them whispering before the faucet ran. Eventually, they turned the water off but didn't open the door. They giggled. Glasses clinked. I wanted to break something. *Take your faces off, assholes.* I should have just said it, even if it was through a goddamn door. *Aidan's a fuckhead* was scratched into the back of a stall door in a boys' restroom at CDA, and I was sure they were saying something similar right then.

There was more giggling, but it came from the hall-way. One of the women who'd seen us come out of Old Donovan's office stood in the doorway and blocked the light coming into the dark bedroom. She beckoned those behind her. "Yup," she said, "they're in here." She leaned against the door frame. I couldn't see her face. She was only a silhouette of a woman speaking to me through the shadows. "Why are you hiding in the dark, Aidan?"

There was something cold and straightforward in her voice that instantly held me. Even though she could barely see me, I felt as if she'd caught me naked, and the emptiness within me was spilling everywhere, running out into the room and staining the carpet and the bedsheets and the wicker furniture. Another woman joined her, and then another, and again, one of them asked me, "What are you doing?"

One of the women pushed through the others and snapped on the overhead light. Barbara Kowolski, Mark's mother, marched forward. She glared at me over her round and flushed cheeks. "What's the matter with you?" she asked.

I remained silent, still fixed in the fear from the moment before. The other women laughed and began speaking with each other in the hallway, but Barbara put her hands on her hips. "Where's Mark? Where are the girls?" She glanced at the bathroom door and pointed. The bangles on her arms clanked as she gestured. "Are they in there? Is Mark in the bathroom with the girls?" I tried to say no, but she pushed past me and tried the door. It was locked. She glanced toward the doorway to the hall. The other women were gone. "Mark?" she said softly.

The faucet ran briefly, and then the toilet flushed. Josie opened the door and stepped out first. "Hi, Mrs. Kowolski." Her cheeks were red. Sophie followed, holding an empty glass in her hands, and Mark followed her with his hands in his pockets. Hunched over like that, he looked much younger, like a dog cowering before a raised hand.

"Young man," Barbara said to him.

None of them would look at me. "Mrs. Kowolski," Josie said, "we're just hanging out. What's up? How's it going?"

Barbara frowned. Her skin was so permatanned and taut that her lips folded her face like an accordion. "Don't play nice with me right now." She turned back to Mark. "Your father was looking for you. There's someone he wants you to meet. But like this?" Barbara glanced at the doorway again and then turned back to us. "This is what is going to happen," she said. "We're not going to speak about any of this. We're not going to say anything to any of your parents. We're not going to mention any of this to Mike. Not any of it. Do you all understand me?"

"It's not their fault," I finally said. "It's my booze."

Barbara turned and pointed her bloodred fingernail at my face. "I know exactly whose fault it is, Aidan."

"Don't take it out on him," Mark said. Although he'd had the least to drink of all of us, his eyes still had a glassy look. I thought tears might have pooled in his lids. "It's not Aidan's fault."

"It certainly is," Barbara shot back. "Enough's enough.

I'm taking you home." She swung her finger around to the whole group of us. "I'm taking you all home."

"Ma," Mark said. "Come on."

"Enough," Barbara said. "This is what's best for you. I'm taking care of this." She pulled Mark in for a quick, lifeless hug. "You know your father, honey. Don't be stupid." She pushed Mark and the girls into the hall as he was trying to say good-bye to me. "Just because your father's not here doesn't mean you get to do whatever you want," she said to me. "Somebody should explain that to you."

She left, and I flipped the light off in the bathroom and then the overhead in the bedroom and sat on the bed in the darkness for a while as the party stormed through the rest of the house. Eventually, I got up, wandered to the window, and looked out to the backyard. The moonlight made the crust of snow look moonlike—a gray, noiseless landscape, something like what I imagined death to be—a landscape where you would inevitably arrive, permanently alone.

I wished I could disappear, maybe even out there, but people were in the hall and on the stairs up to the second floor; they were everywhere. The party filled the whole house, pushing into room after room. *All those bodies and no one to really talk to*, I thought, until I heard a familiar laugh come rolling down the hall from the foyer. I'd known his laugh since he'd first arrived at Most Precious Blood, taking over the Mass from Father Dooley and turning the homily into a stand-up story hour. His voice, thick and low and constant, like a foghorn chanting through the night, had begun to sound like home to me. With relief, then, I steered toward his voice in the party.

Nobody had a laugh like Father Greg, one that bubbled up and gained volume as it stretched out. He stood near the foot of the grand staircase, his ruddy face and silvery goatee shining in the glow from the foyer's chandelier. He palmed a thick rocks glass and swirled the scotch in it as he spoke to the crowd around him. Most of them had to look up at Father Greg as they listened, because it wasn't only Father Greg's voice that commanded attention. I think if you put him in the ring with Coach Randolf over at CDA, Coach would actually have a hard time finding the courage to lace up the gloves. Father Greg looked like a man who had played football in a time before helmets and shoulder pads and had come through it all without a scratch.

He laughed at his own story, and when he noticed me he beckoned me with a nod. I followed immediately. He was a regular on the party circuit, and everyone loved Father Greg. He didn't bother with any of that dancing-is-the-devil's-work kind of ministry. He understood very well that our Catholic town liked Mardi Gras and Easter brunch and preferred to skip the Lent in between. He never missed a party, either.

"But it isn't only about the money," Father Greg was saying as I walked up to him. "Do you know what's hard work? Love. Love is hard work, maybe the hardest, but it's what counts in the end. That's what our work is about with these kids. Teach a man to fish? Ha." He waved a dismissive hand. "Teach a man to love, Richard. Teach a kid to love, to love learning, to love others. Then watch what happens." Father Greg dropped a hand onto my shoulder. "Right, Aidan?" He was the real solicitor at the party—at every party. I was his assistant, and only had been for the six months I'd been working for him.

"Yeah, I know. The kids," Richard said with a hard smile. "That's who I'm thinking of when I write my check every year." Then he aimed that nose at me. "I haven't gotten the call yet this year. Aidan, you going to start making those calls soon? Father, going to put Aidan in charge now?"

Father Greg smiled at me. "Oh, that wouldn't be so terrible. Aidan's not so young anymore. How would I do it without him?" Father Greg put his hand out and I slapped it automatically, as if we were teammates on the field. "Aidan's a guy who knows you need coal in the fire to keep the train running."

I nodded in agreement. I *was* helping him raise funds for Catholic schools down in the city. It was a stretch to call my organizing Excel spreadsheets and Crystal Reports "coal in the fire," but even by opening envelopes and entering gift amounts in the database, I was a part of his vital endeavor.

"I haven't even said hello to my host yet," Father Greg said.

"She's around here somewhere," I said, looking to the library.

Father Greg laughed. "No, I meant you."

"Oh," I said. "Yeah."

He excused us from the group and steered me a feet away, closer to the coat closet. It felt good to get a direction. He smiled, then took on that serious expres he got before he found the right words to set the w straight.

"How are you holding up?"

It was the first goddamn honest question I'd been as all night. I wanted to be somewhere quieter. I wanted be somewhere we could take ourselves seriously, close door on all the gibbering nonsense and speak as two peo who cared about meaningful things. It was about time.

"Look," Father Greg said, "I'm heading outside. I n a break, a little fresh air." He fished out his coat-check and handed it to the doorman. "Why don't we step out f minute?" Father Greg asked me. He took his coat and w it like a cloak, without sticking his arms through the sleev He dug into the breast pocket and pulled out a cigarette. always smelled like them. "Join me. Only if you want to, course." His coat billowed and flowed behind him as walked onto the stoop. I found my ski parka and follow him outside.

He stood beyond the curve of the white stone ser circular drive outside the front door and looked down tl

slope of the snowy front yard. "We have to find a way for you to enjoy your party," he said.

I watched my breath mist and disappear in the cold air. "It's not really my party," I said. I zipped up my parka. "I don't know what I'm doing tonight."

Father Greg stepped closer and put his foot on the stoop. He exhaled from the corner of his mouth and blew the smoke away from me. "Yes you do. You're doing what you always do. You're trying to help. Don't beat yourself up, Aidan." He always said my name a lot, and although at first it had sounded strange to hear myself referred to so often, I actually grew to like it. It made me feel real, as if he genuinely wanted to speak with me, as if I actually meant something to him—as if he might have needed me a little too.

I stared out at the island of manicured shrubs in the front drive. He offered me his cigarette, and I looked away from him as I took a drag. The nicotine went right to my head, and I leaned back against the column. "I'd rather be upstairs, reading for school," I finally said.

"That's my boy, ever the hard worker." I shrugged. "I understand, though. I know how you feel." He gave me another drag. "We've talked about this before," he said softly. "Hard to have meaningful conversations at these kinds of parties. Conversations that people like you and me are accustomed to having. I rarely see many of these people anymore, except at parties like this one. I don't know when I'd see your parents if they didn't invite me to their parties."

"Yeah, and then one of them doesn't even show up."

"There you go," Father Greg said, nodding slowly as he always did when he listened to me. Father Greg rolled the filter of his cigarette gently between his forefinger and thumb, until the cherry dropped to the ground. He tucked the filter into his pocket and glanced toward the front door. "But you're not alone," he said. Father Greg often explained that the presence of God in my life was an assurance, the real stability. God was with me, and yet God had to work through people like him sometimes, he had said, in order to remind me of His presence. God wasn't firmly placed in my mind, but Father Greg was actually there, and something tangible and definite was what I needed most. Certainty.

He blew air into his fist to warm it. "You are doing very well, Aidan, for your father not being here. Nobody wants to feel abandoned. We've talked about this. You know how I worry for you." He breathed softly through his nose and drew that concerned smile again. He sighed. "You're growing up in awfully frightening times, Aidan." He spoke with the knowing tone of a newspaper article and put his hand on my shoulder. It steadied me against the column. "We can't pretend otherwise. And the last thing we should do in times like these is abandon one another." He paused and leaned closer. "But God hasn't abandoned you, Aidan. The Church hasn't. I haven't."

He stepped back. He rubbed at his chin and glanced at the house. "We've been doing a damn good job together, haven't we? This campaign work. You like it, right? You're not bored?"

"No. I love it."

"That's what I thought." Father Greg nodded and turned me back toward the front door. "Strange, then, how your father hasn't given his check yet, Aidan. He usually sends in his gift by now. I'm surprised."

"He's been in Europe all fall."

"I know, Aidan my boy. I know."

He led us back inside and, as we turned in our coats, Father Greg gave an across-the-room nod to one of the men near the library. With a hand on my back, he walked us past the crowd by the center table in the foyer. "Maybe it's not him I need to speak with these days?" Father Greg said. He pushed us back into the thick of the party, to the sitting room. "Let's go find your mother, Aidan." He couldn't see my face because I was in front of him, but he didn't have to. He spoke down to me, over my shoulder. "Don't worry," he said cheerily. "We'll have time to talk more soon. You're scheduled sometime over the break, aren't you? We'll catch up. I know it's been a while. I know you need to talk."

I stopped and turned back to him. He smiled but looked around the room. "We'll catch up over your break," he said. "Don't worry." There was a pause for a second or two in which I wasn't sure what I was supposed to do. I thought he might have been waiting for me, but his eyes rolled up over my head, and he waved to someone behind me.

Farther back in the sitting room, Mother had her own crowd of admirers huddled around her, friends like Cindy, but also other men and women I didn't know. Mother stood on a footstool and drew her arms up in second arabesque, mirroring an image of a portrait of herself that hung on the wall by the narrow staircase in the library. She stretched her arms as she spoke, and looked around the room. I thought she saw me, but she didn't.

"That's how I had to hold myself," Mother said. "Otherwise it would have been sloppy."

"Determination. Stamina," Cindy said. "That's what class is all about."

"Class?" Father Greg said to the group as we approached. "Gwen teaches us about class every year." Mother stepped off the stool, and he gave her a quick kiss on the cheek. "Every year, you set a higher bar. What a party. Only you can outdo yourself."

Mother demurred.

"It's true," Cindy said. "You should plan my parties. I'm serious. Maybe you could consult for my next opening?"

"You make it look effortless," Father Greg said. "It's more than skill, it's art. I'm sure your admirers would agree." Mother bowed in plié. "Some of whom I'd very much like to be introduced to, if you'd be so kind," Father Greg continued.

"The ones you need to meet are in the sunroom," Mother said. She and Cindy laughed, and Father Greg mocked a guilty expression. It made me sick the way they played this game together—as if to be earnest means you lose.

Mother offered to lead the way, and Father Greg took her arm in his and followed her into the sunroom. The doors split open and revealed the men slumped in armchairs, smoking their cigars. Father Greg waved as he descended the couple of stairs, and the men roared their greetings to him. Mother pulled the doors closed. A rich tobacco stink lingered in the air, and Father Greg left behind him that charged negative space an animal creates when it flees into the brush with a snap of sticks and rustle of leaves.

Cindy and I were left standing beside each other, and she looked around the room quickly. "I've heard how much you enjoy working for Father Greg," she said. "I think it's great. James has started working at Most Precious Blood too. He loves it. He's an altar boy now."

I hadn't seen James working there yet, but it again made me realize how many fewer afternoons I'd been scheduled for at Most Precious Blood recently. Of course Father Greg made time for others. Of course he needed assistance with other tasks besides fund-raising. He was our priest. But my stomach dropped as I thought of Father Greg consoling James. Wasn't it okay that I thought I was the one who needed Father Greg the most? He was the only one who didn't speak to me through bars of gritted teeth, as Cindy was speaking to me now—smiling at me in a way that said, *I don't want to be anywhere near you.*

I cut through the dining room to the pantry. When I came into the kitchen, I saw Elena arguing with two of the chefs by the wall ovens. She waved a wooden spoon that looked like it had been charred. She glanced at me but continued her tirade. The chefs weren't listening, though, and she yelled at their backs as they worked. "Elena," I said, but I was too quiet. The room was roaring with commotion. I bumped into one of the waiters coming back into the kitchen and upset the tray of shrimp ends he carried. "Shit," he spat, and I weaved away around the island. I stole an opened bottle of fumé blanc from the ice bucket behind the bartender and ducked out the back door of the kitchen. The noise from inside the house followed me into the backyard, and once I was beyond the circumference of the spotlight over the path, I shouted up into the sky. Nothing responded, and it felt like my voice just disappeared in the darkness.

I made my way across the lawn toward the second garage and walked up the stairs to Elena's apartment. I tried the door. It was locked, but I could still see through the window. Her room was simple and small, like a well-furnished monk's cell: a bookshelf, an armchair, a wardrobe closet, and a crisply made bed. Two frames with pictures of her daughter, Teresa, and her son, Mateo, leaned against the base of the lamp on the bedside table. In the first photograph, her husband, Candido, had his arm around Teresa.

I slumped down, leaned against her door, and drank, staring up into the dark night. I stayed there for a while, and it wasn't until I saw Elena shuffling down the path behind the kitchen and coming up the stairs that I realized how much I was shivering. I hid the bottle of wine behind the flowerpot on her tiny stoop. I was sure she saw it anyway, but it wasn't in my hands so she didn't have to say anything. Instead, she pulled me up into her arms. "*M'ijo,*" she said. "Don't cry. Please don't cry," she repeated as she held me.

She let me in, sat me down on her little bed, and continued to hold me. She mumbled in Spanish and, after a little bit, I realized it was the Hail Mary—*Holy Mary, mother of God, pray for us sinners, now and at the hour of our death.* I don't know how many times she repeated it, but I joined her, in Spanish, although it hurt to pray with a fist-tight throat. "Do not cry anymore," Elena said. "Please." Eventually, she got up and moved her packed suitcase toward the door. She pulled out a toiletry bag from underneath the sink in her little bathroom and packed it with what she needed.

"Why can't you stay the night?" I asked. I hated saying it. It was Christmas Eve for God's sake, and her own family was waiting for her in the Bronx. She was already leaving later than she should have. I knew she wanted to make it to the midnight Mass at her church.

When she had finished in the bathroom, she turned out the light. Only the light outside her apartment door lit up the room. "You can sleep here tonight," she said. "I don't mind. Just please take care of yourself." She stood by the door, and I couldn't see her face. She was only a silhouette in front of the lamplight from the tiny porch beyond. "Please," she said again, and then, without saying any more, she picked up her bag and hustled downstairs to the garage, to get in her car and finally begin her vacation.

A crucifix hung on the wall above Elena's bed, and it focused me for a while as I sat and drank without a glass. Forgiveness, I'd been taught, was the road to peace, but for now, I thought the quiet would do. I felt my tongue go limp and fatten as I lost control. When you drink alone over a long period of time, you're not deluding yourself into thinking you're clearheaded and bright. You're falling apart, you know it, and you just want to slip away, numb as a snowman, melting until you're gone.

CHAPTER 2

Christmas morning, I dragged myself out of Elena's apartment and back to the house to take a shower. I was tender and jumpy, and I stayed under the hot water, hoping I could steam out the toxins. Mother and I suffered our hangovers separately. We had already agreed not to open gifts by the tree. We wouldn't have eggnog at breakfast, or the scones with fresh clotted cream that had been our tradition for so many years before. Pain could strike out from the simplest, most mundane moments, and Mother hid from them under her comforter for most of the day.

I called Father Greg several times. I always got the voicemail but never left a message. It was Christmas—he must have been invited to someone's house. If he wasn't at Most Precious Blood, whom else could I call? Not that I thought Old Donovan wanted to say hello, but even if he had, I didn't know how to reach him by phone. I never really had.

I remembered the morning a few weeks earlier when I'd last seen Old Donovan. He had come back from another long trip to Europe and arrived after I'd gone to bed on a Friday night. I slept late the next morning, and I found him at the table in the breakfast nook with a newspaper in front of his face and a pile of others stacked neatly across the table from him. The last few wisps of smoke rose from a nearby ashtray. He was still in his striped pajamas. I sat down across from him and picked up a section of the *Times* he had already discarded. He cleared his throat and breathed deeply through his wet and heavy lungs.

"Welcome home," I said.

"Yes." He yawned and rubbed his face.

"You missed a lot."

"Yeah? Well, I was shoring up hope among the Europeans. Oil's down, tourism's down, the GDP sank last quarter and will again. Everybody is too goddamn afraid and playing it too close to the chest. How in God's name do you save an economy? Work. Hard work. It's always about work." He looked up at me angrily, as if the recession was my fault.

He was sleepy and disheveled—purple folds sagged beneath his eyes. White chest hair curled around the lapels of his pajamas. He pushed his coffee mug toward the edge of the table. "Mind refilling for me?"

I got up and grabbed the carafe from the island. I poured myself a small cup and brought the carafe over to the table and set it beside his mug. He frowned at me and poured himself another cup. He pushed the papers toward me. "Jump in," he said.

At a certain point, I had gathered from Old Donovan that when he said, *You need to participate in the larger conversation*, he was really saying, *It's time to grow up*. But as I scanned the headlines that morning, I wondered what kind of a world I was supposed to participate in: Everywhere I looked, there was something to fear.

"It's depressing," I said to him at last.

"You sound like your mother. It depends on your expectations. Read your Nietzsche."

I listened to his mucosal wheeze. "Didn't sleep well?" I asked.

"It's hard to get used to some beds," he said. He tried a grin on me, and I wondered what was on his mind. "Sometimes I wake up on a plane and forget where the hell I'm going."

"Yeah."

"It's hard to keep things straight sometimes."

"Yeah."

We sipped our coffees. "I can't keep pace like I used to."

"Yeah."

"Damn it, I'm trying to talk to you here, before your mother comes down and starts up. I want you to know something." He rubbed his forehead. "It's always been important to me to have a son. I've tried to pass things on to you. I've enjoyed that role." He cut himself off as classical guitar music came on over the sound system around the house. He shook his head. "It was important to me to tell you that," he said. "Look. I'd like to be kind for the next couple of days. I'd like for us all to be kind to one another, if we can."

I tensed. He and I hadn't really spoken much since I'd started the school year, and I couldn't remember any time when he'd tried so deliberately to speak with me. "I have to go soon," he continued. "I have to get back to Brussels."

"Yeah, well, that seems pretty typical." I wasn't interested in his conversations anymore anyway. "Look," I said, "I'm going to call a car. I'm heading over to work today."

"Don't you drive yet?"

"I didn't start driver's ed this semester. I've been working."

"You couldn't do both?"

"I haven't seen you in over a month."

He rubbed his forehead again. "What do you expect to gain from a non sequitur like that? You still haven't addressed the question. I know you've been working on the campaign at Most Precious Blood. I admire that work. It's important. You already know that. Let's collect some information we don't know, huh? Do they offer driving classes in the morning, before school? Is there a private company that will do it on the weekends?"

"I don't know."

"Ah! That's the reason for the non sequitur, then. I'm glad we cleared that up." He sipped his coffee. "There's so much of your mother in you."

"I'm going to work," I said. "Welcome home."

"Now hold on," he said. "I'd like us all to stay home today. You'll go off to work, your mother will do errands, and before you know it the day will be over, there will be other expectations, and the weekend will have slipped away. Just stay put here today. Got it?" He tapped his finger on the table. "I know this isn't easy, but I need your help. You can do that, right?" Steam shifted over our mugs. He fished out another cigarette and lit it. He smoked and smoked and let the silence move toward me like a cloud, closing around me until I was completely smothered.

In his years rowing crew he had built up a back that still carried him all these years later. When Mother met him, he had the physique of a man her age but the more determined and wiser mind of a man who had conquered an industry. He was thinner now, but he was still strong, as if he had condensed and ossified. "I'm not going back there for work, not right away at least," he finally said. "I know you're only a boy, but I'm going to tell you something you can't tell your mother. Can you do that? Make me trust you, son."

I stared at him across the table.

"There's a woman in Brussels."

I thought I was supposed to do something now, but I had no idea what. I didn't want to do anything. I wanted to watch him cough again—cough until his eyes blistered red and the veins in his brow bulged.

He stood up and stubbed out his cigarette. "Be a man,

son. Keep this to yourself. Can you do that? Think of it as a kind of contract for the holidays. I'm telling you now because, like I said about the importance of a son? Well, I want to be up front with my son." I nodded, and he smiled to himself as if he'd just walked some blind man across the street.

Later that day, there was shouting. He told Mother he was leaving and would not be home for the party or for the holidays. Then he was gone again—even earlier than he had planned.

That old bastard. He had no idea. I didn't say anything to Mother, but that was easy. Most Likely to Keep a Secret: That could have been my goddamn superlative for the CDA yearbook. To think how valued that skill was, and how I'd learned it so quickly. Days later, over the phone, Old Bastard shared the rest of his story with Mother, and everything finally fell apart.

The past summer, with no one to call, I'd found myself under Elena's feet almost every day and, exasperated, she convinced me to volunteer at Most Precious Blood. She suggested I would find people there with whom I might engage. And not insignificantly to her mind, she thought it would do me good to get a little closer to God. My parents were Catholic in name but not really in practice and, to her, I was moving through life without proper religious instruction. If nothing else, committing to the church community would be more meaningful than lying around the house, waiting for someone to bring me to life.

When I began working at Most Precious Blood, I began attending Mass more regularly too. Our family was "culturally Catholic," as Old Donovan had once said, and we'd rarely attended Mass more than a holy day of obligation or two. Father Dooley had been the priest to lead me through confirmation and first communion, and I knew the value of the rites and the purpose of the prayers, but I went to Mass to hear Father Greg recite them—not Father Dooley. Father Greg didn't just go through the motions like everyone else. He'd drop a fist for me to bump, right there on the church steps after Mass. He'd talk about divine grace in *On the Road*. It was Father Dooley's parish, technically—he was Father Greg's superior at Most Precious Blood—but when we did the rituals and asked for forgiveness for our trespasses and forgave others theirs against us, Father Greg created the real bridge from the person I was to the person I wanted to become. The faith everyone talked about in church was what I found in our everyday conversations: He listened, and by doing so, he elevated me.

The emptiness of the house on the day after Christmas seeped inside me, and I felt hollowed out. I found some stiff, leftover sushi from the party in the refrigerator, and I picked at it while I sat at the island in the kitchen reading *Frankenstein*. It was easy to understand why the monster wanted a mate—without one he was utterly alone. After a while, I decided I wouldn't bother calling the rectory to look for Father Greg. I was just going to show up on my own and remind him I was there.

They were offering late-afternoon services that day, so I thought it was best to find him before then. I had the car service drop me off at the foot of the driveway so I could make the long walk uphill, reciting the lines from Psalm 31 that were earmarked for the day. I'd spent time memorizing the reading and the response. I was not an altar boy, and I had not participated in the rites and rituals of the services, but I'd grown to appreciate them all the more while listening to Father Greg, and I hoped a little extra homework on my part would set the right tone between us.

The door to the rectory banged shut behind me and sent a dull echo up and down the stairwell in the entryway. The main hall was softly lit with only the sconces along the walls and the muted winter light coming in through the windows. Father Greg's office door was closed, and I worried that he wasn't around. I took off my coat and hat and hung them on the standing rack, and Father Dooley shuffled out of the kitchen across from the offices. Although he was old and stooped, Father Dooley never admitted to struggling. He still drove one of the parish cars around town and refused to accept help unless it was absolutely necessary. I walked over to say hello and tried to help him throw open the metal shutters to the service windows. He waved me off and pushed them up with the crook of his cane.

"What's going on?" Father Dooley asked me. He rubbed and flexed his bulbous knuckles. "You're not due today," he said.

"I am," I said.

"You're back next week, I think."

He caught me looking over at Father Greg's door. "I thought I was working today," I said.

"I know the schedule. We have the phone-a-thon tonight. We're hosting the volunteers from Saint Joseph's home."

"Is Father Greg here?"

"He's in a meeting. I haven't seen him much today."

"Can I say hello?"

"Not when he's in a meeting, Aidan. You know that." He looked toward Father Greg's office. "He's not to be disturbed. I'm sorry you came all the way out here."

"I just arrived," I said.

"I know. I know. There must have been some confusion with the schedule," Father Dooley said. "I don't know what to tell you. We're very busy, and I can't look after you. The volunteers will be here soon, and we have today's service to get ready. I'm sorry, Aidan, but you'll have to come back when you're scheduled."

"I'll wait for Father Greg," I said. He hesitated, and I continued. "I can help with the phone-a-thon. I'll start logging thank-you notes in the database. He won't mind." My car had already left and it wasn't coming back for a few hours, and what the hell would I do if it took me back home? "Just tell him I'm here, okay?"

"I can't go barging in," Father Dooley said. He blew out a long, frustrated sigh. "Aidan, we're busy, okay? I'm sorry, but you're going to have to head back home." With his hand behind my shoulder, he guided me back around to the coat rack. He handed me my coat and hat and urged me forward until we reached the linoleum entryway.

"Head home," he said softly, but I didn't like the way he said it. I wasn't used to being asked to leave Most Precious Blood.

He was about to reach for the door when it opened from the outside instead. "Father Dooley!" A man as old as the priest stood in the doorway. He was bundled in a wool cap and a thick overcoat, and the wind rushed into the rectory. Behind him, a line of other elderly men and women slowly made their way to the rectory from a bus in the parking lot. "I hope you have some coffee brewing," the old man in the doorway said. "We need some warming up."

Father Dooley shook his head. "I was just getting to it, Fred." He gestured for me to step aside and let Fred into the rectory; then he turned around and made his way back to the kitchen.

I stood there with my hat and coat in my hands, helping the volunteers through the doorway. One by one, they slowly made their way past me and wandered into the main hall. From behind they looked like a herd of cats, prowling, pausing, and stepping forward cautiously and unpredictably. "It's a little dark in here," one of the women yelled to Father Dooley.

"Then let there be light!" The overheads snapped on, and Father Greg stood by the far wall, smiling. He had the only voice I knew that could fill a room the size of the rectory's main hall, push way up into its rafters and still want to go farther. With its gray vaulted ceiling and simple kitchen off to the side, the rectory could have felt lifeless, but it was filled with the anticipation of his voice.

"The troops are here," he continued. "Ready to bring in the procrastinators?" He held a stack of papers in his hand and waved them in the air. "These folks have five days left to get their gifts in and reap the tax deductions for the year." He smiled. "Hey, even those of us living on fixed incomes can claim the right deductions." There was some mumbled laughter, and Father Greg came around to help them take off their coats and drape them over chairs. He pulled a few seats over to a set of folding tables near the piano and the sound system. A row of telephones ran down the middle of the tables.

I grabbed two folding chairs by the kitchenette and walked across the hall to join Father Greg by the tables. "I thought I'd help with the phone-a-thon," I said.

He glanced at the volunteers taking seats around the table. "You don't have to," he said.

"I want to."

Father Dooley placed a basket of scones on the table and glared at Father Greg. Father Greg sighed and turned back to me. "Not today, Aidan. We're fine. I can't have you underfoot."

"What?"

"Look," Father Greg said abruptly, "why don't you go wait for me in my office."

I did as he told me. In his office, only the desk lamp was lit, and if it had been a normal day working with him, a quiet day, everything would soon wind down and there would be time to talk. There wouldn't be a dozen voices asking questions; there would only be my voice, or Father Greg's—what I was used to and what I needed. Instead, he was in the other room, quieting the elderly volunteers. While he explained the basic script for the phone-a-thon, I stared at the thick Persian rug beneath my feet. The impression of my footprints crushed into the design. They faded as I shuffled and the rug fit itself back into form. I recited the psalm as I waited:

> You are my refuge and defense;
> > guide me and lead me as you have promised.
> Look on your servant with kindness;
> > save me in your constant love.

When Father Greg came in, he flipped on the overhead light and dropped into the swivel chair behind his beveled mahogany desk. He left the door open, leaned back in his chair, and folded his hands over his belly.

"It'll be a good night," Father Greg said. There was no joy in his voice. I knew he had already made his goal for the capital campaign. Whatever the phone-a-thon raised was a bonus. He tilted his head back in his chair and stretched out his feet in front of him. The ceiling could have collapsed right on top of him and he wouldn't have flinched.

I glanced over at the open door. "I was hoping we could talk," I said.

"I know," Father Greg said. "It's a busy day, though."

"I didn't get to say good-bye the other night," I said. Father Greg sat back up in his chair. "I kind of ditched the party."

"It's okay," Father Greg said, and then we were both silent for a moment. I could hear some of the volunteers practicing their scripts in the other room. He smiled at me calmly, almost blankly, as if there was nothing on his mind. I wanted to talk about the cold rushing down into my throat as I yelled into the darkness outside the party, or how I was certain Josie, Sophie, and Mark hated me and how all of CDA was going to make a blood sport of me after winter break.

"Are you too busy? I was hoping you were free for a little while."

"I am, Aidan. Too busy. I have to be out there. That's my role. You know it—parish cheerleader."

"Yeah. Right."

"You should feel good, Aidan," Father Greg said. "This has been a successful year with your help. You're a part of all this." He stood up, came around the desk to the water-cooler beside the couch, and pulled a plastic cup from the sleeve. He sat on the arm of the couch and handed me a cup of water. "You're such a special young man," he said. "You have to start feeling better."

"I do."

"You don't look it."

I glanced toward the open door again. Normally, we'd close the door and Father Greg would open his desk drawer and pull out the bottle of Laphroaig. I'd grown used to seeing the amber bottle glow in the lamplight. But the rhythms were all off today.

I had so much I wanted to talk about, and yet I didn't know what to say. I wanted Father Greg to sit back down at his desk, to find a way to carve out a quiet space for the two of us. But by sitting on the arm of the couch, he seemed like he was hovering, as if he was going to spring to his feet any second.

"Aidan, we'll have more time," Father Greg said. "I promise. Have I ever not kept a promise?"

I drank the cup of water in one quick gulp.

"You are going to be okay," Father Greg said. He leaned over and gave me an awkward one-armed hug. It held me tightly all the same, and I let him hold it for a moment because it felt like he meant it. "You have to start trusting me, Aidan," Father Greg said, pulling back.

"I do," I said quietly, like I did every time I told him that I did.

"You have to really trust me. This is all going to be okay."

I reached toward him, but he put his hand out to stop me. He leaned back, keeping the distance between us. It sounded like there were a million people talking out in the rectory and they would be there all night, like one of Mother's goddamn parties. I thought I had wanted to stay, but now I wanted to get the hell out of there. Something was wrong. I wanted to go home, but not because I wanted to be at the house, really. It was more the idea of home.

"I have many people to take care of, Aidan," Father Greg continued.

"But you said you'd always make time for me."

"Yes, yes." He glanced in the direction of the doorway. "You're also becoming a man now, Aidan. Suddenly, and so strongly, you've become a man. I'm so proud of you. Don't you know that?"

"I still feel alone."

"We've talked about that, Aidan. You're not alone. That's what faith is all about." I didn't respond, and he sighed. "Look, we'll talk more about it later."

I hunched forward with my elbows on my knees and stared at the floor between my feet. "When?"

"I don't know. We have to look at the schedule."

"I'm never on it anymore. Please. You promised. You said you'd always be here."

"And I am. We'll talk, Aidan. I promise."

"When?"

"Let's just see."

"Tomorrow!" I shouted.

Father Greg grabbed my arm. "There's no need to yell." He looked to the door. "Tomorrow, fine. Tomorrow. Just stop all this yelling and get ahold of yourself."

I nodded, and he got up and sat down again behind his desk. He crossed his arms and shook his head at me. "I think it's time for you to go now," he said.

I was about to say more when he held up his hand and pointed at me. "Aidan," he said, looking me in the eyes, "remember that you made a promise to me, too. You wouldn't break your promise, would you? After all I've done for you? After all we've discussed?"

"No."

"Good," he said, and nodded toward the door. I hesitated. He calmly folded his hands together and placed them on the desk. "Don't make me ask you again, Aidan," he said, looking at his hands.

I stared at his hands too, until we both heard Cindy's voice in the hall, shouting hello to Father Dooley. As usual, she was so wound up, she stuffed four syllables into the word "hello." Father Greg looked up at me and for a moment was speechless. Cindy knocked on his door and poked her head into his office. "We're here!" she shouted through her bullhorn smile. "James is ready for his first service, aren't you, honey? Oh. Are we interrupting?"

"No," Father Greg said quickly. "Not at all."

"Good!" She pushed James forward and stepped into the office behind him. The electric blue in her scarf and pumps accented the cool light in her eyes. She was "fierce," as Mother called her. "Come on, honey," she said to James. "Speak up. You're ready, aren't you? Tell him what you practiced."

James had changed his look since I'd seen him last. He was still shorter than me, but he was much skinnier now, with the pale, gaunt features of a goth rocker, and a wild nest of dark hair, but he was still the timid, twitching little boy I'd always known him to be. "Is Aidan helping too?" James asked quietly.

"No," Father Greg said.

"But," I said, looking at Father Greg, "it's the Feast of Saint Stephen. I know what you'll read in the service:

> "When they bring you to trial, do not worry
> about what you are going to say or how you
> will say it; when the time comes, you will be
> given what to say."

"Aidan," Father Greg said, cutting me off. "That's enough." The room was quiet. I'd memorized it specifically to impress him, but instead Father Greg stared at me silently, and he aimed at me a tight, cheerless smile. Cindy was behind him, though, and couldn't see him. "See, honey?" she said to James. "You'll be as good as Aidan in no time. Can you imagine?"

"Aidan," Father Greg said, "apologize to James."

"What? Why?"

"Nobody likes a know-it-all. That's not welcoming. This is church, Aidan, and in it we behave in a way that makes everyone feel welcome and respected, don't we?" He turned to Cindy. "I'm sorry. Please forgive my tone, but occasionally a child needs a bit of discipline."

"Oh, I understand, Father," she said. "Hear that, James? You listen to Father Greg." She patted her son on the back and pushed him forward again. "He'll be good. He always is!"

Father Greg stood up and ushered Cindy and James into the room. "Please. Take a seat," he said, gesturing to the couch. He became more animated and enthusiastic as he spoke. "Aidan was just on his way out." He looked at me with one of his party grins. "I have a meeting with Cindy and James. What a big day!" Father Greg clapped once and then, with one hand on my back, steered me out of the office. "All right. Let's go," he said as he closed the door. Through it I could hear him clap again and then say, "You are going to be great, James! Let's run through the rites to make sure you remember."

In the main hall, the geriatrics dozed over their phones

and coffee. I knew the damn script better than any of them and yet, nobody wanted me there at Most Precious Blood. Even with all the holiday adornments, the statues, the paintings, and the people positioned around the room in chairs, or leaning over tables, the church felt cold and empty, and the pageantry could not hide the lifelessness behind it. It reminded me of my own house, a giant dollhouse perfectly appointed to pretend something real existed where nothing did. I didn't want to wait around for the afternoon service to watch James wave the incense or hold up the book while Father Greg raised his hands in prayer and smiled down at him. Prayer was a sacred trust, Father Greg had told me, and there was nothing that could break it, if I had faith.

> *For the words you will speak will not be yours;*
> *they will come from the Spirit of your Father*
> *speaking through you. . . .*
> *Everyone will hate you because of me. But*
> *whoever holds out to the end will be saved.*

I repeated the passage to myself as I got outside and took off, on my own, down the long slope of the front lawn to the street. I couldn't understand: Was it really love if it was so often being tested? Hadn't I endured? I had, and I would hold out to the end, I told myself. I must. What else did I have?

CHAPTER 3

The car service had been scheduled to pick me up later, but I left without calling to cancel. I walked home, letting the cold air sting my face and eyes. When cars passed me, I tried to keep my head down. I felt like a stain on their gorgeous country view, and I wanted to be a mark that could be dissolved with the blink of an eye. I could only imagine what I looked like, leaning into the wind with my overcoat billowing behind me, my face wind-burned and splotchy. I could just hear those people asking as they passed me, *Who is that? Does he belong here?*

Well, *go take your faces off*, because I am just one of you.

When I got home, I threw off my coat, made a snack in the kitchen, and prepared to barricade myself in my room for the rest of the afternoon and evening; and that would have been the end of my day had the phone not rung while I was still downstairs. I ran to get it, thinking it was Father

Greg calling back to apologize, calling to tell me to come speak with him after the service, calling to tell me he was proud of me, calling to tell me that if a man can reach out to another man in his time of need, then he is bringing God into both their lives and they are both the better for it.

But the voice on the other end was not his. It was Josie, and it took me a few seconds to collect myself. I was suddenly embarrassed, and I didn't know why.

"Good break so far?" she asked.

"Oh, yeah," I said.

She hesitated. "Actually, isn't it always kind of a letdown? There's all this buildup and expectation, and then it's, like, where's all that fun I'm supposed to be having?"

"Yeah."

"Oh my god, Mom. I don't need an audience!" Josie breathed harder, as she must have walked away and tried to find privacy in her house. I waited. "Actually, I was having fun at your party, for a little bit," she said finally.

"Me too."

"Even though Mark's mother was a total psycho and made us pull a Houdini for no real reason. We weren't even drunk yet. Anyway, it's kind of bugged me how it ended. I mean, we didn't even say good-bye to you."

As she spoke I walked out of my own kitchen and cut back toward Old Donovan's office. "It's cool," I said.

"Actually, it wasn't. What was cool was how you handled the whole thing. You just stood there calmly, taking the heat for all of us. We stood there doing nothing. When I got home, I was, like, *Why did I do that? I suck.*"

I was quiet on the other end. I couldn't believe what I was hearing.

"Seriously," Josie continued. "You didn't fight back. At first I thought that was weird, and then I thought, *Oh my God, he's just going to take all the blame*—for us."

"It was my fault, I guess."

"Hello? Let's get real here. We were all there together."

"Get real? People do that?"

"Jesus, you're cynical."

"Look," I said, trying to sound a little warmer. "I didn't think it was a big deal."

"Well, I did," she said. "I thought it was cool. I thought you were pretty cool."

As she spoke it felt like she reached through the phone and brushed my chin with her fingertips. I had to pace while we talked. "Thanks." I could barely say it.

"I felt bad"—she lowered her voice—"like I was a stuck-up bitch. And then I figured we got you in serious trouble."

"I don't think that. Besides, nobody said anything to me. Believe me. Remember? None of us were supposed to say anything. You, Mark, Sophie, me. I don't know, dumb, deaf, blind, and dumber?"

Her laughter came through the phone like a hug. "I'm glad you're okay," she said.

Neither of us spoke for a moment. There was only her breathing, and I could picture her running her hand through her hair while she was thinking. I could see the tilt of her head and that slope of neck I was so used to studying in Mr. Weinstein's class. I waited. "Listen," she finally said, "I'm trying to get a jump on my New Year's resolution. I've decided that I need to become less of a bitch. It's hard, because everybody else around me is one, but I want to try. I don't want to be like that. I want to be different, you know?"

"Yeah. I know how you feel. I want to become someone else too."

There was a pause. "So, listen. Sophie and I were going to call Mark and hang out today. You want to come?"

And, all of a sudden, I had plans. Not an activity, not a job, not some prearranged social disaster waiting to happen that Mother had set up. I had plans to hang out like a normal kid my age. I'd been invited. *Get real,* Josie had said, and I wondered if that was what they were when they all hung out. *Real.* In school there was a script. I could talk about the homework, or the books we were reading. I could talk about geometry theorems, but I never talked about how they twisted together in my mind like the braids Josie sometimes wore in her hair. I would never tell her how I noticed that. Was that what I was supposed to talk about now? What I really noticed? I did want to get real, but what had they noticed about me? What was real about me? This was what I thought I had wanted, but now I wondered.

+   +   +

Josie and Sophie picked me up a little while later, and we headed to Josie's house. Ruby, Josie's family's housekeeper, made us hot chocolate while we waited for Mark. Even though our families had once been close, I had never really hung out with Mark alone. As far as I knew, neither he nor I hung out with many of the other kids at CDA, but his cultivated distance somehow gave him the appearance that he didn't need anybody else. I admired that more now.

When he arrived, he came right in through the kitchen door without knocking. He kissed Ruby hello. He kissed Sophie and Josie hello too. "Donovan's in on this too?" he asked the girls, but it was a rhetorical question. "Good to see you again, dude," he said to me. He stuck out his hand, and I took it.

"Sorry about the last time," I said.

"Dude," Mark said, "it was all my mom. She flipped. Let's not even talk about it."

Josie led us out the back door and up the hill to the pool house. We turned on the stereo and sat on stools around the bar. Mark stood behind the bar, packing a bowl. He got it cooking and passed it. Josie had us exhale through a little cardboard tube filled with dryer sheets.

I hadn't said much since I'd gotten there and, after the weed, Sophie and Josie wrapped themselves up in private conversation. Mark played with the soda gun behind the bar, so I turned on the TV. I stood a couple of feet away from the screen and flipped through the channels. There was something satisfying about watching people appear and disappear instantly on my command. A sullen and spooked John Walker Lindh stared into the pool house from the TV. It was a still photograph, the one all the news stations had been using since they'd caught him running through the tunnels of Tora Bora in December. Behind the smeared soot and the scraggly beard, his eyes glowed intensely white. A subtle smirk rose in the corners of his mouth. Everyone knew his story: He'd been caught with a bullet in his thigh, burrowing through the hills of Afghanistan like a mole, the wayward American fighting for the Taliban. He stared out like he was waiting for me to get the joke.

"Dude's fucking crazy," Mark said from across the room. I turned around. "Not you, Donovan." Mark laughed. "Fucking Lindh."

"I don't know," Josie said. "There's something so sad about him."

"Well, turn it off," Sophie whined. "He looks like a monster."

"He's just scared," Josie continued. "That's what I see."

"Oh my God," Sophie said, pointing behind me. "Now, *that* woman is crazy. How is she going to let her marriage with Michael Jordan end?"

"Does that mean Michael Jordan is single?" Josie asked, and both girls laughed. The news had jumped to another story already. No time to linger or ask questions or analyze or develop. Move, move, move. On to the next suggestion.

"Turn that off, man," Mark said, holding up the empty bowl. "Let's repack this." I snapped off the TV and joined them at the bar.

"I think that Lindh guy thought he was doing the right thing, even if he wasn't," I said.

"They should name a prison after him," Mark said, sparking the bowl.

"That is *not* funny," Josie said.

"Oh my God, enough about that guy." Sophie pouted. "I hate it."

Mark took a big hit, and when Sophie handed him the tube to exhale, he waved it away. He leaned over the bar to Sophie and looked her in the eye. She giggled and leaned forward. They kissed, and a little smoke slipped from between their open mouths. Sophie broke from the kiss and exhaled through the tube. "Why waste any of it?" Mark said, and slapped me a high five above the girls' heads. Sophie took a hit, and she and Josie followed. Josie exhaled a tiny stream through the tube. "Think that's hot?" Mark asked. I nodded while my heart raced.

Josie looked at me. "Have *you* ever recycled?" she asked. I had never smoked pot before that afternoon, but I hadn't admitted that, either. Alcohol and pills were so easy; they were in every house I'd ever been in. I was too slow to answer Josie, though, and when she took a small puff, she pulled me to her lips. The smoke came into my mouth, followed by her tongue, which flickered gently, then slipped out. I held my breath and tried to smile, which was harder than I thought because the smoke burned more than the cigarettes I'd had, and worse, I thought my stomach was going to explode. How many times had I stared at the back of Josie's head and wondered what it was like to be close to someone so beautiful? But there was more. She was looking at me. My eyes began to burn, too. I froze, and my neck and shoulders tightened. *Get real.* What did Josie see? There were so many Aidans, stacked like Russian nesting dolls within me, who I never wanted her to meet or know. I exhaled through the tube and coughed.

"Nice one. When you cough, you get off," Mark said. "And fuck it, by the way," he added to Josie. "Dustin can suck it."

"Dustin?" I asked, desperate to swing the spotlight somewhere else.

"Yeah, I guess I've been dating him for a couple of weeks," Josie said.

"*Trust in Dustin* Dustin?" I asked. Sophie and Mark laughed.

"All right, that was lame, but he won, didn't he?" Josie was right, but Dustin had become the junior-class representative because the whole baseball team had done a shakedown to get votes for him.

"But he's not going to know about that," Josie said. "Or any of this." Then she smiled at me. "Got it?" I nodded. "Okay," she said, pointing from me to Mark, "your turn."

"No. That's cool," I said, glancing at Mark. "I should just come back the way I came, right?"

Mark leaned back against the shelves behind the bar, with a wry half smile.

"No way," Josie said. "This is a circle."

"Yeah," Sophie said. "Girls do it all the time. What's the matter with you boys?"

"Nothing," I said.

Sophie and Josie protested and, still amused, Mark watched us bicker. A dull ache gripped me. I couldn't look at him again. My body felt like a machine. I could respond any way I was asked to. Don't ask me to start. Just kiss me and I'll kiss you back. A kiss was nothing—I knew that. A kiss was so simple. It was what followed that frightened me. I didn't want to move, but I wondered if I could end the debate right there by kissing Mark, and then we could all get back to feeling like we were getting away with something together. That's all I really wanted—for the circle to continue and for me to remain a part of it.

"You're acting a little uptight, man," Mark finally said. The girls laughed.

"No, I'm not," I said. I hesitated while they looked at me. "I think I'm stoned," I continued. "Am I supposed to do something now?"

"Listen," Mark said to the girls. "You all need to ease up. You're going about this the wrong way."

He stepped forward, away from the shelves, and pointed to the bowl in my hands. "Hit that, dude. Before it goes out." I did, and as I took the smoke down into my lungs, he reached across the bar and pulled me by the shirt collar toward him. He yanked me to his lips and popped open my mouth. The smoke rushed out of me. He huffed it in, pushed me back across the bar, pumped his fist, and exhaled through the tube into the air above us. His lips had been dry and firm, and I couldn't tell if he had wanted me to press back. I didn't know if I wanted to or not. Static buzzed through me, and I had no idea if he had it humming down in him as well. His face was cool and collected as if it were chiseled out of stone, and I felt like I was melting with sweat. Eyes were all over me, watching me, eyes in the room—eyes across town, floating closer, hovering like gigantic birds outside the windows, watching, waiting for the moment to crash through and strike.

"Like I said before"—Mark grinned—"why waste any of it? This is premium bud, dude. It's not every day we get the budalicious from the BC." He put his hand back up in the air above the bar and I slapped it again, quickly and automatically and with a giddiness loopy with fear.

The girls hooted, and the room spun a little. "Budalicious," I mumbled. "Yeah."

Mark and the girls laughed. I hoped they couldn't tell

I was trembling. I was dizzy and damp with sweat, and I braced myself against the bar. *This is what I want*, I kept telling myself. *This is different. Keep it together.* If one little Aidan doll cracked, so would another, and I'd fall apart one shell at a time until they saw the tiny, terrible nugget at the heart of it all. I'd never thought of myself like that before, someone with a pit of darkness at the center of me. I didn't want to think about it. I slumped down onto a stool and forced out a loud *I-dare-you-to-doubt-me* laugh I stole directly from Father Greg.

"Are you totally stoned?" Sophie asked.

"Yeah," I said.

"Good," Mark said. "Relax into it, man. Welcome to the group." We slapped hands again, and this time like we meant it.

Josie grabbed the bowl from me and lit it. I wasn't sure if I was supposed to lean in to her or not, and she knew it. She wagged her finger and grabbed the tube. She blew right at me through the shit-brown dryer sheets, and the smoke washed over my face. She walked behind the bar, next to Mark. "Tell you what?" she said to all of us. "I know my dad watches this stuff like a hawk, but we could pour out just a little vodka, then refill the bottle with some water. I bet he'd never have a clue."

"I'm not having anything to drink," Mark said. "I have to see my parents later. They want to have another *family night*, whatever the hell they think that is."

"You just smoked a bowl," Sophie said.

"That's different," Mark said.

"Everything's different to you, Mark," Josie said.

"I'll have some," I said to Josie.

"Yeah?"

"Yeah, and I won't spit it all over anybody this time either."

Josie burst out laughing, and Sophie did too. I puffed my cheeks and made a big scene, and Sophie pretended to get showered with my spray. She laughed so hard, she started to cry.

We drank and the afternoon became hazier, punctuated by Josie's and Sophie's laughter. They barely had to exchange more than a few words for one to know what the other was saying, and it set them off again and again. It swept into me. I was still nervous and confused and not sure if they were making fun of me or not, but I began to feel like I could really be a part of this.

I tried not to look Mark in the eyes too much, but when we spoke together, he was completely calm, the same disaffected-smile-wearing Mark I always saw around school, but with less distance than usual—as if that smirk wasn't aimed at but instead included me. And later, when he decided it was time for him to start walking home, he asked if I wanted to join him.

"I'm supposed to see Dustin later, but maybe I'll skip it," Josie said. "Skip your *family night*," she said to Mark.

"We've got our own thing going on here. We're like a perfect square."

"Nothing's ever perfect," Mark said. "That's what my dad says. Thinking something's perfect is a sign of laziness. It's not working hard enough to find something better."

"What the hell does that mean?" Sophie asked.

"Never settle. That's what," Mark said. "I mean, *chill out*, right? Last time I said that in front of him, though—not even to him, just in front of him—he went on a fucking tirade."

Josie and Sophie gave him a hug. I kissed Sophie on the cheek and leaned toward Josie. She held my arm. "You're coming to the New Year's party, right?" Sophie giggled behind her. It was strange how I suddenly felt like I knew what I was supposed to do, and I kissed her good-bye on the lips. She kissed me back and smiled.

Mark put his hand on my shoulder. "He'll come with me," he told Josie. We turned to leave. "It'll be interesting," he said to me quietly. "Dustin will be there."

We left through the back door of the pool house, then cut along the low stone wall to a small wooded patch. Mark pulled a one-hitter from his pocket and we took turns with it. When we were finished, we continued along the wall and emerged onto the street on the hill behind Josie's house.

"Dude," Mark said after a while. "It's nice to have another guy in the mix. It's always just me and the girls."

"That's cool."

He laughed. "No. No, I didn't mean it like that." Then

he added, "I'm just saying that it's nice to have another guy around. The perfect square. I like that."

"Suits me," I said. "Obviously."

He laughed again. "You're all right, Donovan. You're all right." He shook his head, smiling, and I didn't know what else to say.

We walked along in silence. I was in a fog—still trying to figure out what had happened all afternoon and how the hell I'd become a part of it. We were cutting downhill, beside the back nine of Stonebrook Country Club. While a lot of the snow had melted around town, there were still drifts of it clustered in the sand bunkers spotted over the course. As clouds passed by overhead, the sun occasionally broke free, and bursts of light ignited and glistened on the hard crusts of the embankments.

At the bottom of the hill we curled around the other side of the country club and came to the short bridge that was just a ways up from the harbor. To get to our homes we had to go in opposite directions, but Mark didn't seem to be in a hurry anymore. "So, this party . . . ," I finally said to him.

"It'll be cool, I guess. Kegger over at Feingold's. Everyone's going. It'd be too weird not to go," he said. "I don't know. I'm going to this one, but I don't go to most of the parties. They can be lame. Everyone's there, but nobody is really talking to one another. Like none of it's real." He waved his hand in the air in front of him. "I don't know. Sorry, man. I'm stoned."

"No," I said, "you're probably right. But maybe it's because everyone is too afraid."

Mark looked at me. "Of what?"

"I don't know. Everything. Maybe everyone's just faking it because that's all there is."

"So they can't get real?" Mark asked. "That's depressing."

"Tell them to take their fucking faces off," I said, but it felt weird now to say that so casually. "They can't, right?"

Mark gazed down into the river, and I did too. The chunks of ice and dead foliage floated from beneath the bridge and zigzagged out to the harbor. "But we can," he said. "We are."

I nodded but didn't say anything else. I was too locked away in myself. I had to be. I was afraid to speak anymore for fear of saying something I didn't want to. We were both quiet for a while. Mark put his hand on my shoulder again. "Dude," he said. "I have to get going here. I'm totally late." We cupped each other's hand and pressed shoulders into each other's chests the way I'd seen athletes do on television.

Mark went the other direction on the bridge, and I let him go on ahead of me. I waited, hoping the dope would wear off and I'd sober up before I got home. I stood on the bridge for a while and looked down into the black slick of river that tumbled forward into the saltwater harbor beyond. I thought about Josie's tongue and humming lips, Mark's voice springing from his strong jaw, and Sophie's laughter. I jumbled all their body parts together in my mind like a fractured Picasso, shifting the images so they split and re-formed into a new shattered mosaic like a kaleido-scope shifting colored crystals. I wanted to keep shuffling the pieces—tongues, lips, fingers—until I found some language to the pattern—because there was something deeper than only sex, wasn't there? I had to believe that when our bodies came together, it was a bridge to something deeper and more meaningful, a conjoining of parts to make a fuller whole, just as a breath is not only an inhale and an exhale but one act in which they complete each other. That was all I wanted: a sense of stability, of completeness, an assurance that any fear could be dissolved, that loneliness was a sick-ness cured when someone else's exhale became my inhale and, together, neither of us could ever feel alone.

As I stood on the bridge I began to feel sick. I only wanted to be told everything was going to be okay. I could give and give and give, and go and go and go, but I would wander aimlessly forever unless I had a road map that said, *Aidan, go straight ahead, turn right, then left, then left again, and you will be where you want to be.* Isn't that what Father Greg kept promising? "A better home," a way to feel at peace wherever I was? *This is what our Lord asks of you, Aidan. This is what I ask of you. Shhh, shhh, soon you will feel much better. Soon everything will be better. You'll know love. This is love, Aidan. This is love.*

I kept hearing his hush in my head as I stared down into the river from the bridge. His voice was in me, endlessly shushing. Occasionally, a shaft of ice shot out from beneath the bridge and cut through the river until it passed out of sight into the dark distance. I couldn't stay focused and fixed. I wanted a sense of direction, to be able to see myself clearly and say *Yes, yes, yes, this is me,* but my thoughts emerged and rippled over one another chaotically, and I couldn't see through the mess.

CHAPTER 4

"The most important things in life require a leap of faith," Father Greg once told me. "Jesus did not turn stones into bread when he was starving in the desert, nor did he throw himself off the temple to prove he was the son of God. He knew he could survive on faith, not bread, and he knew he need not test his faith to believe in it. You must believe in me, Aidan. You must believe that I love you. Everything will be okay if you have faith in this love between us. Love is God in action."

And I did. I believed him. I continued to believe him when he was the only person to give me a birthday card in September, and when he gave me a copy of a photo he'd taken of Saint Aidan in a stained-glass window in England, and when he tore a clean handkerchief so we could each have a half one day when we both were sneezing, and when I laughed because he made me, and when he told me

I would not feel this way forever, and when I cried and he held me and didn't say "don't cry" or "take care of yourself"; I believed him when he said "I will take care of you" and that it was okay to cry because it gave him the chance to take care of me more. There seemed like nothing else other than the strange, painful gravity he could provide.

I was certain we had agreed that I would return the next day, the day after he'd asked me to leave his office for the first time, and I did not want to disappoint him. I left earlier than I had the day before, and I had the car service drive me over to Most Precious Blood again, with instructions not to pick me up until that evening. On the way, I thought about what I was going to say to Father Greg. I wanted to talk about Josie and Mark and Sophie, but I also didn't. It meant I had something against which to compare, something that frightened me more and more on the drive over.

When I got there, the lights were dimmed in the rectory, and it was quiet. The gate to the kitchenette was closed, and no one moved around in the main hall. The remnants of the phone-a-thon from the day before were littered about the far end of the hall. An easel held a poster of a schoolhouse lined with hash marks indicating escalating amounts of money. Across the top, scrawled in marker and in big, green handwriting I knew was Father Greg's, it read ST. PHILLIP'S IS NOW A REALITY.

The light in Father Greg's office shone through the cracks around his door, and Father Dooley's door was open.

I could hear the mumble of his low voice on the phone, and I didn't want to walk past his office and have him see me. Father Greg knew I was coming. If I didn't knock on his door, he'd know where else to find me. I turned and went down the stairwell to the basement.

At the foot of the staircase, a dim overhead light showed the cracks and damp blisters in the walls along the hallway to the storage room. The gray metal door looked heavier than it really was, and I realized that I'd never actually opened it before, Father Greg always had. Inside, the naked bulb swung loosely when I tugged on the chain, and it cast a jaundiced glow around the entrance to the storage room, the faint light reaching only as far as the workbench in the middle of the room. Underneath the workbench, the orange coils of the electric heater glowed, and I knew Father Greg would be coming down later. He had set up the room like this before. He wouldn't push me away again.

The boiler murmured in a dark corner. Banging and hissing pipes crisscrossed the ceiling, hushing the room. Clutching my coat and hat, I walked over to the two small, barred windows in the far wall that looked up into foxholes in the yard alongside the rectory. Through them, afternoon light faded into the makeshift workshop. Other guys my age would have looked out this window and wanted to go surfing down the long slope of the icy lawn on cafeteria trays, but I just waited and let my eyes adjust to the darkness of the basement. I preferred where I was: the cold comfort of the shadows. The pipes finally settled down, and in the stillness there was nothing but the heater humming one long buzzing note. For once, doing nothing seemed like all that was expected of me. He would be down here soon; there was nowhere else for me to go.

I was still standing under the windows, in the shadows of the metal shelves, when I heard the door open. I pressed back against the wall and hid myself beside the shelving unit in case it was Father Dooley. I was relieved to hear Father Greg's voice instead, but he was speaking to someone else. They made their way toward the workbench, and although I couldn't see them, I knew he was with another boy, one younger than me.

"Is it okay to be down here?" the boy asked.

Father Greg laughed. I heard a thud on the workbench and glasses knocking against each other. "This is where we have to come," Father Greg said. "Remember, this is only between you and me. This isn't for anyone else. No one else can know. No one."

"I remember," the boy said, and I recognized the timidity. It was James, the eighth grader, Cindy's son.

"This is a man's drink," Father Greg said to James.

"I can take it."

"I know."

"But I don't feel well," James said after a moment.

"Come on. Go ahead. I like sharing this with you."

"No, it's just that I don't feel well, I think. That's all."

"You're fine."

"No. Maybe I should go?"

"There's no one else here," Father Greg said. "We don't have to be afraid. This is all right. You don't have to be afraid when you're with me."

"I don't feel well," James said again. "I'm sorry." There was a moment of silence and then a glass coming down hard on the workbench. "No," James said. "Please."

"It's all right," Father Greg said. "It's all right."

I couldn't see anything, but I didn't have to. I knew then that Father Greg was pouring out two glasses of scotch—more for himself and a smaller one for James. Even without standing next to him, I knew how it smelled on Father Greg's breath; I knew the heat; I knew how his breath would soon blast against the shoulder and move slowly like a hot wind up along the neck to the ear and stay there, making you wonder if it was ever going to run out.

"We've talked about this," Father Greg said to James, and as the familiar words rolled out of him I was gripped with a fear I hadn't felt since the first time Father Greg had walked me down into the basement. "This is part of what makes what we have together so special," Father Greg continued. "It's only you and me, James—that's important. You don't want them to take that from us, do you?"

"No," James said.

"I care about you, James. I don't want to hurt you. You don't want anyone to hurt *me*, do you?"

"No."

"Shhh," Father Greg hushed. "I can help you. You'll see. Shhh."

I slid down the wall and tucked my knees to my chest. I jammed my fists over my ears and squeezed my eyes shut, even though I couldn't see anything anyway. I didn't have to see—I knew how Father Greg's embrace swallowed you, took the air away until your breath was something you gave him, too. Father Greg was twice the size of James. I knew the earthy air that was up around James now. I knew how to take it all in silence, and I held myself tightly in a ball while it lasted. I couldn't hear anything except the voice in my own head, Father Greg's voice telling me, *This, too, is a part of love—this is love, our love—only for the two of us.*

There were tears in my eyes when they finally began the Our Father, and I said it along with them to myself. Father Greg made him repeat it until James said the words loudly and clearly, with force, as if he meant it, or at least had calmed down. Then, in silence, Father Greg switched off the heater and the light and urged James upstairs, beckoning him with those words I'd heard so many times before. "This is only between you and me, James, remember that. No one else can know."

I stayed squatted in the dark corner beside the shelves, and tears slid down my face. I hated James, and it wasn't even his fault. *No,* I could hear him say. It repeated within me.

I hadn't been able to find that word last summer, when

Father Greg had led me down to the workbench and offered me that first sip of scotch. I had just let him come up against me as I closed my eyes and sank into myself. Father Greg's thumb had pressed up against my Adam's apple and I had wondered if that was it—if Father Greg was bringing me right up to the end of my life—but a glow of pleasure had washed across Father Greg's face and I felt strange and oddly important because I knew I had given it to him. I took it, again and again, until it seemed familiar.

I sat there, listening to my own teeth chatter, until the beams of a car's headlights shot through the foxhole window above me. I didn't know how long I had been down in the basement. When a horn beeped out in the parking lot, I knew it was my car returning for me. I couldn't stand the thought of climbing into the car and trying to make conversation with the driver, but I had to get the hell out of there. It beeped again, once.

Still clutching my coat and hat, I ran to the door. It swung open and smacked against the brick wall with a hollow bang that clattered up through the stairwell. The hallway was dark, but light filtered down from the rectory above. I took the stairs two at a time but came to a stop at the landing.

Father Greg stood in the doorway to the parking lot and looked outside, one arm holding the door ajar. I could see the headlights of the livery cab shining in the darkness, out toward the lawn in front of the church. I heard a voice in the parking lot, but it was too far away for me to hear what it said.

"No, I'm terribly sorry," Father Greg called out. "He wasn't here today." He turned around. His frame nearly filled the whole doorway. He wore a wool, knit hat and a flannel shirt without his Roman collar, and his overcoat was open and loose. He glared at me for a moment, hesitated, and then turned back to the parking lot. "No. No, he definitely wasn't here today. Sorry I can't be of more help." Father Greg waved. "That's right. All the best. Merry Christmas."

He pulled the door closed tightly and clicked the lock. "Aidan?" His eyes were red, and he breathed heavily. "You scared the hell out of me. You're not supposed to be here."

I didn't say a word.

"What are you doing here?" he asked me. "Were you downstairs?"

"You told my driver I wasn't here," I said. "You saw me. You looked right at me."

He folded his arms. "Calm down," he said. He scratched his jaw. "We should talk. I'll drive you home."

"No," I said quietly.

Father Greg straightened. "We need to have a talk in my office," he said.

"I want to leave," I said with a little more volume.

Father Greg relaxed his shoulders. He peeled the wool hat from his head and stuffed it into his coat pocket. He flattened the tousled hairs on his head. "Aidan, come on," he said. "You know who you're talking to here."

"No," I said again. I looked out toward the main hall. It was completely dark except for a broad pane of light spreading out from Father Greg's office.

"The driver said he dropped you off earlier. Have you been down there all afternoon?" He wiped his face and sighed. "Okay, all right. Calm down. Calm down, Aidan. Calm down." His voice had the whoosh and hiss of too many drinks. He approached me as he spoke, and before I could move, he took hold of my arm. I tried to jerk away, but I couldn't free myself. He marched me through the rectory to his office and shut the door behind him.

"Have a seat."

"I don't want to be here anymore."

He took off his overcoat, then took my coat and hat from my hands. "Now, look," he said as he draped them over his desk chair, "just calm down. We can talk about this."

He walked me to the couch, but I wouldn't sit. I rubbed my thumb over the dull copper studs that lined the seam of its arm. St. Augustine stared at me from his small portrait on the wall. The reading lamp on the desk cast a dull cone of light over a stack of thank-you notes Father Greg had written. They were waiting for me, I realized, to fold, stamp, and send out. Father Greg moved the bottle of scotch and brushed the two rocks glasses across the green desk pad with the back of his hand. He leaned on the edge of the desk and crossed his arms over his shirt in a way that pulled it taut against his chest.

"Why don't you take a seat?" he said.

"No," I said.

"Easy, Aidan, easy. Calm down. Just take a seat."

"No," I said again, louder.

"We are going to talk about this. I didn't know you were here."

"I thought you expected me. You told me to come."

Father Greg rubbed his face. "Oh, Aidan."

"Yesterday. You said, 'Tomorrow.' I came."

"You wouldn't leave."

"I don't understand anymore!"

"Aidan, calm down."

"I thought it was different. I thought I was different."

"You are. You are. Let me explain, Aidan."

I stepped toward the door, but Father Greg pushed me back. I fell onto the couch. "Enough!" Father Greg shouted. He leaned against his desk and rubbed his face. "Just stay seated while we think about all this."

I was quiet while I tried to catch my breath. Father Greg stared at his feet and nodded to himself. "You don't want to go home. That's not what you want, right? You know that."

I said nothing.

Eventually, he looked up at me. "You are going to be okay."

"You always say that."

"Because it's true, Aidan. It is."

"No," I said. "You lied."

"No. That's not right. Let me explain this all to you."

"You lied."

"No. I didn't," Father Greg said. His voice sounded younger—pleading. "I need you to understand me." He approached me, put his hand on my shoulder, and leaned in closely. He spoke softly, hovering just over my head. "Shhh. Shhh. Hold on. You know who you are talking to here. I've never lied to you. Shhh. I care too much about you, you know that. Shhh. Shhh." He wiped his face with his hand and pulled on all the sagging skin. "There. Settle down now. Good. Just breathe awhile. Good. Yes, good." He reached up to my face and wiped at my tears with his thumb. He pressed against my cheek and rubbed right down into the corner of my mouth. "You are special, Aidan," he said softly. "Don't forget how much I care about you. We just need to remember this. We can understand, right?" His hand went around the back of my head and clutched my hair. He tugged gently. The cloth of his shirtsleeve brushed my forehead. His sweat. Hushed, scotch-stinking breath. I trembled and, after a moment, he continued. "You've never told anybody, have you? You've never said anything, have you?"

I shook my head.

"You know what they would do to me?" he continued. "You don't want them to hurt me, do you?"

He leaned back, and I saw the wall beyond him again,

and the pictures on it of his worldly travels—El Salvador, Kenya, Senegal, Cambodia, the people, the children, smiling around him. Now Father Greg stood smiling down at me. He touched my forehead with the back of his hand. "You're on fire, Aidan," he said. "You're shaking. Let me get you a glass of water." His hand felt icy. I couldn't feel it again.

Father Greg stepped beside the desk. I looked again at the bottle of scotch, and Father Greg followed my glance. "Are you okay?" he asked. I nodded, and I stood. "I guess that'd be good. We'll both have a little. We understand each other?" I nodded again, and Father Greg relaxed his shoulders. He smiled more as he poured. We swallowed quickly, and I stared down into my empty glass. There were tears in my eyes. "Easy," Father Greg said, and I listened to that tone shift in his voice again. I squeezed at the glass with both hands and shook. "Aidan. Please."

When he reached for my shoulder, I smashed the glass down against the edge of his desk, and the shards exploded everywhere. I backed away, and it wasn't until I saw the blood in my hand that I felt the pain.

Father Greg grabbed me before I moved farther away. He repeated my name again and again with panic. He pulled me closer as he opened drawers, and I wiped my hand down on the desk pad and the notecards and cried at the pain.

"Please," Father Greg begged. "Let me help you."

I coughed and tried to pull away, but Father Greg's grip

was too strong. He had no other directions for me, no more words. He pulled a tea towel from the drawer and dabbed my hand. "Aidan, Aidan." He repeated my name over and over as if it were all he had left to hold on to. I grunted. He looked at my hand and tried to examine it for slivers, but I kept tugging back. It was bleeding quickly, and I turned it and wiped at Father Greg's sleeve—the pain burned again. "Aidan," Father Greg said. "Please. Let me take care of you."

In response, there was a shout from outside the office. "Greg!" The door swung open, and the bright overhead lights from the rectory's main hall lit up the room. "What the hell is going on here?" Father Dooley asked as he came in.

"He's cut himself," Father Greg said.

Father Dooley stared at Father Greg.

"Aidan. He cut himself. I'm trying to help." Father Greg dabbed at my hand again with the towel and then wrapped it tightly. I couldn't speak.

"Greg. Stop," Father Dooley said.

"No, no. No, it's not that."

"Shut up," Father Dooley snapped. "Stop talking. You're sick, Greg. You're not well." He trailed away and shook his head.

"No, no. He's only cut himself."

"Greg! Enough!" Father Dooley said. "Aidan," he continued, "please don't be afraid. Nothing else is going to happen." He waited for me. "Please. Let me drive you home."

Father Greg began again, but Father Dooley cut him off.

"Damn it, Greg. This is too much. Let go of him!" Father Greg was about to speak, but he hesitated. His grip slackened, and then he finally let go of me.

"Everything is going to be okay. Please, Aidan. Come here. Come here right now."

I stepped forward, but as Father Dooley gestured for me, I pushed past him and ran out through the rectory, to the driveway, and down to the sidewalk. The snow-covered lawns looked like a desert. Ornamental bushes became cacti casting hazy shadows across the sand and dust, and I was out there in it like some creature seen only by the light of the moon, wide-eyed, loping through the yards, a pale shadow passing through town.

Blood pooled in my hands and dried in brown threads around my wrist. It was mine, I was sure, cut from the glass, but somehow it felt like his, like he was reaching out, grabbing me, and pulling me back. *Aidan.* I stuffed my hand in a snowbank, and the cold bit at my skin, but it stopped the bleeding. The wind howled around me, and in it I thought I heard his hushed breath whispering at my neck. I screamed to keep his voice out of my head, and I kept running while the low moon burned an orange ring through the clouds and hovered, like an eye blinking down on me and following me into the night.

After a while, my throat went raw and my face stung with the chill. I found myself standing, shivering, in the pale light beneath a Mobil sign. I had left the church without my coat, gloves, and hat. The smell of gasoline cut through the air, and I realized I had walked out of town to a rest stop near an on-ramp to the highway. Only a few cars were in the lot outside the McDonald's attached to the gas station. It wasn't all that late, but there were only a few people inside. My teeth clacked uncontrollably, and I couldn't hold my hands still. I went into the Mobil Mart and walked up and down the aisles a few times. I bought a burrito and an Irish Crème coffee. I warmed up the burrito in the microwave and watched it grow in the yellow glow.

The attendant didn't give a shit about me. She sat behind the counter on the other side of the Mobil Mart, talking on her cell phone. I wasn't even sure there was someone on the other end of the line. She just kept going and going. I took my burrito and coffee over to the window and used a short tower of beer cases for a table. Cars whipped by on I-95. Thoughts charged all around my head, and I kept picturing little objects in Father Greg's office: the small portrait of St. Augustine on the wall, the jar with pens beside the desk pad, the dull copper studs that ran along the seams of the leather couch—the little things I had stared at so many times, focused on, and known the texture of.

A white bus pulled off the highway and rumbled down the road. It bounced into the parking lot and dropped off its passengers in front of the McDonald's. They all got in line behind the counter. Another cup of coffee would have done me good too, or a tab of NoDoz, like truckers pop as they floor it across the country in the dead of night.

The bus rolled forward and parked in front of the diesel tanks. When the driver got out, started the pump, and then made his own way into McDonald's, I made a break for it. On the side of the bus, bright green and red Chinese characters were painted around a blue sign with double arrows pointing to New York and Boston: the express bus, even more run-down than Greyhound's.

I kept looking over my shoulder, thinking the driver was going to come out of McDonald's, but when I hopped on the bus and looked out from the coach, I could see the driver buying cigarettes at the Mobil Mart counter as if nothing was the matter. The back of the bus had a cramped, windowless closet of a bathroom, and I snuck in. It smelled like somebody had just taken a piss in there, only he'd sprayed down the whole room and gotten it everywhere except the pot. Strands of toilet paper stuck to the walls in dissolving clumps. The door didn't have a lock either—you got it to stay shut by hooking a bungee cord around the handle and stretching it over another one along the wall. I stood there, terrified and paranoid the driver had seen me, until the bus finally started and lurched forward. It stopped again, and I heard people climbing back on board. I stayed in the bathroom until we were rolling down the road and onto the highway, and once we'd been cruising for a while, I opened the door. The bus was mostly empty. People dozed in their seats. I sat down near the bathroom and hugged myself tightly as the bus slowly warmed. It was heading south. The engine hummed, and the tires zoomed a rip-and-thump beat along the road. The seats smelled like Windex and Bounce and some fruity bubble gum air freshener, but nothing felt clean. When I breathed it in, I felt propelled—hurtling forward toward nothing.

The highway was swallowed by the city as the expressway dipped down between high concrete walls and sliced through the neighborhoods. Eventually, the bus came to a stop at a clustered corner beneath the massive steel structures of a bridge. Every sign hanging over doorways or taped to storefront windows was written in Chinese. Passengers filed off the bus, and eventually, I did too. I walked through the warren of streets that smelled of fish and gasoline. Fire escapes ran like zippers up and down the tenement building facades. People yelled and shouted over one another everywhere. I was bumped and ignored. My nose hurt in the cold, and no matter how much I wiped at it with the sleeve of my sweatshirt, I couldn't clear the snot from my lip.

I wandered through the barricaded downtown Manhattan streets, avoiding the clusters of National Guard soldiers around the financial buildings. It was Old Donovan territory, and I pictured him sitting at a desk near one of the windows high up in the office towers, peering out over the glowing city beneath him—lording over the landscape and seeing nothing within it. I yelled, then listened to my voice echoing among the canyon of buildings, but nobody found me or heard me, and eventually, my voice was too raw to leave my throat.

I was exhausted, and I felt noise in my head like the glass that had been in my hand. Dusty tracks of blood still wound around my fingers. I stared down at my hands as if they belonged to someone else. I found a quiet, cobble-stoned street and a steam grate for the subway near what looked like an old, unused, brick doorway. I held myself in a ball, but as the gray huffs billowed up from below, I never really fell asleep as the machinery of sirens, brakes, and hissing hydraulics crept inside me like the cold air.

CHAPTER 5

I awoke amid an air of violence. As I crawled out from my little hovel, it all came back to me in flickering bursts: the warm shade of the desk lamp; the green desk pad; glass exploding; Father Greg pressing a tea towel into my hand; a bloody swipe across his shirt. Father Dooley called to me, but somehow it felt like he had been calling to someone else, a stranger—a stranger who'd been keeping all my secrets for me, as if they weren't mine, as if they'd been locked up inside somebody else, until now.

I cleaned myself in the bathroom of a diner downtown. After breakfast, as I wandered north through the city, I admitted that I didn't have any other real option: I needed Elena. I'd never been to her home before, but I knew where she lived. It was late afternoon when I finally mustered the energy to descend the stairs of the subway pavilion at Union Square and look for the 4 train to the Bronx. Everywhere, packs of three or four National Guard soldiers stood in their spread-eagled stances with their guns strapped to their shoulders and the barrels pointed toward the ground. They scanned the crowds stoically, waiting patiently for a violence their very presence made seem imminent. The more armed guards I passed in the subway station, the more I glanced around, wondering if they could see something I could not.

It was twilight when I found her street. On the corner, I stopped at a bodega and bought a giant armload of flowers and marched up the street without waiting for my change. I didn't know what I was doing. Eyes were on me from every direction. I'd never felt my whiteness so strongly until I stood there as the only white person, waiting for the light to change, waiting to find her front door and close it behind me and lock out the rest of the world.

Undercliff Avenue curled away from the bustling neighborhood near the train and wound around the foot of a large hill clustered with old clapboard houses. Like the houses around it, Elena's had a garage that stood a few yards back from the sidewalk, and a stone staircase climbed a steep slope up to the front stoop. Two stories rose above the front door, and it looked like a little lighthouse on a precipice, if a lighthouse could be a cube with a gabled roof. Even in December, the three-tiered garden embedded in the slope beside the stairs was colorfully alive. Ivy clung to the rocks and evergreen shrubs.

From inside the house, the voice of a swaying balladeer gently rocked. I held my breath and rang the bell. Teresa answered. I recognized her immediately from her picture. She was two years ahead of me in school. A naked strip of scalp divided the perfectly parted hair that fell over her shoulders, but I fixed my eyes on her vibrant sneakers. She crossed one foot over the other as she leaned on the handle of the wooden door.

"Oh my God. What are you doing here?" She looked at the flowers skeptically, and I remained silent. "You okay?"

"I've seen your picture," I said. "You were on the volley-ball team this fall."

She looked at me with a confrontational smile. "Yeah, I've seen yours, too," she said. "You always look like some-body just died." She cocked her head over her shoulder and yelled up the stairs behind her. "*Mami*, your other boy is here." Teresa turned back to me. "She's on vacation, you know."

"I know. I just have these," I said as I held up the bundle of flowers.

Elena came down the flight of stairs from the second floor wearing a snug sweater and powder-puff, fuzzy slippers. She beamed, and her smile comforted me, but I could see the anxiousness in her eyes. "Tere, step back. Let him in," she said.

"*Bienvenido al* Bronx," Teresa said sarcastically.

I squeezed past her, and Elena quickly embraced me.

She held me for a while. *"M'ijo."* I could feel Teresa staring at my back. I began to release myself, but Elena hugged tighter. She only let go after Teresa pushed by us.

Elena tut-tutted and drew me by the arm into the living room. The smell of sizzling onions was in the air. The crooner's song ended, and a more bubbly merengue began as I surveyed the couch, the armchair, and the tall, free-standing birdcage by the stereo cabinet. A small forest of plants surrounded the front window that looked down onto the street. A large painting of Mother Mary hung on the wall over the armchair. The gold disk of her halo glimmered faintly. Although her head was humbly pitched down, her eyes looked askance, as if she peered out into the house. Round and bright, they followed me around the room.

"What a surprise," Elena said. She was nervous. "Are you here alone?"

"Yes."

"I don't know what to say."

"How about 'Why are you here?'" Teresa said as she leaned against the doorway to the kitchen.

I handed Elena the oversized bunch of flowers. "Happy holidays," I said. *"Feliz Navidad.* I never gave you a present."

Elena gripped the hem of her sweater. "What a surprise," she said again. *"Gracias. Gracias."* Her hair was down too, and it made her look younger. "I wouldn't have expected you to give me anything."

"And come to our home to do it," Teresa added.

I nodded and wished I had thought of something more to say when I arrived, something to whisk away their questions. I had the urge to speak only in facts. *This is a birdcage. There are two birds. Yes, one is blue and one is yellow.*

"Tere," Elena said, handing her my flowers. "Find a place for these."

"Did you buy the place out?" Teresa asked me, but she took the flowers and stepped into the kitchen.

She banged around the cupboards as Elena walked me to the couch and sat me down. *"M'ijo,"* she said with a sad smile, "I'm happy to see you." She hugged me again and then sat back. "Why didn't you call to tell me you were coming? Your mother . . . ," she began, but she trailed off. She sighed and looked toward the front window, a dark wall now, speckled only with a few dots of light from other windows down the hill and the faint orange glow from the streetlamp. "I am confused," Elena said.

"Me too," I said softly. I wanted to lean on her again but wondered how weird it would be to continue doing that in her house. We were quiet for a moment, like we were watching TV together up in my bedroom, eating dinner on little folding tables. Elena grabbed my hand and patted it gently. There was something so warm about Elena's house, I felt snowed in, and when Teresa marched back in I could have pictured her carrying two steaming mugs of hot chocolate, not the vase cramped and bursting with my flowers.

Teresa set it on the coffee table and looked at her mother.

"No boy ever came here to give me flowers," she said with her hand on her hip. Elena smiled up at her. "Caz," Teresa went on, "that boy wouldn't know where to buy flowers even though he lives right next to the store."

"Aidan is not Caz," Elena said.

"Don't I know," Teresa said. "I've heard how wonderful you are," she said to me.

Elena had told me about Teresa's successes at St. Catherine's too, but watching her rock her hips as she spoke with me, I wanted to talk to her, but I didn't know how. I'd never known how to talk to girls, no matter how much I wanted to. I liked girls, didn't I? That's what I'd always told myself, but who the hell had I been with Father Greg? Was that me too? I felt dizzy and rested my head against the back of the couch.

"Okay," Elena said. She stood and wiped her hands down her hips. "Tere, go add another place at the dinner table."

"You're staying for dinner?" Teresa asked me.

"Yes," Elena answered. She snapped her fingers, and Tere went back to the kitchen. "*M'ijo*," she said softly to me, "this is not okay. How did you get down here?"

"Thanks for letting me stay for dinner."

"What is your mother going to say?"

"Please don't make me leave."

"No," she said as she pulled me close. "I'm happy you came to me."

My head sank into her. The edge of her sweater's neckline itched at my eye. "I'm sorry," I said. I shook out a few tears and held back everything else I could.

Voices mumbled on the stoop, and the screen door wheezed open. I broke from Elena's embrace so quickly, I startled her. She still held my hand in her lap when Candido let his younger child, Mateo, run into the room. Mateo bounced a basketball once. "Hey!" Candido shouted after him. They both stopped and looked at me. Mateo backed up and pressed into his father's jeans.

"We have a guest," Candido said, glancing from me to Elena.

Elena walked over to her husband and kissed him on the lips. "There's room for one more," she said in English.

Candido nodded. "Why is he here?" he asked in Spanish. "What's wrong?"

"He speaks Spanish," she replied.

"I forgot," Candido said. He smiled. "*Lo siento*," he said to me. He took his time hanging up his leather jacket.

"Aren't you still on vacation?" Mateo asked Elena.

Elena shushed Mateo and pushed him forward. "This is the boy whose family I work for," she said.

"I know," Mateo said.

Candido came up behind him, and I stood to take his hand. "I've heard a lot about you," Candido said. He had a belly that spilled over his belt, but he was taller than I had pictured him, and he made the room seem smaller and more cramped. He and Elena exchanged glances. "Welcome to our home," he added. He excused himself and took Mateo upstairs to wash before dinner. Elena patted my shoulder and followed them.

I dropped back onto the couch and stared at the ceiling, not wanting to bring my head back down and make eye contact with Mother Mary. I closed my eyes and listened to Candido's and Elena's voices upstairs. It was hard to hear exactly what they were saying, especially with the radio playing a few feet away from me, but I didn't have to hear the words, I only had to hear their chatter to know they were used to talking over each other and listening at the same time. I heard my name, but it didn't concern me. I was at Elena's house, and without Mother and Old Donovan around it was peaceful.

"Hey," Teresa said. She hovered next to me, behind the couch. "Don't fall asleep. You just got here." She shook my shoulder.

"What's for dinner?" I asked.

"Not what she cooks at your house." She came around the couch and sat down next to me.

"She makes this chicken, red bean, and rice dish sometimes," I said. "If it's just me and her for dinner. I love it."

"You mean, like, her Dominican food?"

"Yeah, I guess."

"I don't know it," Teresa said, playing with the little gold cross on her necklace.

"Does she teach you any recipes?"

"Irish stew. Lasagna. Soups and chili. You know, stuff we can pick at all week."

"Oh, yeah."

"But one time she showed me how to make *lengua picante*, and *lambí guisado*."

"Those sound cool," I said, hoping I could get out of this conversation. "She never made those at my house."

"Yeah, I'm just playing," she said. "She never made those here, either."

I laughed uneasily.

"But my friends love coming here to eat. We'll do our homework, and then I'll heat up some leftovers. They all know how good a cook she is."

"She could work in a restaurant."

"Yeah, she should." Teresa's glare challenged me.

I nodded in agreement. There had been plenty of nights growing up I had fantasized that Elena was my actual mother. I had come to envy Teresa and Mateo, thinking they were lucky to have such a devoted and caring mother, but as Teresa stuck her nose down into one of the bunches of flowers, I wondered if she felt differently about Elena. She'd seen her mother less than I had, for God's sake.

"These must have been crazy expensive," she said sullenly.

It had been the wrong gift to the wrong person. It frightened me to realize how much I knew about her mother and that there was no way for me to share it with her. It was easier to pretend all my memories with Elena didn't exist. Teresa turned the vase in a circle.

"I should have gotten more," I said. "I should have gotten some for you, too."

"Oh my God, did you just say that?" She laughed and shook her head. "Damn, I thought you were supposed to be shy." She smiled as if she knew something I didn't and was waiting for me to catch on. Maybe it was just like her laugh, an easy openness that said something like, *Hey, buddy. Relax already. Tranquilo.* She put her hand down on my thigh and smiled. "Why don't you help me fill the water glasses for dinner?"

"Yeah, of course," I said, standing up quickly. I was as surprised as she was that I had said what I had said. It felt good, though, and safe, but I wanted to get busy doing something before I blew it and said something stupid. In the kitchen, she handed me the glasses and talked about her classes at St. Catherine's. It was good to be a senior, she kept saying. Her whole life was going to change in just a few months, and she was excited. She wanted to face it head-on. I was jealous of her breezy confidence: I admired her.

Before we could eat, the Gonsalves family and I gripped hands around the table, the hot food only a foot away, tempting us. My hands were in Elena's and Teresa's. The food was blessed, and God was thanked that I could join them. I hazarded a blink and opened my eyes: Steam rose off the plates in the dim air, wavering to the incantatory tone of Candido's voice, thanking the Lord for his guidance and his strength. I couldn't follow along with Candido, because I had my own prayer, and although they usually felt so empty, just chants to beat away the pain, I had something I wanted to shout: *Christ, leave me alone with this family.* I closed my eyes again as Candido ended the prayer. *"En el nombre del Padre, del Hijo, y del Espíritu Santo,* amen."

Elena sat between her boys, Mateo to her right and me to her left. She cut her meat delicately, taking her time, as Candido talked to his children. She occasionally offered some advice, but she mostly ate in silence, smiling, watching Candido and Mateo slap hands as they talked basketball. Candido winked at Elena occasionally, when she hushed him.

"You should have had that game against St. Mike's. Coach Carney's an idiot."

"Candi," Elena scolded.

"What's that lesson you were getting at before, *Papi?*" Teresa asked. "Play a team sport to learn how to be indignant?"

Candido stuffed a forkful in his mouth and chomped it slowly. *"Mira, la pequeña maestra.* You can add something to this conversation after you've come and watched one of your brother's games."

Teresa sighed with what seemed habitual melodrama. "Jesus Christ, *Papi.* Always with the guilt."

"Eh! Watch your mouth," Candido said in Spanish. "There are rules in this house."

Elena reached across the table in front of me and touched her daughter's arm. "Please. Listen to your father," Elena said in Spanish.

Teresa got up to get more water for the table. "Whoa," Candido boomed as he leaned back in his chair. "She lifts a finger!" She bumped him with her hip as she walked past him to the sink. He laughed.

When we were finished eating, Elena grabbed my plate and stacked it on top of hers. Candido leaned back in his chair, threw his napkin on the table, and picked his teeth with his tongue. Before Elena could reach for the others, I stood and asked if I could clear the plates. I couldn't stand the thought of Elena slipping on her rubber gloves in her own house. Everything seemed upside down anyway. Why couldn't I do the damn dishes for once? But Elena waved me off. "Please," I said. "I want to. I want to do something."

Candido sniffed.

"There's no need," Elena began, but I ignored her. I stacked the rest of the plates and carried them over to the sink.

The phone rang. "Don't anybody answer it," Candido said. "We're still eating. We haven't had dessert."

Elena hung her head and sighed. The answering machine picked up after four rings. I snapped the rubber gloves over my hands as the message began. "Elena? It's Father Dooley again. I'm worried now. Have you still not seen him? He's still missing. Please call me as soon as you get this. I'm with Gwen. She is about to call the police. Please, call me."

My back was to the rest of the room, and I couldn't bring myself to turn around. I just stood against the sink, gripping the edge.

"What the hell is going on?" Teresa asked. She stepped back toward the table.

"This is what I was talking about," Candido said. "I said something was seriously wrong." His chair squeaked against the floor as he pushed it back and stood. "What did he mean, *again*? Again what?" His voice grew louder. "You knew about this?"

Elena shook her head. "I'm sorry. He wasn't here when Father Dooley called before. Then he came." She wiped at her face. "He came to me."

"Eh, *Mami*?" Teresa said. "You knew and kept it a secret from us? What?" She pushed my shoulder. "You think you can buy my *mami*, rich boy? Come in here with your flowers and your mopey-ass face. Go get your own *mami*, eh, rich boy." She hit me again.

"Tere!" Elena yelled, but Candido stepped over and grabbed Teresa's arm. "Okay, okay. That's enough," he said without much force. He stepped between us and pointed at me. "Are you bringing trouble into my home?"

"Please," Elena said. "Please. He hasn't done anything," she said in Spanish. "He wouldn't."

"You don't know that," Candido said.

"Yes I do!" Elena yelled back. "Yes I do." She stepped between me and Candido. When I turned around, he reached beside her and grabbed the cordless from the wall. "He hasn't done anything," Elena pleaded. "It's his parents. I've told you before. Look at him. What could he do?" She reached for the phone. "Let me call Mrs. Donovan."

"Yes, you will," Candido said. "And the priest."

He handed the phone to Elena, and she stared at it absently for a moment. Then she turned to me and lifted her hand to my cheek. "*M'ijo.* It's okay. It's okay. You'll be okay."

I slumped over her, letting her embrace me. Her kids stared at me. *Don't worry,* I wanted to tell them, *she has enough for all of us,* as if I knew and as if that wasn't an insult.

Elena called, and paced by the sink as she spoke on the phone. We could all hear Mother's shrill invectives screaming through the earpiece. "No, ma'am," Elena got out occasionally.

Elena put the phone out to me, but I didn't want to take it. I held it in my hands and looked down at it. "Honey?" Mother squeaked across the distance. "Honey?" I put the phone to my ear. "Are you safe?"

"I'm with Elena."

"I know that, but, honey, are you safe?" Her voice was raw. "Are you okay?"

"Of course," I said. "I'm with Elena."

"I know. I know. You're with Elena now, but you were missing!"

"No. I left."

"Can you imagine what I was thinking? Father Dooley has offered to come down to pick you up. I don't think I can drive—the state I'm in." I didn't know what to say. I could hear Mother sniffling.

"Father Dooley?"

"I'm grateful. He has been so kind. I didn't realize how much I needed someone until he was here." She breathed deeply. "I'm relieved." She continued more calmly. "I'm glad you'll be coming home."

I put Elena back on the phone. After she hung up, she went straight to Candido, and he wrapped her in his arms. "I was wrong," she told him. "Please forgive me. I should have said something right away."

"You don't need this," he said. "You never needed this."

"I don't understand," I choked. "She barely noticed that I was gone. She probably didn't care."

Elena pushed out of Candido's embrace. "She misses you," she said to me.

"Why now?" I asked. "When has she ever missed me?"

"You came here. You left and you came right here, to me. She misses you, *m'ijo*. I know. Father Dooley will come pick you up," she added. "He's driving down now."

Candido shook his head. "God is looking out for you," he said to me. "Always."

I think he meant to inspire me, as if that invisible, omni-present eye was protective, but I saw Father Greg's eyes, bloodshot from scotch, bleary with pain and rage. "No," I said. "No, I'll take the train. I'll call for a car. I don't want to go back with him. Please."

"I'm doing what he asked me," Elena said. "You'll leave with him. You need help."

"I can't. I don't want to."

"Enough," Candido interrupted me. "Stop yelling. You don't tell her what to do in this house." He stepped to me and grabbed my arm. "You came to my house. And in my house, you will do by my rules." He shook me and then calmed himself. He let go. "We will do as the priest has asked us, and you will go home with him tonight."

A cold emptiness opened in my stomach and crept through my body. I rocked in place for a moment, and I heard my name but didn't know from where. It sounded familiar, as if Father Greg was in the room with us, saying my name, calling me to him.

Elena directed Candido to take Mateo upstairs, and she allowed me to help her with the rest of the dishes. Teresa hovered in the doorway, leaning on the molding. "You can't be that bad," she said. "You're, like, barely in the room. You're like a ghost. How could you do anything that bad?"

"Tere! Upstairs. Now. Leave us alone." Teresa caught the fright in her mother's voice and obeyed. She stormed upstairs. A door slammed.

"I'm sorry," I finally said. "I didn't know where else to go. I had to leave."

Elena held a dish under the water for too long, staring at it. "Your mother is very upset." She shook her head. She turned off the water and passed me the last dish. "Your mother? She's not just upset with you, *m'ijo*," she said. "With me, too."

"I'm sorry," I said again. "I thought it would be all right."

"It is," Elena said. "With me." She mustered a smile, but one that wasn't genuine. It was imported from some dying expression I might see on one of my teacher's faces at CDA, or maybe one that a guest at Mother's parties might have offered me before she disappeared into the ever-circulating crowd.

"Please," I said. "What if I didn't go home?"

"No. You have to go home."

She led me into the living room and directed me to sit on the sofa. She stood by the foot of the stairs for a while, looking up to where she had banished the family. She seemed to be standing guard, or at least like that was what she wanted to be doing but she wasn't sure who needed protection from whom. I lolled my head on the back of the sofa and stared at the ceiling and at the lumps and cracks in the paint, the touches of age and natural decay. Through the window, a streetlight below the house flickered, then went out. I felt Elena's eyes on me, and Mary's, too, casting down from the wall.

Upstairs, Mateo whined and complained that he didn't want to go to bed, but Candido had him quiet in less than a minute. He didn't yell at his son, but there was something resolute and demanding of respect in his voice. I don't think Candido hated me as much as he wondered why it was too easy for me to bust up his family's life. I wanted to tell him that I hadn't tried to. If I'd had anywhere else to go, I wouldn't have come into his house like a criminal, or I wouldn't have come to New York, but what else wouldn't I have done? Isn't it crazy to keep walking back in time and asking yourself to correct this choice and that choice? You could probably walk yourself all the way back to the beginning and say, *Fuck it, why get involved with this mess in the first place—look what's ahead?*

When Father Dooley arrived, we heard his car doing a three-point turn. Elena walked me down the long staircase to the street. "We'll come to you, Father!" she shouted. He stood motionless beside the car, stooped forward onto his cane. The streetlight had come back on but it flickered and went out again. I could only make out his silhouette as his coat ruffled slightly in the breeze. I wanted to take the stairs two at a time and bust down the street to the elevated train. I couldn't see into the car, and I wondered if Father Greg had come too and, if they were together, what they would do to me. That familiar sense of inevitability swept through me, that sense that I was being guided down the stairs into the deeper darkness to a place where I had no control.

"God will help you," Elena said as she brought me down the last few steps and ushered me ahead of her. "He will take care of you. Father Dooley will help you. You need him, *m'ijo*."

Father Dooley stepped toward us and glared suspiciously. "Thank you," he said to Elena. He stuck out his hand to shake hers, and he relaxed a little when she took it and spoke to him warmly. There was reverence in her voice, and it pleased him.

"Please, Father," she said, "don't be upset with him."

"He gave his mother quite a scare," he said. "As I'm sure you can understand."

"Yes, of course, Father."

He urged me into the passenger seat, but before he could close the door, she pleaded with him again. "But, Father, you understand too, right? No one is to blame here. No one."

He knew quite well that Elena had been the one to urge me to look for a job at Most Precious Blood. He knew a deeply committed Catholic when he met one. "We are all partly to blame, Elena, are we not? Now and always. God knows and God will do the forgiving. Let's pray for His guidance as we think about all this." He turned to me, and with confidence he added, "You, too, Aidan."

Elena nodded. Before she could say more, Father Dooley continued, "I'm to remind you what you discussed with Mrs. Donovan on the phone. Let her call you before you head back up."

"Yes, Father."

"She needs some time alone with her family."

"I understand, Father."

Father Dooley nodded, and I didn't like the condescension in his voice. "Hey," I said. "Don't take it out on her. She didn't do anything!"

Father Dooley smiled. "Please, Aidan. No one's yelling. Elena understands. Isn't that right?" he asked over his shoulder.

"Yes, Father." She backed up and then hesitated before retreating up her stairs. "*M'ijo*," she said. "I'm glad you are okay. You will be."

She stood her ground for a moment, but Father Dooley said good-bye and sent her back up the stairs. Her overcoat came down so close to her heels, it was as if she floated up the steps. She climbed and climbed and didn't look back. Father Dooley started the engine, and the streetlight flickered again and came back on, and it was impossible to see her behind it.

Father Dooley navigated the streets of the southwest Bronx and found his way to Route 95 quickly. As soon as we were on the highway he relaxed. His confidence scared me. He didn't look at me. He kept his pale, deeply wrinkled face pointed ahead. Nausea crept over me, and I cracked the window. The breeze filled the car with welcome noise. When I put my head against the window, I could feel my pulse thumping in my temple. At least he'd come alone.

"We expected you'd go there," he said after some time. "She was the first person we called. I'm surprised she didn't call us as soon as you arrived. She should've known better." He glanced at me. "I'm glad, however, that we can straighten this all out."

"Are you taking me to Most Precious Blood?"

"Absolutely not," he snapped. "I'm taking you to your mother. Do you have any idea how she feels right now?"

"Did she call you?"

He took a breath and waited. "No. I called her, and we discovered you were missing."

"Yeah." I sniffed. "'Discovered.'"

He breathed through his nose and waited. "You hadn't shown up for work today, remember? You were expected at work, so I called to check on you. She was terrified. I offered to help. Why go to the police? Why start up the gossip?" He glanced at me again and continued with emphasis, "Especially after your father left home, Aidan. Your mother didn't need more of it. I could help. And with discretion, you understand."

We passed effortlessly through the city limits up into a greener stretch of highway. I listened to the rhythm of the tires on the pavement. "I'd like for us to come to an understanding," Father Dooley finally said.

My nausea worsened. Sweat stuck to me everywhere. "I've straightened things out at Most Precious Blood. Please listen to me, Aidan," Father Dooley said, slowing down. I looked out the window as we drove past a Mobil station along the highway, but I knew he glanced at me occasionally. "This was quite an act. Running down here. I can appreciate the pressures you're dealing with. It's too much for a young man. Too much. I want to help alleviate some of it. What I'm saying is, don't worry about coming to work on the campaign anymore. You've done enough."

"What?"

"There's no need for you to come back to work, Aidan. Don't even come to Mass for a while. Take a break. Please." Father Dooley kept his eyes fixed on the light traffic and waited for me to respond. The silence between us grew. "Aidan, please talk to me. I'd like us to work through this. You can trust me." His voice became more agitated. "Now, wait. Let's be clear. Are you hearing me? I'm telling you all that is behind you. I'm trying to reassure you, Aidan, and I want to know you understand that. It's time to move on."

"Did you talk to him about it?"

"Aidan," Father Dooley snapped, "do not come to Most Precious Blood anymore. Do you understand?" He lowered his voice. "You're a bright young man with a future ahead of you. I don't want anyone to take that away."

We pulled off the interstate. The smaller highway wasn't as removed from the suburban neighborhoods, and I watched the darkened houses and businesses go by. It wasn't long before we were on my side of town.

"Your mother is very fragile right now," Father Dooley

said. "She is distraught. She's trying to rebuild your lives. As I understand it, your father's moved to Europe permanently." He paused and glanced at me. "Aidan," he continued, "I know you want to do what is right for everyone here. I want you to listen to me. I want you to search deep in your heart and ask yourself if you want to hurt anyone. What I mean is, that can be avoided. You and I, we can talk about this."

"But you want me to be quiet."

"I'm trying to get you to think about the larger picture. There are consequences to everything."

"Yes. I understand," I said with more volume than I intended. "I understand consequences."

Father Dooley looked at me coolly. "I don't think you do, Aidan. There are consequences in this for you, too."

The winding road had unlit patches between the street-lights, and the interior of the car lit up and darkened as we curled around the corners. I couldn't be sure, but I thought I saw Father Dooley smile. He turned onto my street, the green gate swung open, and he pulled up the driveway.

"I'd like to know I can trust you, Aidan," he said when the car came to a stop. "We've come to an understanding, right? Tell me I can trust you."

"You can't," I said. "Because I can't."

I opened my door. Mother came out to the stoop hugging herself, and she didn't have a drink in hand, which surprised me at first. I moved toward her and left Father Dooley muttering behind me. He had misunderstood me. I didn't want to look back either. If I no longer spoke about Father Greg, maybe he would disappear and, with him, the parts of myself I didn't understand.

Mother came out into the driveway to meet me and pulled me close into a tight hug. She said nothing and simply squeezed. She wore no makeup, and while she smelled of cigarettes, I couldn't smell any booze. Instead, there was a sweet hint of diet soda on her lips when she kissed me. She thanked Father Dooley over my shoulder and told him we'd call him tomorrow. Once we were inside and she'd closed the door behind us, she put both hands on my face. Her eyes were wet and fatigued. "For God's sake. Do you have any idea what I have been going through?" She stepped back, wiped her eyes, and led me into the living room.

"You have no idea what I started thinking," she said. "I thought you might be dead." She stared at the floor beyond me as she spoke. "I thought you were going to work, but Father Dooley called and said you never showed up. I thought you were up in bed. Can you imagine?" She gripped the belt of her robe. Her tiny knuckles yellowed against her pale skin as she squeezed. "He asked me to bring you to the phone. He was upset. Your door was open, and when I looked in, I realized you hadn't been there. Do you know how terrified I was? Where were you, I kept thinking. And I had no idea. I had no idea. Who could I call? Father Dooley was still on the line. You didn't go to work. More than a day had passed. Was it two days? I had no idea where you had been, where you might have gone. I didn't know what to do. Father Dooley came over right away."

"Father Dooley came here? What did he say?"

"She was the first person he called, you know—Elena. The very first person. Can you imagine the embarrassment? What were you doing down there? Why didn't you tell me?" She breathed hard. She chewed on her lip and stared straight at the floor by my feet. "I didn't even know you were gone," she said more softly. "Honestly. Can you imagine how I felt?"

Father Dooley and Father Greg were still telling people I hadn't been to Most Precious Blood. They flat-out lied to Mother. Father Greg was as scared as I was.

Mother put her arms around me. She rocked us gently. "Don't you ever leave me again," she said into my shoulder. "You can't leave too."

"I'm home now," I said. That was all she wanted to know, and it was the easiest fact I could share. That seemed to be all anyone desired—a sense of hard and fast certainty. It felt good to finally be the one to provide it.

CHAPTER 6

For the next couple of days, Mother and I sat in her bed watching movies like *It's a Wonderful Life*, *Mr. Smith Goes to Washington*, and *Pocketful of Miracles*, and if the predictability and dependability of those sweetly upbeat endings aren't a sedative, then I don't know what is. After watching a couple in a row, you get the feeling that everything you want in life is easier to attain than you ever realized, like it's on sale at Macy's and the only trouble is getting down to Thirty-Fourth Street before your dreams are sold out. My new life, however, wasn't going to start with a slip-sliding run down Main Street, waving my hat, letting everyone at the coffee shop and the post office know that I was gloriously in love with myself. I still had the scar on my hand I couldn't wipe away, and Father Greg's voice still spoke in my head.

On Sunday, I stayed in bed for a while listening to the

news. America was winning the war on terror; Karzai was our man in Kabul. Frank Capra would have been proud; promises were made that order would be restored soon. When I made my way downstairs to the kitchen, it was almost noon. I found the surface of the butcher block scattered with flour. A bottle of vanilla extract stood next to a large mixing bowl, and a fat, pristine cookbook was spread open near the edge. Mother stood over a pan, flicking a wooden ladle to the beat of the synthesized eighties music playing over the stereo system. A subtle bounce traveled from her hips to her feet. "I have some errands to do today, but I didn't want to take off before you got up."

"What are you doing?"

"Waiting for them to bubble. Once they bubble, they're ready to be flipped."

"No. I mean you're making pancakes."

"I like making breakfast."

"But usually in a blender."

She flicked her wooden ladle toward me. "Enough. You got up late. You don't get to make fun of me. I've done my forty-five on the elliptical and made my shake, thank you very much. I'm making these for you."

Mother had one of the flapjacks too, but without butter or syrup. She sat across from me at the butcher block, sipping the mossy dregs of her health shake, and told me more about her business plans. Cindy had suggested it at the Christmas party, and Mother had taken it seriously.

"A body in motion stays in motion," Mother said. Simple law of physics. Start marching forward and don't look back. Cindy's suggestion was for Mother to start her own event-planning business, and since she'd heard it, Mother hadn't looked back. Only a week had passed, and she was already wrestling with the paperwork.

"Nobody throws a party like you," I said to her.

"It's exciting, isn't it?" There was a hint of mania behind her eyes as she continued, but she did have a plan, and I admired her determination to create a new life. Cindy had started her own art gallery years ago, and now that it was a thriving business in town, she had the right friends to help Mother get organized and begin. Mother already had a list of clients to approach, opportunities to pursue, and locations for a small storefront. "I couldn't possibly work out of the home. It'll be my business. I'm not going to hide from everyone. I'm going to plan the parties everyone attends, and they don't even have to be at my house."

"It's all happening so quickly," I said.

"It's happening, Aidan. And I'm going to take care of this family."

Maybe, I thought, but it would be easier when Elena came back too. She could help bolster Mother's new pioneering spirit, or at least help me find a way to match it. I wanted a little of Mother's courage and enthusiasm, but I didn't know how to do it alone.

Mother made a number of phone calls, and by the

time she was finished it was already late afternoon. She found me in my bedroom reading. "I have to get moving or I'll never get out of here," she said. "Are you coming with me?"

"I should finish some homework. I guess I have a job to do too. Break a leg. You'll be great," I added.

Mother grinned. She came over to the armchair and hugged me. "Thank you," she said softly.

The doorbell interrupted us. Mother went down to the foyer to open it, and I followed more slowly. The light was already beginning to fade outside, but through the narrow window beside the front door I saw the powder blue Lincoln Town Car parked by the front stoop, and I began to shake. The broken glass was in my hands again. His breath was hot and close and rank beside me. I braced myself against the banister of the grand staircase and tried to hold still, drifting inward as if I were suddenly watching what was happening in front of me on TV, not there in the room with me being a part of it, too. Mother opened the door, leaned back, and gave him a canned, happy greeting. His voice preceded him into the house, and it held me firmly. Mother ushered him in and beckoned me to come greet him as well.

I couldn't drag myself any closer. Instead, he came to me and offered me a cold handshake. He squeezed quickly and let go. The three of us stood together near the table in the foyer, and it reminded me of being at the party together and how long ago that seemed.

"I missed you at Mass today," Father Greg said. His voice moved slowly within me.

"I'm sorry," I said automatically.

"No." Father Greg laughed. "I was speaking to your mother, Aidan. I thought she might come. It's been a hard holiday season, hasn't it, Gwen? I thought you and Father Dooley discussed that."

Mother nodded. "Thank you for your concern."

"Of course," Father Greg said. He fidgeted and laughed a little nervously. "Here's one of my favorite families, and Frank's doing all the consoling. I didn't want you to think I was neglecting you. I wanted you to know my concern too. I'm here to help."

"You're too kind, Father."

"No, no. It's my responsibility. I'm always here to support you. Both of you. You know that. I don't mean this with any disrespect, but sometimes when we have all that we need, materially speaking, we forget to tend our spiritual and emotional gardens. Sometimes we still need to be cared for in ways we don't fully understand. This isn't a lecture, Gwen," he quickly added. He put his hand on her shoulder. "We're part of a community. You can let yourself be helped." He laughed, genuinely and confidently. "We've been doing it for nearly two thousand years. We have a little practice."

"Again," Mother said, "thank you. But Aidan and I needed a little family time." She put her arm around me. "Didn't we?"

"I'm glad to hear it," he said. He nodded and reflected for a moment. I wanted Mother to keep talking, to steer the conversation up and away, back to her business, anything to push him out the door and out of the house. I was too frightened to speak, and my palm was still clammy from our brief handshake. But Father Greg spoke. "Gwen," he said, "as Aidan knows, we are all one family at Most Precious Blood. You have always been a generous person. Allow yourself some of the generosity of others. You'd be surprised how freeing it feels." He reached out to me and closed his hand over my shoulder tightly. I felt it in my stomach. "You want to support your mother, right? And you will. I know you will. But you'll need support too, Aidan. We're the place for that, aren't we?"

My insides shook violently, and I wanted to sit down. I leaned on the marble tabletop for support, but Mother held herself perfectly still. She only blinked as Father Greg spoke to her. She swept one foot in front of her and planted it firmly. "Why, Father, that's exactly what we have been talking about all day. While we've been here. At home."

Father Greg drew back. "I'm only offering advice," he said to Mother. "I'm glad to find you both doing so well."

"Yes," Mother continued. "And thanks for your advice. However, there are many things I have to do today. I'm sorry to rush you."

"No, of course," Father Greg said. "Of course." He looked at me. "I haven't seen Aidan at work, though, for a while. There are some things we should touch base about.

Shouldn't we, Aidan? Maybe you'll come down to the rectory?"

They both stared at me for a moment, but it was Mother I looked at, even though I spoke to Father Greg. "Actually, I was talking to my friends," I said slowly. "There are some projects at school I'd like to get involved with." Sweat ran down my back. I wiped my hands on my pants. "I don't think I'll be coming back to work at Most Precious Blood. Besides, my mother might need a hand with her new business, and I want to be able to help her if she needs it."

Father Greg cocked a half smile. "If that's the case, I'd like your help tying up some loose ends, then. Can we discuss it more back at the office?"

"I need to get my homework done before going back to school," I said. "I'm back at CDA on Wednesday."

"As he should," Mother said. "I'm glad."

"Well, I see. Fine. But then there's another matter I'd like to discuss with you," Father Greg said to her. "Especially if Aidan isn't coming back to work. And since Jack isn't around, I suppose I need to be speaking with you. It's the matter of your family's gift this year."

Mother sucked in a breath and straightened. Father Greg put up his hands defensively. "No, I don't mean right now, Gwen. I only mention it because Jack usually prefers to get it on the books before year's end. Tax purposes. You understand. Maybe this is something useful for you, too, when thinking about your new business?"

Mother stared him down. "I understand perfectly well. I'll be making the decisions now, Father. I'm sorry, but you'll have to excuse us. It's getting late."

"I'm glad to see you moving forward with such determination, Gwen." Father Greg smiled. "A role model."

We were all cordial and pleasant as we said our good-byes, and I even mustered something that resembled a smile as I shook Father Greg's hand again. It was so familiar; I almost wanted to lean in for a hug. How many times had I allowed myself to fall into his embrace? I felt sick and left for the bathroom before he'd closed the door behind him.

Whatever whiff of confidence I'd had while he'd been there evaporated when Mother left. It was dark out when I watched her car disappear down the street, and although I went up to my bedroom, in my mind I was back in Father Greg's office as he quoted Matthew 28:20: *"And I will be with you always to the end of age."* Then he was up and around his desk, perched on the edge of it, leaning forward, his breath close to me. He reminded me that God worked through him and that he would in no way abandon me, and that love, like faith, is being sure of what we hope for. I believed I was loved.

I still had the throbbing wish that things hadn't changed—that we were still at the Christmas party and he was leading me outside and there was no one else around and he was making me laugh and giving me advice so I wouldn't hate Old Donovan or Mother, and advice to help me cope with my new friends—and even more, a wish that I'd never seen him with James, and after that, that I'd never wiped my blood on his shirt. Why did I have to accept the truth that I'd been a part of it all too? When I thought of Father Greg now, I felt his hands on my arms, pulling me closer, bruising me in a squeeze. There was so much more. The truth doesn't always have to get smashed into us for us to recognize it, does it?

I stared at my bedroom walls and hoped something would jump to life. I wanted the sheets of computer paper stacked up on my desk to lift and spin up in the air, a voice to emerge from within the whirling dervish and speak to me, tell me what to do, for all the books to fall off my shelves and highlighted passages to reveal themselves to me as they spread out on the floor. It was a kind of prayer, I think, or an all-out begging, for words to find me—the words I knew I needed to deliver to Mother. But they never appeared. Instead, I could only see the monster she'd see me as, if I told her, and I wanted the strength to avoid that for both of us.

I sat in my reading chair and cried, until I pictured Mother onstage, Odette in *Swan Lake*, the glistening white costume, legs intertwined, both feet balanced on her toes, prepared for her aggressive pointe-shoe attack across the stage. She seemed so much stronger to me now. I could see the ferocity in her eyes. *They were my eyes too,* I thought, and like her, I would have to push forward.

CHAPTER 7

Mother and I prepared separately for New Year's. Her countdown began sometime in the early afternoon as she modeled a number of outfits and asked my opinion. A friend of hers had planned a night down in the city. She had reserved two spots at a cocktail bar, called in a favor to get a table at a small Italian restaurant I'd never heard of, and accepted invitations for the two of them to attend a party thrown by one of Mother's former dance colleagues in an apartment on Seventy-Second Street with views over the park. Mother's anticipation of their plans derailed her decision-making abilities. She showed me formal gowns I'd never seen her wear. She paraded a small army of boots, pumps, flats, and heels that looked impossible to walk in, although she marched back and forth across the balcony above the foyer with renewed confidence. *Fuck. You!* the heels shouted, as if they were calling all the way across the Atlantic to Old Donovan.

"Is this me?" Mother asked as she walked past me.

"Who do you want to be?"

"Just like that." She laughed. "I get to choose, don't I?"

They took a car to the city and were gone shortly after dark. Instead of deciding how to present myself, I spent my time figuring out which small bottles of liquor to take from Old Donovan's bar, which cigars to take from his humidor, and how to fit them all in the pockets of my coat with the last of my Adderall and whichever other pills I found in Mother's cabinet without looking like a kleptomaniac clown waddling around a psychotic circus. Loaded down, I sat on the stoop smoking one of Mother's cigarettes and waited for Mark to pick me up.

I almost thought Mark wasn't going to show up, but eventually his Audi sped up the driveway and hugged the curve around to the front of the house. The music was loud in the car. He opened the passenger door. "Do you mind putting that out?" he said, pointing to the cigarette. "It's supposed to be my car, but it isn't, if you know what I mean." I flicked it away and got in. He didn't say much as we took off through town, only asked if I'd mind making a pit stop before heading to the party. He left the music blasting, and we cruised over by the golf course and parked on a spur just off the bridge. It was a dirt lane leading down to a spit along the river that was just large enough to be a put-in for a rowboat. Mark cut the engine. We got out and leaned back against the front grille, surveying the river as it emptied into the harbor. He lit a thin joint and nursed it to life.

"Dude," he said. "I apologize for my mood. I was a little fucked off earlier. God was pronouncing his commandments today. I can't even get in my own car without thinking he's in there watching me sometimes, following me everywhere with that fat fucking frown of his."

"God?"

"My old man. He thinks he is. He expects us all to obey his every breath."

"That sounds familiar," I said. I inhaled and held it for a moment before exhaling, like I'd seen him do earlier. "Only, mine is gone for good now."

"You're lucky, then."

"Maybe," I said.

Once Mark and I had finished the joint by the river, we were back in the car and on the way to the party. Feingold's place was a couple of towns up the coast and only a few blocks from the ocean. The houses in his neighborhood were nearly as large as mine, but they were stacked more closely together. The lights were out in most of them, but Feingold's illuminated the neighborhood. It sat on a hill, and cars lined both sides of the street and packed the driveway, too. Mark drove past it and parked around the corner, away from the rest of the cars. I didn't notice my leg was bouncing until Mark glanced down at it, and when I stopped I felt the urge welling up in me again quickly. I took a breath. Before we got out, I showed him what I had on me.

"I'm a goddamn pharmaceutical convention tonight," I said. "Do you want anything?"

"Nah, dude," Mark said. "I just smoke pot. It quiets me, in a way." I nodded, but before I put the baggie away he added, "But go for it if it's your thing, man."

"I have Vicodin."

He nodded. "Maybe later."

"This is me," I said, shaking out an Adderall. "It makes me feel prepared."

"Yeah." He was quiet while I crushed the pill on a piece of paper on the dashboard, rolled the sheet into a cone, and did the whole thing in one big bump. Mark nodded his head as if there was still a beat in the car that he was following. I balled the paper up and pocketed it when I finished. "Everything's cool," Mark said when we got out of the car. "Let's just have each other's backs tonight. Never know at these things." We gripped hands in that way that looks like we were about to arm wrestle, and I was relieved Mark was taking me along with him to the party and I didn't have to go alone.

As we climbed the driveway the music and noise grew. On the porch, a group of kids stood around smoking, and Mark introduced me to a couple of seniors from CDA I didn't know. He knew them from the swim team. Mark hit the joint that moved around the crowd, and I bummed a cigarette from someone else. Through the windows on the first floor, I could see people dancing, and more were standing around the windows of the second floor. Mark leaned back against the side of the house, smiled vaguely, and let the conversation roll. He nodded occasionally, as if he knew something we all didn't. I did my best to join in but found myself talking quickly. After another cigarette, I asked Mark if he wanted to go find Josie and Sophie, and we made our way into the crowd.

The rooms were lit by dull lamps with green-, purple-, and yellow-colored bulbs, giving the house the atmosphere of a phosphorescent-lit greenhouse. In the semidarkness, people shouted over the hip-hop blasting from the living room, and some were dancing, writhing with their legs squeezed between someone else's. Plastic cups swayed overhead. The kitchen beyond was slightly brighter, and three guys I didn't know circled the keg and rapped along with the lyrics of the song. One held the tube from the tap in front of his face and shouted at it. Sophie sat on the counter, her big, searching eyes fluttering at two guys who leaned toward her. Her hair was shorter than it had been a few days before, and it made her look older, or at least less innocent. One of them had his hand on her jeans. "They *are* soft," he said as we approached.

She laughed quickly and dismissively. She was backed up against the cupboards, and she held a fake smile. When she saw us, she brightened. "These guys go to my school," she said as an introduction, pointing to us. She kicked forward, jumped off the counter, and threw an arm around each of our necks. "Oh my God, get me out of here," she whispered.

Mark got a hand beneath one leg, I copied him, and we carried her across the kitchen, back to the keg. She held her cup aloft like the queen of Egypt. Eventually, she found a clean one for me, and after we'd filled our cups we ducked back into another large room with a television showing the celebrations in cities across the world. It was just past midnight in Rio de Janeiro, and the streets were packed with colorful revelers. As Sophie caught us up on what we'd missed, I looked around and wondered if this was how everyone else but me spent most of their weekends. Most people were shouting nonsense at one another, but what did it matter? They were all doing it together, weren't they? No one feels lonely at a masquerade, even if no one really knows who each other is. I was at a party. People wanted me there with them—this was real. I felt like Mother, rising and spinning and spinning among the other dancers.

When our cups were empty again, I asked if we should go find Josie. Sophie rolled her eyes. Mark laughed genuinely for the first time since we'd gotten to the party. Sophie looked at him. "She probably needs the company, though, even if she doesn't realize it."

I followed them as they wound through the party on the first floor. We found her on the screened-in porch smoking a cigarette with some other girls from CDA. Her eyes caught the lights of the party inside and glinted like ice in the night.

"Feingold's letting you smoke in here?" Mark asked.

"I don't know. It's kind of like we're outside."

"Where the hell is Feingold?" Mark asked. "Guy's throwing a party, and I haven't even said hello to him yet." He looked around the porch. "I know I sound like a weirdo, but maybe we should find out from him if it's cool to smoke here. I mean, it's his house."

"No, you're right," Josie said. She put out the cigarette in the base of a potted plant, opened the back screen door, and flung the butt into the backyard. "I just bummed one of these to take a break, I guess. The cold air's nice."

"Yeah." Sophie grinned. "Where's Dustin?"

"He took off somewhere. I'm sure he'll come looking for me later." She wrapped arms with Sophie. "Especially after he's had a few more drinks."

Josie suggested we get some more of our own, and we slipped back through the party and went down to the dimly lit basement. Dustin wasn't there, but we did find another bar, and more people mixing noxious cocktails with whatever the hell they wanted. After the four of us huddled around the bar and I fixed everyone except Mark a drink, I felt a hand come down on my back and the deep voice of Craig Riggs over my shoulder.

"Dude," he said quietly. "Nice to see you here. You interested in anything?"

I thought about stepping away, finding somewhere private like we usually did at CDA, like his car in the junior parking lot or in the locker room while everyone else was out at practice, but Riggs tucked a long brown curl behind his ear and leaned closer. "Everybody here cool?" he asked.

I bought another stash of Adderall from Riggs, and still feeling vaguely in charge, I marched the four of us to the bathroom in the basement. Once inside, with the door locked behind us, I broke up what was left of my old stash, ground down a few of the new pills, and laid out the lines on the back of a box of tissues. I rolled up a bill and busted the first rail. The girls followed me, but not Mark. He wouldn't touch it. He took a hit of weed from his bat instead. We each did a second round before we left the room, and I felt a pop and gush stronger than any high I'd had before.

The four of us climbed back up to the living room and discovered that the New Year was about to arrive off the coast of Canada at St. John's. We danced with one another feverishly, grinding our teeth and talking faster than words could make it to our lips. Mark and I traded off dancing with Josie and Sophie, and at one point Mark and I danced together too, an awkward brotherly shuffle in which we clashed forearms like a pair of victorious gladiators. The four of us were sweaty and thirsty, and only after we stepped onto the back porch again, with fresh drinks, did we realize it was nearing midnight in New York.

"I guess I should go find my boyfriend," Josie said. She'd gotten half a pack of cigarettes from a girl who was now throwing up in the backyard behind a bush, and she and I stood on the step below the open door and shared one.

"He should be looking for you," I said.

"Oh my God." Sophie laughed. "The thing is, Josie, Aidan's right."

"You know what?" Mark said. "Fuck Dustin, all right?"

Josie sighed. "Please don't say that."

"No." Mark stepped down to her and held her by the arm. "I'm serious. Fuck him."

Josie smiled and tipped her head to the side. It was the side I never saw in English class, the underside, the track from the chin to the base of the throat. *Why, I wondered, are our most vulnerable spots also the most seductive?* I looked up into the sky, wanting to be made to feel small enough that my memories would be insignificant against the vastness around me. I searched for stars through the light pollution. Mark kept talking.

"Look," he said, "we're all right here. We're having a great time without him. So are you."

From inside the house, people shouted that it was almost time. The television was turned up, and the music turned off. More and more people crowded into the large back room with the TV. I reached over to Josie. "I'm starting over this year," I said. "It's all my mother talks about, but I see her point, I think." She shivered, and I put my arm around her. "Let's all go in," I said. "It's freezing out here."

The room off the porch was jammed with people cheering at the television, yelling back at the crowds that flashed in Times Square. Little jolts from the Adderall still buzzed through me, and I felt confident holding Josie's hand as we walked. She withdrew it as we entered the room, and Mark put his arm over my shoulder instead. Sophie squeezed between us, and we lifted her again so she soared over the bodies. She pumped her arms and rallied the crowd, and I wondered if this was how everyone else felt most of the time and why, although I was a part of it now, hollering at the television with everyone else, I still felt a hole widening within me. I shouted "Three minutes!" with everyone else, and yet that hole was like the tunnel left behind by something burrowing within me. I could picture that thing inside me, a small beast chomping and gnawing its way from my stomach up to my heart. I didn't want to think about Father Greg. I didn't want him anywhere near me. I only wanted crowds and cheers and Josie, Sophie, Mark, and me in a knot of linked arms, but he was inside me, his whisper, *I know you, I'm here for you, Aidan. I'm here.* It was like there were two Aidans at the party: the one stomping and shouting and chanting "New Year, New Year, New Year!" and the one standing quietly in the darkness, listening to Father Greg, being told how the secret makes it meaningful.

Bottles of beer and wine and champagne went around the room. Cups sloshed and banged together prematurely.

There was too much noise, and it took me a few seconds to realize that Mark was shouting at me. "Where the hell is Feingold?" he repeated, and I tried to scan the crowd, but Sophie wavered on our shoulders. We shifted our balance and kept her propped up as people began the countdown. As the ball dropped on television I thought of Mother down in the city, the same energetic recklessness doing a dervish spin through everyone at her party, the same hope and resolution repeating in her as was repeating in me: *Please please please, everybody, see the cheer. Nobody notice anything else.*

When the ball dropped and the room exploded, Sophie leapt off our shoulders and showered the crowd with the contents of her cup. She kissed Mark with an open mouth, and then she kissed me the same way. I was jealous of her freedom and her liberty to celebrate, as if sadness was an illness she was immune to. Josie watched us. I leaned close to her, but she turned her cheek. She pulled away, flipped her hair to the side, looked around the room, and then turned back to me and kissed me on the lips. She laughed nervously and looked at Mark. He pushed toward her and she accepted his kiss too. Mark glanced at me when he pulled back. He put his arm around my neck and said, "Donovan, you are all right, man."

"Kowolski," I said, mimicking his voice, "you're all right too. Seriously," I added. I pulled him into a hug. My hand reached a little high and I got the base of his neck as I brought him in close. He was damp with sweat.

For a second or two we hesitated awkwardly. Then he broke free. "This is the world we live in, man!" he shouted. "It's totally fucked. All the wrong people are in charge. Welcome to 2002. We're Generation Fucked—everyone's fucking us."

"Especially the ones who say they have our best interests in mind," I said.

"Yeah," Mark agreed. He lost some of the ironic joy in his face. "Yeah. They are."

"At least we have what we have," I said.

"What's that?" Mark asked.

I pulled Josie into the conversation by looping my arm through hers. "At least we have this. Us, I mean. Something."

Josie raised her cup and tapped it against mine. "Here's to us. All of us. Where's Sophie?" We drank and looked around for her. She pressed back through the crowd with two glowing bands wrapped around her wrists.

"This is the best party!" she screamed as she ducked forward and surfaced between other people's limbs. She had lost her cup but gained a bottle of wine. She poured too much into my cup as the stereo kicked back on with a funk song that got everyone dancing.

I passed Mark my cup, but he waved it off. "Have you seen Feingold anywhere?" he asked. The rest of us were bopping up and down, but I saw the look on his face and stopped.

"Let's go find him," I said.

He led the way as we weaved through the room and out to the front, where there were other people dancing too. We asked around, but nobody seemed to have seen him, although it occurred to me that few of the people we asked even knew who he was. Fewer and fewer of the people at the party looked familiar to me. I stuck my head out the front door and surveyed the porch. Feingold wasn't there. Mark walked upstairs, and we followed him. A couple was making out at the top and didn't stop as we passed. In the hall, Riggs leaned against the wall beside the closed door to the bathroom. His eyes were open but droopy, and he didn't notice us. His lips were parted, and he nodded as if he was being pushed around by a weak breeze. At the far end of the hall, a door was ajar, and I had a sinking feeling as Mark charged toward it.

Dustin and two other guys from the CDA baseball team circled the bed with their crimped and fraying ball caps pointed down at a naked Feingold spread-eagled across the beige comforter. He was tattooed in permanent marker—FAGGOTS FALL FIRST was scrawled up his arms and legs, and a series of cheap doodles of shit and piss were drawn on his stomach. Toothpaste streaked his hair. The bed was soaked around his waist and beneath his legs, and his crotch was painted with stripes of lipstick. The tube was jammed in his belly button. Dustin, laughing, pointed a camera toward his friends, Nick and Andre, who hovered over Feingold. Nick held a Bic razor poised over Feingold's eyebrow, and Andre gave a thumbs-up and held a marker in his other hand. They both smiled for the shot, and Dustin snapped it as we entered. He turned to us, and when he saw Josie he lifted his cap and wiped the thin blond hair back on his head. The boyish giddiness in his face dropped immediately into guilt. He turned back to his buddies. Nick was about to begin with the razor. "Hey, hold it!" Dustin yelled.

It happened quickly. Mark sprinted toward Nick. He pushed Nick away from the bed, into the dresser, but as he looked down onto Feingold's closed eyes, he was pulled back by Andre and pinned with his arms behind him. Sophie and Josie yelled at them. Nick got up in Mark's face. "Take it easy," Nick said. "We're just fucking around. It's his own fault. He passed out. He passed out first." On the other side of the bed, Dustin tried to comfort Josie, but she shook her head and backed away.

"What the fuck?" Sophie said.

Mark wrestled to free himself but couldn't. Locked in Andre's arms, he cursed the three of them. Nick yelled back at Mark, and I finally made a move, but Dustin caught me by the arm and pulled me back too.

"Calm down," Dustin said to all of us. "It's not a big deal."

"Why would you do this to somebody?" Josie asked him.

"Assholes," Mark said.

Nick squeezed tighter. "Shut the fuck up."

"Everybody, calm down!" Dustin shouted. "We're just having a little fun."

"Fun?" Josie repeated. "Don't you dare touch me," she said to him as he stepped closer to her.

"Oh, come on." Dustin sighed. "What the fuck?"

"No. What the fuck?" Mark said, nodding at Feingold. "You get off on this?"

"I will fucking deck you if you don't shut up," Nick told him. "What's the matter? You and Aidan coming to jerk Feiny off or something? Is that why you're here, looking for him? I know what you are. I know what you like."

"You wish you knew something important," Mark said. "You wish."

"Shut up, faggot," Nick said. He punched him in the stomach.

"That's enough!" Dustin shouted at Nick. He eased his grip on me as he yelled. I broke free. "Calm down," Dustin told the room again, but I didn't need his direction. I didn't think I was going to throw punches and knock anybody out. I'd never been in a fistfight before, but it didn't matter. I could still do something.

I went after Nick, but he pushed me to the side, and I fell toward the bed. He punched Mark in the stomach again, and I found my footing quickly and charged him. Nick turned, swung at me, and hit the side of my face hard. He grabbed me as I fell and hit me in the head again. I stumbled toward Mark, but with his arms pinned back he couldn't catch me. I rolled off his shoulder and fell to the floor. The girls screamed, and I lost sense of where I was or what was happening for a few moments.

When I came to, I was on my back. Dustin had Nick pinned up against the wall. My head throbbed, and Josie and Sophie were yelling at Andre. Mark was free again, and he stooped down to me on the floor, pulled me to the bed, and propped me up against it. To my right, Feingold's fingers dangled in my peripheral vision, but I couldn't see much to my left. I couldn't open my eye any wider. There were more people in the room now, and though the chatter built to a louder and louder buzz, the room was calmer than it had been before. I looked up at Nick. I smiled. It stung, but I held it. Blood dripped off my chin to my lap.

Josie and Sophie crouched down in front of me and asked if I was okay. I smiled again. "Cover Feingold," I said. Mark leapt up immediately, and Sophie helped him.

Josie touched my face and shook her head. She stood. "What the hell is wrong with you?" she asked Dustin. He let go of Nick and turned around.

Nick stepped around him and pointed across the bed to Mark. "I'll still floor you too."

"No one's flooring anybody," Dustin said.

"Fuck you," Nick said. "Change your tune the minute your girlfriend walks into the room. We were just talking about that guy."

"Seriously," Dustin said. "Shut up." Andre grabbed Nick

by the shoulder and dragged him to the door. They pushed their way through the crowd to the hall. "Let's find some place to talk," Dustin said to Josie when they were gone.

"I'm not talking to you," she told him.

He reached for her, and she batted his hand away. "Hey, come on," he said. "It's not what it looks like. You have to understand."

I tried to stand, to get between the two of them, but I was weak and dizzy, and he'd already stepped around me. He pursued her halfway around the room, begging her to take it easy. When I finally got to my feet and saw my swollen eye and bloody mouth in a mirror, I knew it wouldn't heal quickly, but I wondered if it was still worth it. Two guys and a girl started tending to Feingold. I coughed. A girl I didn't know came forward with a damp cloth from the bathroom and pressed it gently to my face. She was shorter than me and had a hairdo like a sponge. I wanted to lean down into it and fall asleep, but I still rocked with Adderall and adrenaline, and my pulse nearly kept pace with the thoughts exploding in my mind.

Josie suddenly had me by the arm. "Do you want to get out of here?"

"Nobody has to leave," Dustin said in the background.

"You should," the sponge told him.

"I'm not going anywhere. Everybody is fine. Let's just get back down to the party."

"Look around you," I said. "Nobody's fine." He made

a move toward me, but Mark grabbed his arm. Two other guys charged Dustin and held him back too.

Sophie walked up to him and pointed her finger in his face. "You are who your friends are," she told him.

Then she stepped over to me. With my arms draped over Josie and Sophie, I shuffled to the door. They called to Mark, and the four of us squeezed down the now-crowded hall to the stairs. He spoke to a few other guys from the swim team and sent them back to look after Feingold. Then we found our coats and a bag of frozen peas for my busted face and made our way out to the front porch, where, with a little indulgent flourish, I milked the injury and bummed a couple of cigarettes for the road. Everyone was eager to share.

Back in the car, Josie and Sophie kept saying I should go home, but I didn't want to. When they finally consented, Mark said he could take us to the beach where he had done lifeguard training the past summer, and I reminded them that the party didn't have to end. I was still loaded with liquor and pharmaceuticals. "Maybe we could watch the sunrise," I suggested. "I've never seen the sunrise, and we live right on the damn ocean. It'd be a hell of a way to start the year." I popped a Vicodin, leaned back in the front seat, and let them discuss it.

It wasn't too long before we made it to the coast. Mark cut the lights and pulled into the shadows of a parking lot down the road. We walked quickly along a path that ran beside a few dark and quiet houses and emerged onto the beach. The surf roared, and a freezing wind shot along the shore. The moon had been full the night before, and even though it was high and distant in the sky, it still cast a pale luminescence over the beach. Milky waves tumbled up the sand, and we walked only a few feet above the tide line, in order to not draw attention from the road. The noise drowned out any conversation, and we were too cold to talk anyway. Josie took my arm and huddled against me. Her thin arm squeezed mine through the jackets and guided me across the hard-packed sand. I was half-blind and listing back and forth between pain and delirium, and her support didn't correct my steps as much as lift me from within.

We were heading to the lifeguard station, and when we got there, Mark ducked under a ramp that led to the short porch. I peered into the window. The room was big enough to hold a couple of chairs, a narrow table, and a row of floating tubes and boards. When Mark reemerged and let us in, we were grateful to get out of the cold. It blocked the wind at least. Once we had all stamped our feet a few times and gotten the blood flowing again, I pulled a small bottle of Midori from my inside pocket and passed it around. Its sticky sweetness tasted awful, but the heat that came with it made it worth it.

The wind found its way through a few cracks in the flimsy house and whistled in the corners. "The house is creaking," Sophie said. "I feel like I'm on a boat."

Mark lit a joint and passed it to Sophie. She took a hit and beckoned Josie closer. They kissed and recycled. Josie took a hit and leaned toward me. Her tongue moved gently into my mouth, and though my jaw throbbed, I didn't pull away. The smoke leaked out, and we kissed for what I thought seemed a long time, though I only realized that when we'd finished. Sophie grinned, and Josie's eyes sparkled back at me. I was a little embarrassed. I took a big hit, and with it all down in my lungs I leaned toward Mark. I kissed him and exhaled as quickly as I could. He took it in and worked his cheeks like bellows on the other end. His lips weren't all that much different from Josie's, a little thinner and tighter, but he worked back against mine as Josie had. He pulled away and exhaled the recycled smoke in a thin stream through the corner of his mouth. He smiled and looked away. Sophie and Josie giggled.

"Yeah!" Sophie said.

"Can't leave anybody out, dude," I said.

"Left out?" Mark laughed. "Thanks, man, for caring." He reached for me, and we gripped hands. He laughed harder and pulled me into a one-armed hug. "Seriously. Thanks, man. I should be the one with a black eye tomorrow." He kept smiling, and I wasn't sure, but I thought he was going to kiss me again. The room tilted around me, and I held on to him for balance. "You okay?" he asked me.

"Yeah. I could use some water, though. My throat kind of burns." I took another sip of Midori, which didn't help, then wobbled over to the table by the wall and scrambled onto it so I could lie down and look out the window. The moon was high enough that some stars were visible too. "I'm okay," I told them. "Don't worry."

Josie followed me. "You talking to yourself?" she teased.

"No. I don't know. Maybe. I think it runs in the family."

She hopped up next to me. She sat crossed-legged, lifted my head, and scooted closer. I put my head back down on her thigh and smiled up at her. She took the bottle from me, sipped again, and we stared out the window in silence for a while. She put her hand down through my open coat to my chest and rubbed gently.

"Are you in a lot of pain?" she eventually asked.

"Not a lot," I lied.

"Another painkiller?"

"I don't know," I said. "I don't have any idea how much of all this stuff I've had tonight. I guess not too much."

"Maybe I'll have one too—just 'cause. I feel like I'm floating. I don't want it to end."

"Don't take too much. You've been drinking."

"Wow." She laughed. "You sound like you care or something."

"I do. I mean, it's like sliding over ice. It's hilarious and fun until it suddenly isn't and you crash down into the water."

"And you might die."

"Don't do that," I said. "We're just getting to know each other."

She leaned down and kissed me softly on the lips. "You're going to look like a monster tomorrow. You realize that? Like, really bad."

"Yeah," I said. "But if you kiss me again, I won't care."

"Oh my God," Sophie whined. She was across the room, standing next to the other window. "I can hear you from over here. Please."

"Seriously, dude," Mark said. He broke into a cough. Sophie patted him on the back. "Seriously, dude," he wheezed again. She laughed and took another hit.

Josie smiled. "Don't mind them."

"I don't," I said. "This is perfect."

"Yes," she said. She looked up toward the darker waves farther out to sea. "We could stay out here forever, except we'd freeze to death."

"Not if we stayed this close together," I said. I enjoyed saying it and liked the sound of my voice with hers, but I began to have the strange feeling that it was someone else speaking, that I was, in fact, hiding under the table, listening to this other puppet talk, because the me that was under the table had a premonition of things to come, as though somewhere, just beyond where I could see, something or someone was waiting for me, coming to take this all away from me, and it was inevitable.

I lit a cigarette. We shared it and listened to the surf thump and hiss along the shoreline. I wondered if I could somehow erase all the events of my life so far, as though

I could call in a flood, wash it all away, and begin anew. I imagined the ocean rushing up the beach, surrounding the little house, submerging the neighborhoods and towns behind us, the water level rising and lifting us up above the tumult. I'd save two of the important things: two joints, two martinis, two girls, two boys. We'd stare out the window, watching the dark water slog and gurgle, our boat creaking and groaning above it, moaning, writhing over the water with a slap and a splash in the crests of the waves. We'd purge all the junk overboard, the shelves loaded with bullshit trinkets at home, our computers, sheets of practice music, our clothes and uniforms, the whole Latin language, our worst memories. What else was necessary other than the glow of Mark's skin, the hum in Josie's lips, and the way Sophie squinted when she laughed? When it all subsided, everything else would be washed away and we could emerge from the muck and bloom. And something new might grow.

But there wasn't any flood, and we didn't even stay for the sunrise. At a certain point, Josie slipped out from underneath me. She kissed me on the forehead and went over to the others. I dozed off while they talked, and soon I found myself dragged out into the freezing wind and marched along the beach to the road. Mark staggered like the rest of us. I thought he was only having trouble in the sand, but I noticed his steps were heavy on the sidewalk, too. I smoked a cigarette to wake up, and I finished it before we got to the car. On the way home the girls fell asleep, and Mark and I talked about Feingold a little. He was sure nobody else had fucked with him for the rest of the night, but he was worried for the state of the house. "Nobody was in charge," he kept saying. "It was total fucking chaos."

Mark took his corners too widely, and my nerves kept me awake. Twice I rolled down the window to blast my face with cold air, and Mark did the same. He dropped Josie and Sophie at Josie's, and they stumbled up the rest of the driveway after barely saying good night. Mark and I didn't say much as he turned out of her neighborhood and headed back to our side of town. As he came around the corner at the bottom of the hill we found ourselves on the wrong side of the road. Another pair of headlights blinded us. I yelled, and Mark jerked the wheel just in time, but we swung into the shoulder of the road and bounced up into the wooded patch beyond the sidewalk.

Mark still clutched the wheel. "Oh shit, oh shit," he repeated. We got out and surveyed the car and found that we were lucky. He had been going slowly, and there wasn't much damage we could see other than a few scratches and dings that could be explained away easily. Still, he leaned back against the car and held his head in his hands for a moment. "I swear, one of these days it's all going to catch up with me. I fucking feel it, and they are going to be standing there with those fucking grim pouts, all disappointment, and shaking their heads like they're saying, *Yup, we knew he wasn't going to turn out the way we hoped, we just knew it.*"

"Who?"

"My parents."

"Hey, man," I said, pointing to my face, "at least you don't look like this." He laughed with a sniff. "Seriously," I continued, "don't they want you to have a little fun? I mean, I'm going to have to come up with something about this busted face, but my mother will hear I had a fun time with friends and be relieved."

"I'm not even talking about fun," he said. "That's not even a part of it. Fun is something you earn, like fucking paradise at the end of your life, and I haven't earned it yet. I have to become a senator or something first."

"They know how to have fun," I said.

"Hah," Mark said flatly. "Anyway, we don't have any of those in the family yet—it's all business. My father thinks it's time the Kowolskis moved into politics."

"Why doesn't he do it, then? Why does he have to put it all on you? Do you want any of it?"

"I don't know what I want. I just don't want to disappoint anybody while I'm still trying to figure the rest of it out."

"I know how you feel," I said, but as I did I wasn't thinking about Mark. I thought about how often I'd heard that line before and what it meant to me now. It felt like one of those things you intend to be a truth but that can't be anything but a lie. I wanted to offer more than bullshit.

Mark cupped his chin with one hand and hugged himself with the other. He stared at the ground by our feet. I had nothing else I could say to reassure him. I was better at taking a punch in the face than trying to impart a sense of hope. *What the fuck, man,* I wanted to say. *Just get a grip—fucking learn to cope.*

"Let's get out of here," I said instead. "But don't drive me home. Let's make sure you get home."

He was grateful, and even more so when we pulled back onto the road and he realized the wheel alignment was off. It was still drivable, and he decided he could get it fixed without his parents knowing, but the details were piling up, and Mark was beginning to worry he couldn't remember them all. We pulled up the long slope of his driveway and around to the side of the house. The car rolled onto the lawn, but he didn't notice. He cut the engine.

"Where do I say we went again tonight?"

"You came to my house." I opened my coat and fished out the baggie. "Listen, do you want a sleeping pill? Something to calm you down so you're not up all night like a madman?"

"You do a lot of these," he said, taking two pills from my palm.

Mark knocked one back and put the other in his pocket. He sat there waiting for it to take effect, like he'd just taken a hit from his bowl. I smiled and leaned back too. I wanted an ice pack, but all I had was another Vicodin, which I swallowed. I thought about saying good-bye, but I didn't want to go home yet, so I stayed there with Mark in silence for a while.

"You should go inside," I said eventually, but he didn't move.

"Hey? Do you like Josie?" he asked, lifting his head slightly. "I think she likes you."

"Jesus, I don't know, man. And there's her boyfriend."

"Yeah, right." Mark laughed sleepily, and I began to worry, but I couldn't move either. My body was slowing down too quickly. "Bet he's out of the picture now," Mark said, slurring. "Watch."

"I don't know."

"I thought maybe you were gay?" His voice rose at the end, as if he had asked a question, but I didn't answer right away, because I didn't know how. I knew I wanted Josie, but I couldn't trust what I'd wanted. All that time with Father Greg, I'd never considered it sex. My body had worked on command. But it was different with Josie.

Mark dropped back and to the side, against the headrest. He smiled at me dreamily, moved his hand over the gearshift, and it fell on the seat beside me. His eyelids drooped and bounced. He fought to stay awake. "Are you?" he asked. He looked younger, less sophisticated and jaded than I'd ever seen him. Maybe the drugs had stripped him down, or it was because he was on the brink of sleep, or maybe it was an act of courage it had taken him all night to muster, or for me to notice, but I thought Mark might have looked at me with something close to hope.

"Didn't you see us?" I finally asked. "Me and Josie?"

He didn't respond. He let out a puff of air. His cheek sagged into the headrest, his shoulders sank. His lips remained slightly parted, his breath moist against the leather of the car seat. I'd never watched a person fall asleep before, never witnessed such vulnerability.

I wanted to crash as well, and I could have, even in that cold, but I lifted myself heavily and climbed out of the car. It would have been easy to abandon him, but I couldn't. His parents weren't expected home until the next day, but I couldn't let them find him out in the car in case he slept through until they arrived. I took the keys from the ignition, pulled him out, and tried to wake him. He mumbled with his eyes closed. I wrapped his arms over my shoulders and lugged him to the side door of the house, with his feet dragging behind us.

He woke slightly and asked if we could sit down. I put him down on the stoop and he leaned toward the bushes and vomited. I looked away so I wouldn't do the same, but when I turned around he'd dropped into his own puddle, face-first in the dirt. I rolled him over quickly. "Oh, shit," he mumbled. His sweatshirt and pants were soaked with what had come out of him, but his jacket was open and seemed relatively clean, and I peeled it off him. He didn't respond when I asked him if he was feeling better. He only smiled up at me with his eyes still closed.

One of his keys worked in the side door, and I eased him

onto a bench in the dark mudroom. As in my house, it led to the kitchen. I found some paper towels and cleaned him up as best I could, but his clothes still reeked. "Mark," I said. He was completely asleep. With some effort, I took off his shoes, and then his pants and shirt. I grabbed the loose bag of marijuana from his pocket and put the clothes in a trash bag. Stretched out on the bench, it was easy to see how by anyone's standards Mark was the kind of attractive we all aspired to be. His shoulders and chest muscles pushed an outline into his T-shirt, and the bulge in his briefs was evident. I could have run my hands up the long lines of his leg muscles, touched him there, anywhere, because in his state, I could have done anything to him, or with him, molded him like clay to whatever purpose I wanted, and oddly, although he was asleep, he still smiled up at me shyly, as if he wanted me to act—the Bronze Man glowing beneath me, an air of supplication and eagerness humming somewhere between us.

And then I did. I slid my hands against his skin and cupped his crotch. I held him for a moment and then let go when nothing moved inside me. I wanted Josie. I could have kissed Mark again, if I'd been asked to, if it was a game and it included the girls—but I didn't want to. I didn't want Mark's body; I wanted his friendship. We were just beginning to see the world. I wanted his opinions about it; I wanted to experience it with him. Wasn't that a kind of love too, a kind that had nothing to do with sex and, instead, everything else important that commingles between two people?

I got him up under my shoulder again and hauled his nearly naked body through the kitchen and down the hall to a den with a huge flat-screen TV. I flopped him onto the couch, covered him with a blanket, and slid down in front of the couch to the floor. I looked back at his sleeping, peaceful face. I couldn't meet Mark where I thought he wanted me to, but he was my friend. I admired him, but I didn't know how to tell him.

The remote was nearby, and I switched on the TV. Confetti, fireworks, concerts, crowds loosely whipping their heads to a beat: The parties were on their last breath in New York, but the day hadn't ended elsewhere. The celebrations continued across America, and I didn't want to knock out yet. I thought that somewhere Mother was still up too, not sleeping so she didn't have to wake, holding back tomorrow and its inevitable loneliness with her thin, birdlike arms wrapped around someone else's body. I didn't mind. It was my hope for all of us that we'd each have someone again soon, someone to cling to, however briefly, to remind ourselves we were alive.

CHAPTER 8

I was mid dream when I woke up with a start. My head was dropped back onto the couch, resting on top of Mark's shin. The television still blinked, but the voices I heard weren't coming from it, they were coming from the kitchen. They were shouting for Mark, and they entered the room before I could really move and process what was happening.

Mike Kowolski swelled into vision, a lavender polo shirt drifting in front of the television. "What the hell is going on?"

Barbara came into the room a moment later and let out a yelp of shock. Mark quickly squirmed into a sitting position and tried to blink himself awake. Sunlight blasted in through the windows. I still had on my jacket, and a film of sweat stuck to me beneath it. Barbara stooped and grabbed the bottle of Midori that stuck out of my pocket. I hadn't realized it was still there, and I didn't remember us finishing as much as we did, but its syrupy aftertaste coated my mouth. She held it in the air and showed her husband.

"Pathetic," he said.

"Dad," Mark began.

"I don't want to hear one excuse. I don't want to hear what happened. Look at the two of you—Jesus Christ, Mark, where the hell are your pants? What are you doing?"

Mark blushed deeply and threw the blanket back over his waist. "No, but Dad—"

"No. Bullshit, bullshit, bullshit. That's all you have to say for yourself right now. Bullshit. The car is a mess, and you parked it up on part of the lawn. You are lucky to be alive. What a waste. That's what you want—to waste it all away?"

"Michael," Barbara said, but she stopped when he looked at her. None of what he was saying was how I remembered it. At the time I thought we had managed all right. I turned to look at Mark, to see how we should respond, but my neck hurt too much.

"Dad," Mark said again.

"I don't want to hear it! I don't want to know how you embarrassed yourself, your name, and mine. This is what I worked for all my life? So you can bring your deadbeat friend to my house and parade around in your underwear? Is that what you think? That you can squander it all away and shit on everything I've done?"

"Michael!"

"Dad!"

"Enough," he said to Mark, and he thrust his stubby forefinger at him.

Barbara stepped over me and sat on the arm of the couch, next to Mark. She put an arm around him and whispered into his ear, "You can tell me what happened, honey. I'll try not to get too mad."

Mike paced and muttered. "Completely disrespectful. Completely." He shook his hand and balled it into a fat fist, and Barbara rocked her son gently.

Mark gazed wide-eyed at the floor. His hands were in his lap, his thumb twitched slightly, and his mouth was drawn into a comatose, flat line. Shouting behind me, Mike asked me to hurry up, and Barbara nodded along, but their protests didn't scare me as much as Mark's distance. It was as if he had abandoned his body, left it behind as collateral in the noisy violence of the room, and fled to somewhere silent. It was a retreat I knew well, and I wanted to follow him. I climbed to my feet wearily.

"Maybe I should call my mother," I said.

"Yes. I'd like to speak with her," Mike said. "She probably gave you the booze. You want to drag my son down into your family's problems? Is that it?"

"My family?"

"Yes." He stepped closer. "You have to take someone down with you. Is that it?" Mike continued.

"Like you'd say that if my father was around," I said, pointing back at him.

"How dare you speak to me like that."

"Look at me." I pointed to my swollen eye. "Think I care?" Mike stormed over to the phone and dialed my mother. Barbara chastised me, but I didn't listen. "I'm sorry," I said to Mark. "I'm sorry, man."

While we waited for Mother, Mike gave me a lecture in the front hall. I apologized, but my tone of voice belied everything I said. He tried to explain to me why we should be afraid of the things people like him tell us to be afraid of and why we should listen and respect the people whose responsibility it was to protect us—and what he said had the dull echo of words Father Greg had once shared with me, which rang more and more hollow as I heard them again.

I thought Mother would have sent a car to pick me up, but instead she came herself, and even more surprising, when she arrived she got out, left the car running, and bounded up the walkway. She called to me, and when she reached me, she stood poised and deliberate for a moment, surveying my swollen face. Then she took me by the arm and pulled me into a hug. Mike hung back, and I watched him deflate.

"Gwen?" he said weakly.

"Oh, deary," she said to me, ignoring him. "What happened? Are you okay? We should get you to the hospital right now. You didn't tell me he looked like this," she said to Mike over her shoulder. "What's the matter with you? Just let my son bleed to death on your carpet?" She turned around and stepped closer to him. "Where do you get off calling me like that? Where's your son? Do I need to take *him* to the hospital too?"

"Now, Gwen, hold on. Just hold on a second. There's really no need."

"You're not a medical expert, Mike Kowolski."

"Gwen, please," Mike said. "I thought we could talk about some rules."

"How dare you condescend? I'll take care of my son from here, thank you." She pulled me down the walkway. Mike called after us, but Mother hurried me into the car. He apologized repeatedly, and she paused by her car door to let him stutter impotently for a moment. "Mike"—she cut him off—"thank you for calling." She chiseled each word with an exacting politeness. "It's good to know you have friends you can trust. Tell Barbara not to worry. I still want to share with her some ideas about her next party. I'll invite her to my office when they're ready." The old pro, she tucked away any pain or frustration and wore a mask of indomitable cheer. I couldn't help but admire its efficacy. She silenced him, and each time she smiled, she pushed Mike back closer to his house. She closed the car door, shifted into drive, and angled us down toward the street without saying good-bye.

I told her how I'd been thumped in the face but that

it had been in solidarity with my friends, and she nodded with a kind of grudging understanding and pride. Still, she was worried for me, even though I told her it looked worse than it felt. I had to beg her not to take me to the hospital.

She also explained her phone conversation with Mike, and how he referred to her as a "single parent." "Men," she said. "They just assume they know better. As if I needed advice now that your father has gone. As if your father was ever around!" We stopped at a red light, and she again asked if she could take me to the hospital. "Please," she said. "I'd feel much better if we went."

"No, I don't need to. Elena will take care of it tomorrow when she's back."

"Elena?"

"Yeah," I continued, "she'll know what to do. Let's just go home."

"Elena? You're thinking about Elena right now? Why can't I just take care of you?"

"C-Come on," I stammered. "You know. She's her and you're you, and—"

"What the hell does that mean?" Mother shouted. She paused and breathed and became quiet. "You know, I'm trying here, Aidan. I'm trying. How about a little support from your end? I'm putting this family back together, even if it is just you and me, and a little pat on the back from my own son might go a long way. And anyway, I dismissed Elena. So you'll have to get used to that."

"You can't fire someone who's a part of our family."

"It's already done. We'll find a day when she can come collect the rest of her things. She's not family, Aidan. That's precisely what I'm talking about."

I wanted to yell at her, but I wasn't sure what to say. If it had been Old Donovan who had named me, it had been Elena who had raised the boy he had named. But where did that leave Mother? "She might as well have been family," I said. "You can't do that to a person."

"Oh, Aidan. Grow up already."

"I liked having her around," I said.

"I've thought about that."

"You have?"

"That's right, I have." She shook her head and then smiled. "Look, I had an instructor," she said. "A mentor. I thought I could never dance without her. I was young, and I thought I was nothing without her guidance. Then, for family reasons, she moved back to Vienna. I thought I was going to quit dancing altogether, but I decided to train on my own until the auditions for Juilliard. That's life, Aidan. I got in. We can get better. We don't always need the people we think we need. I was still young when I learned that, and I was lucky. Just imagine. To think I almost forgot that lesson. Your father has left. That's a fact. But here's another: I don't need him."

+   +   +

Mother's attempt at a pep talk did little to rally me. We avoided each other in the house, unless I was getting fresh ice for my face, but eventually, I decided I needed to get out of the house, and I went for a walk. I knew I was hungover, dehydrated, and dizzy from the blood throbbing around my black eye, but a deeper, more profound uneasiness shook through my body. I wanted to see Josie, Sophie, and Mark again, right away, but I was also nervous and afraid to go back to CDA. All the people staring at me in the halls would see below the black eye. They would read my thoughts, and the thin mask, the puffy face, was a useless disguise for the damaged, demented, crazy, fucked-up boy beneath it. They'd all point to me and say, *See, we knew it, we knew you were a freak, a jack-off boy, a doll for a priest. What are you, Aidan?*

I didn't have an answer. I was a somebody to Josie now, and the taste of her lips still lingered on mine. As she'd leaned over me in the boathouse, I smelled the vanilla shampoo in her hair, the hints of cocoa butter on her skin. I still hadn't showered, and I wanted to find those smells still on me, wrapping me in the memory of her lap. But who was I, really, to her? She knew so little about me, and if she knew more, what then? Why would she waste her time with me? I was fixed on her in a way that felt so new and jarring, in a way that drove me crazy for more, and it hurt to think of Mark, instead, looking up at me from the bench in his mudroom, and my cold hands sliding over him to prove to myself that his body couldn't warm them. How much did he remember? Couldn't he ask me too? How could I answer in a way that wouldn't make him run away?

As I walked, I drifted across town in a familiarly beaten path, circling and circling with those same questions until I found myself standing across the street from Most Precious Blood. Just as the hands and fingers remember a song on the piano long after you forget you know the piece, I didn't realize I'd walked there until I was staring up the long drive, wondering how I could address questions I found too difficult to answer by myself. He was in there, wetting his lips, musing over the same trite maxims he'd probably used on innumerable boys. I wanted to scream and roar and tear the place apart stone by stone with him still in it, and yet a dull ache still rumbled inside me, the memory of a time when his voice calmed me, his words assured me, and my belief in him guided me. All that was gone now.

I don't know how long I stood in the street, staring at Most Precious Blood, but eventually, I became aware that the afternoon light was fading, and I could only think of how I'd watched it disappear in the basement the afternoon James had been there. It seemed unreal that I had been that boy too. I started to feel my mind spin through a zoetrope of other memories, and I couldn't stop thinking about my time with Father Greg. I pulled an Adderall from my inside jacket pocket, tried to crush the pill in my palm, and snorted the uneven chunks up off my fingertips. They burned like I'd stuck a Zippo up my nose. I tasted something like baking soda dripping down my throat, and I let the tears come down, telling myself it was only the Adderall and nothing else.

My head rocked, and as I tried to gather myself, I realized the taillights of the parish Lincoln Town Car had lit up and the car was backing out of its parking space. I took off down the street, hoping whoever was in the car hadn't yet noticed me. I walked quickly downhill, toward the center of town, and as I rounded the corner onto North Street, I caught a glimpse of the Town Car behind me. It changed lanes, slowed beside me for a moment, then passed on ahead. I couldn't see who was in the car, but now that I was on this side of town, I had no choice but to round CDA, swing past Stonebrook, and cut back along the roads closer to the cove to head back home. I could no longer see the car, but I broke into a dead run.

I got all the way to Stonebrook before I saw it again. I was on the bridge, down by Mark's neighborhood, when I saw the car appear at the top of the hill in the direction I was heading. It had its headlights on now, and as soon as the beam swept down the street and found me, the car accelerated. I took a few more steps but then realized the Town Car was gunning right in my direction. I turned and ran back across the bridge and heard the car approaching. There were no houses along this stretch of the road. One side of the street was a thin band of trees on a slope that led down to the harbor, and the other side of the street was the grounds of the country club. The car beeped. I leapt off the shoulder of the road, into the line of trees bordering the golf course.

"Aidan!" I heard behind me.

His voice still stung.

"Aidan," I heard again, and I knew he was out of the car. He repeated my name as I broke through the tree line and jumped into the first sand pit. I thought if I took it directly I'd get farther up the hill faster, but it slowed me. As I climbed out of it, I heard him again. He was on the golf course too. He took the long way around the pit, which cut me off from making a break across the fairway. He was dressed in his usual black pants and shirt, buttoned to the throat, with the Roman collar crisply fitted at the top. He lumbered after me. His gait was awkward, but his speed was surprising. By the time I was out of the sand pit, he was close. Flushed and breathing heavily, he called me again.

"Please!" he yelled. "I need to talk to you. Stop. Please."

I cut right, toward another stand of trees, and pushed as hard as I could uphill. Once I was back in the grass, I put more space between us, but he kept up. Just before the top of the hill, I ducked into the cluster of trees. They lined the quickly flowing river that ran downhill and slipped under the bridge and poured out into the harbor. The river narrowed along the golf course, then widened as it flowed toward the street and the bridge. I jumped down the slope, springing wildly, using spindly trees and limbs to break and guide my near fall to the riverbank. I looked back up when I'd gotten to the bottom. Father Greg appeared at the top, where I had been standing moments before. He paused, leaned on his knees, and briefly tried to catch his breath. "Aidan," he growled. He couldn't say much else, and he began his descent.

I scrambled along the river toward a large tree that had fallen across it, roots twisted haphazardly into the air. The churned soil near the base was darker than the ground around it. I grabbed hold of a root and swung onto the trunk. Father Greg crashed through the thicket above, and as I began to slowly make my way out over the river, I heard him fall. He moaned as he hit the ground and tumbled. His back finally slammed into a tree, which kept him from rolling into the river. I paused on the trunk, and a rich stink of dank earth and crisp, rushing water overwhelmed the silence as I waited for him to move. He sat up and wiped the debris from his face and clothes. His face was lacerated, and as he tried to stand he clutched his side and cried out. He didn't get up. He leaned against the tree and stared at me. He coughed and groaned, and I waited.

"Please, Aidan," he said. "Please listen."

He could barely move, but as each moment passed he seemed to gain more control of himself. His focus came back and he looked at me without bobbing his head. It had only been this past summer when I'd found bruises on my shoulders where he'd squeezed me while I'd obeyed him and held him as he'd directed. I pictured myself grabbing a thick stick and whipping him; I pictured stoning him. Somewhere else, deep within me, I could see our hands reaching out for each other, slipping behind each other's back and pulling close—the image still warmed me. The thoughts rose and died in my mind, and all I'd wanted was to feel less afraid, to not feel as lonely as I had, as non-existent. Even if he had breathed a kind of life into me, what did I owe him now?

"I need to talk to you," Father Greg said. He rubbed his head.

"No," I said.

"Listen to what you're saying. It doesn't have to be this way."

"You made it this way!"

"I expect more from you, Aidan." He shook his head.

"Please. Stay away from me," I said.

Father Greg leaned heavily on an elbow and adjusted himself. I began again, but he held his hand up. "No. Listen. You misunderstand me."

"I can't. I won't. Don't touch me. Don't get near me. Stay away."

He coughed. "Nothing will ever happen between you and me again. I don't want it to. It's over, Aidan. It's over."

"I don't want anything to do with you."

"No, no. It was nothing."

"What?"

"It was nothing, wasn't it? Inconsequential. A passing thing. It's over. It's behind us. It's as if it didn't happen, Aidan. It was nothing." He cleared his throat and used both hands to push himself into a more comfortable sitting position.

I struggled to speak. "It happened. It happened."

"No, it didn't. It didn't mean anything."

"Yes, it did," I said. My throat tightened—it was out of my control. "Yes, it did. It happened."

"It's over. You have to understand that, Aidan. It's over, and you need to move on. Be a man about it, Aidan. Forget it. It was nothing."

I crouched lower on the tree trunk as my arms began to shake. "Why are you talking to me? Stop talking!"

"I'm trying to protect you, Aidan. Remember all our conversations, how I helped you think about your family? Think about all the work we've done together too—think about all those kids, the schools they'll have now. We've accomplished so much."

"Stop," I begged. "Please stop." All of that was true. It was all that I had been proud of, all that I had been dreaming might be the springboard from which I'd leap forward into the rest of my life.

"No. I'm concerned," Father Greg continued. "If you tell people things about me, they'll find out about you, too. What will they think of you, Aidan? It's just like I always told you: They won't understand." He smiled. "See? I didn't lie to you. We have to be careful. I'm getting older. But what will happen to you, Aidan, if you tell anybody? What will happen to your mother? What will they all say about you if they find out? Have you said anything to anybody?"

"No."

He smiled and shifted his weight but did not get up. "What about your friends, your friends from your party? You haven't shared what was between us with them, right? You haven't said anything to Elena or to any of your friends, right? Protect yourself. Don't speak to anybody." He leaned forward off the tree. "You haven't, right? Not to Mark, or any of the girls?"

"No. No one."

"Not about anything?"

"Nothing."

"Good. Then you're safe," Father Greg said, leaning back against the tree. He took a deep breath. "As long as it stays that way. I care about your safety, don't you see that? I've always cared about your safety, Aidan. And think of what we accomplished together. That's what is important. All that we've done for others, I mean." His voice sounded automatic, as if it was an old recording and not the man I once knew.

"I can't," I said. "That's meaningless too. It's all meaningless now."

"You can't mean that," Father Greg said. "You don't."

He looked up at the darkening sky. He sniffed after air, growled, cleared his throat, and spat into the dirt. He wiped at the blood from a slash across his neck and then wiped at the blood on his fingers with his thumb. So many times I had sought out his voice, listened to it with an eagerness, hope, and desire that I had called love, and still now, that thing that tugged me toward him must have been some-thing like love, or what love leaves in its wake when it is gone.

I remained on the trunk, listening to the rush of the river beneath me. Eventually, Father Greg used the tree to pull himself off the ground. He staggered toward me, losing his footing but grabbing hold of another branch to steady himself. His hair was a mess, and his shirt was ripped and soiled from his fall. One of his legs bothered him enough to make him limp. It struck me that Father Greg was a man who would someday die—and if things worked out the way they should, he would die long before me. The haggard old man stumbled to the base of the trunk and took hold of one of the bigger roots. He looked at me and tried the root to see if it moved the tree at all. Nothing happened; the root only bent slightly with his pressure. "I wanted . . . ," he said quietly, and then he stopped. He searched for words and nothing came to him. "This will all just go away, won't it?" He tried the root again, and I knew with a strange assurance that he wouldn't climb up onto the tree, and that even if he did, I could move more quickly now, get across the river, and make it back down to the road in no time. He turned around and picked his way uneasily back through the thicket to the edge of the golf course. His shoulders shook and trembled. Father Greg was broken, and yet, I thought, more right than he had ever been.

CHAPTER 9

My busted face wouldn't heal in a day, of course— a crescent of jaundiced skin cupped the blue and purple bursts around my eye—but Mother let me skip school on Wednesday anyway. I knew I couldn't stay home forever, however. The longer I was alone, the worse I felt. No matter how many painkillers I popped, they only numbed the sting in my face. I couldn't hide. On Thursday when I woke up, I knew it was time to go back to CDA. I sat on the edge of my bed listening to the news for a while. Another mosque was vandalized and ransacked, this time in Columbus, Ohio. Jury selection began in Cambridge, Massachusetts, for the trial of the father who beat another father to death at a hockey practice. How do we all go on with our lives?

I called the car service before I changed my mind, and threw the phone across the room when I was done. I needed to move forward, and enforcing an absolute silence was the only way I could hope to feel safe. What if there was only one story to tell—that nothing had happened?

I didn't make it to school on time, though. My driver took his sweet time crawling along at the actual speed limit on every road. But as we turned onto Mulberry, a powder blue Lincoln Town Car pulled away from the curb across the street from the driveway up to CDA. I couldn't see who drove the car, but I couldn't help but think it was the car for the priests at Most Precious Blood. It shot up Mulberry, ahead of us, and as we turned into the driveway, I lost sight of it.

I fidgeted with my backpack in the backseat until my driver cleared his throat and asked me in broken, Slavic-clipped English if I would kindly step out so he could get to his next passenger. He stood on the curb and held the door open, but I couldn't get out of the car. All I could see in my mind was Father Greg standing beyond the double doors to the lobby, leaning on Mrs. Perrich's desk, entertaining a crowd that had gathered around him, waiting for me with his broad smile, and him reaching out between their shoulders to grab me and pull me into his story.

I was about to tell the driver to take me home immediately, but Mrs. Perrich came out onto the stoop to see what was going on and why the driver was waiting around so long. She held down the points of her pashmina so it wouldn't blow away in the breeze, but then lifted one hand and waved to me. She waved again, like we were old friends, but when I finally climbed out of the car, she pulled back as if my bruises were viral. She recovered quickly and wrapped an arm around me and walked me up the rest of the stairs, offering her sympathies.

"I fell out of bed," I told her as we entered the lobby. No one was there. She didn't buy my excuse, but she didn't press me any further, either.

"I hope it didn't ruin your break?" Mrs. Perrich asked me.

"This? Oh, no. This was nothing. No big deal," I said. It was my mask, a way to present myself without having to talk about anything else.

She made me sign the late sheet and ushered me off to English class, saying, "When you have a minute, come back down and tell me about your break. Wasn't it wonderful? Did you travel?" I looked back at her before I left, wondering about her chipper world. Like Mother, Mrs. Perrich seemed to be able to smile her way into the world she wanted to believe in. I flashed one at Mrs. Perrich, just to try it. She smiled back.

When I opened the door to Mr. Weinstein's classroom, everyone stared at me. I came in and took my seat on the other side of the room. The questions would come later, questions I could handle. Questions Josie, Sophie, and Mark could answer too. Mr. Weinstein perched on the front of his desk and waited for me to take my seat behind Josie before continuing with his lecture.

"And what did the creature want most?" he asked the class.

"A partner," I answered without raising my hand. Josie's shoulder bounced in front of me, and I knew she was smiling.

"Mr. Donovan, did you forget your manners over the break? We raise our hands in this class." Mr. Weinstein rubbed the hollow of his sunken cheek. "That, and you're late. One more strike today and you'll be out of the class." He paused and looked at my face. "Are you okay?"

I smiled.

It was soon clear that I had missed a quiz on *Frankenstein* the day before. I didn't raise my hand, and Mr. Weinstein didn't bother to call on me as he asked questions. I didn't take notes. I scribbled the pen down until it broke through the pages and left blue-black craters in my notebook.

The sunlight through the windows found the auburn hints in Josie's hair, and I played my game of watching the shades shift from dark to light when she moved her head, but when first period ended, instead of dashing out into the hall as usual, she turned around. "Hey," she said. "It doesn't look as bad as I thought it would. We were all talking about you yesterday. We wanted to know how you were doing. We wanted to see you."

"Like this?"

"Seriously, it's not that bad. It's kind of cool, actually." She grinned and stood up. "You missed out yesterday."

"Yeah? What did I miss?"

"Me," she said.

I laughed. "That's true."

"Or at least the new me," she continued. "The single me. Dustin's history, FYI." She bumped me with her shoulder. "So what's next? I guess my future's pretty open right now," she teased.

"You're free," I managed to say.

"For now." She zipped up her bag and swung it over her shoulder. "Anyway, I just wanted to tell you. See you around." She left quickly and met Sophie outside the classroom door. They linked arms and headed off down the hall. It was a gift. She might as well have slowly unbuttoned her shirt and revealed the lacy edge of her bra. What was the point of dreaming all those dreams while I'd sat behind her if I didn't try to make them a reality?

I packed my bag slowly, however, and slumped out into the hall, because as much as I wanted to get excited about Josie, I couldn't help thinking about some of the other people I'd see at CDA. I made it through chemistry class only because there was a surprise quiz and I had nothing else to think about except formulas, but after fourth period Nick finally found me. I hadn't noticed him coming up the stairs in the stairwell by the gym. He threw his arm over my shoulder and walked us into the corner of the landing, by the window that looked out to the lacrosse and football fields. "You tell anyone I did that to you?" he asked.

It was tempting. Fighting, whether on campus or off, was automatic grounds for a disciplinary review at CDA. "No," I said. "But I could."

Nick looked around quickly. He pinned me back against the wall with his forearm. "Don't be a dumbass. If you say anything to anyone—any teacher, fucking Berne, anyone—I'll tell them and everybody else we saw you and your faggoty friend, Kowolski, up in the bedroom lathering up Feingold's naked ass and painting his drunk dick."

"That was you."

"No. We saw you. Get it? Fucking circle jerk over the passed-out kid. I'll tell everyone. Dustin will too. And Andre, and anybody else we make be a witness."

I struggled against his arm, but he was too strong. "What the hell are you talking about? People saw us downstairs. I was dancing with Josie. People saw us."

Nick grinned. "Your word against mine. And Dustin's, and anybody else he tells. Don't you get it? We make the rules. Not you." He pushed harder. "I get to say what happened."

My legs felt shaky. I might have collapsed if he hadn't had me pinned to the wall. He said something to me again, but I was somewhere else, back in the woods along the stream in Stonebrook, thinking about how a story can be rewritten. "Nothing happened," I mumbled.

"That's right," Nick said. He laughed. "Unless I say it did."

"Nothing happened," I said again.

Nick gave me one hard thump in the chest. "All right. Good. I'm counting on that. And for now, I'm not saying anything about what I saw up in Feingold's room, and neither is Dustin—got it?" He stepped back and crossed his arms. "Your secret is safe with me, lover boy." A couple of freshmen passed us as they came down the stairwell. Nick glanced at them, and they kept their heads down. He looked back at me.

"Nothing happened," I said so other people in the stairwell could hear. Nick's smile dropped. "Don't you get it? There's nothing to talk about because nothing happened." I was shaking, and dizzy with a kind of weightlessness.

"You better not say a damn thing," he said quietly. "Or I will make your life a fucking hell."

"Nothing happened, Nick, so there's nothing to talk about!" I was shouting now, and Nick shook his head. He looked around at the other kids now filing into the stairwell.

"Freak," he muttered.

I tried to find some quiet place to calm down. I was on fire, still riddled with fear from Nick's threats, but I knew that I'd scared him a little bit too, and deep down that felt good. I'd survived, and more important, I could again. I ditched lunch, but Sophie found me before last class and slipped me a note from Josie. *I've never kissed a guy with a black eye before, not until the other night. It was kind of hot. Do you have time for me this week?* I managed to nod and mumble an affirmation. Sophie didn't notice; she giggled and took off down the hall with her message.

I was exhausted and sweaty as Dean Berne delivered the end-of-the-day announcements over the loudspeakers, and I drifted out of school like a zombie. Josie, however, caught up with me down by the junior parking lot. She had a bashful smile in her doughy cheeks, one that anyone would stop to appreciate to let it linger on him a little longer, as I did, slightly shocked that she had searched for me.

She looped her arm through mine and dipped her head against my shoulder. "I thought you'd nearly forgotten about me," she said, looking up at me and veering us in a diagonal line until we nearly slipped off the sidewalk and into the trees beyond the lot.

"Just one of those days."

"Oh, I know. Hey, I have to get home, but we can take a while to get there. You don't mind, do you?"

"I want to," I said, and I kissed her. She hummed as our lips met, and it moved into me like the heat from a warm shower. We hadn't gotten all that far from the parking lot, and I was sure that people could see us. I didn't care. In fact, I wished we'd been even closer, right there in the middle of the junior parking lot, on the hood of somebody's car.

I didn't really know what I was doing, and after a while saliva smeared around our mouths and pooled on our chins. Josie pulled away and laughed. "Wow," she said. "I think I need some air." She turned away to dry herself, and

I did too, looking back into the parking lot. There were a couple of classmates, but mostly a lot of juniors leaning up against cars, talking. Others had formed a circle and were playing Hacky Sack, passing the beanbag from foot to foot in a slow, undulating dance. Riggs's car had the windows rolled down, providing the parking lot with a soundtrack, Bob Marley singing that the soul shakedown party was happening tonight, and standing next to Riggs, leaning against the hood, two girls who'd played on the field hockey team with Josie were pointing over at me and Josie. They weren't snickering, and it was a small victory I was glad to finally have. I felt like a new person—the kid with a black eye like an eye patch, writing his own new story for everyone to see.

"Come on," Josie said, taking my arm again. "Let's get out of here."

We walked out to Mulberry with a lazy stride, locked side by side at the hips, and even though my legs were much longer than hers, we found a rhythm that suited us. We stopped and kissed a few more times along the way, and by the third and fourth times we weren't slobbering all over each other. We found a calmer, slower pace, gently chasing after each other's breath. They were kisses mixed with smiles, and when I realized she had to push herself up on the balls of her feet to reach me, I cushioned one arm behind her head and the other around her back to support her, and we relaxed into each other naturally.

Between kisses, we fumbled our way through conversation, trying to find topics that would stick for long enough, but none of them did, and whether it was against a mailbox, beside a tree trunk, or right on the wide curb of Halverson Road, the conversation fell away and we pressed against each other, grinning in silence. We shared an unspoken understanding that the point of the walk seemed to be the kisses themselves and all the time in between a distraction.

"Did you read the article in the *Times* yesterday about face-recognition technology?" I asked after we peeled ourselves off the stone wall at the foot of her neighbor's yard. We were nearly at her house, and I didn't want the afternoon to end.

"No. That's so funny. Do you read the paper every day? You're like an old man. It's so cute." She smoothed the lapel of my overcoat with her glove. She sighed and pecked me on the nose. "I wish my mother wasn't home."

"Yeah."

"She's going to hover over my shoulder all night to make sure I do my homework. It's like a prison in there," she said, jerking her thumb toward her house. The trunks and limbs of a cluster of thick trees obscured a clean view of the house. A last dirty crust of snow still clung to the foot of the trees, and alongside one of the larger trunks a film of ice glazed the bark. Our faint gray outlines hung in the ice like smoke meeting smoke in a still and heavy air.

"She's even told Ruby not to let me have people over anymore on the weekdays," she continued. "We're going to have to find someplace else to hang out. I don't know what her deal is these days, but she is going crazy. I wish she wasn't home. I'd sneak you in anyway." She giggled. "That'd be fun."

"What if your mother is one of those people who supports all this extra video surveillance? She could have cameras all over your house. She could have cameras down here. She could be watching us right now." I ducked and pulled the collar of my coat over my head. Josie giggled again. She unbuttoned my coat and slipped in close, and I wrapped it around her, too. "She might have a camera in my coat," I whispered.

"Then she's going to have to watch us make out for a minute."

We kissed again, for a while. I shook the coat off my head, and we held each other tightly in the cold. Eventually, she stepped back and thanked me for walking her home, and I watched her head around the trees to her driveway and make her way up to the house. When she was gone, I looked back into the ice, but nothing was there now, only the rough bark beneath. A cloud had passed in front of the sun and absorbed all the brilliance. I almost didn't believe there had been a trace of us there before; I didn't see myself kissing Josie, it was too new for me to fully accept. But others had. They could be called upon as witnesses. There was some record now, one I could cling to, a story I wanted to tell and wanted to believe.

That was all I could think about on the way home: the possibilities. It was suddenly easy to imagine Josie and me holding hands on our way down into the cafeteria, the way she might rub the underside of my chin in the hall when teachers weren't around, and her tongue moving gently against mine—all of it right out there in the bright sunshine. Mother wasn't home, but she left a plate of cookies on the butcher block with a little sign next to it that read YOUR FAVORITE. Cinnamon chip. It had been once, but I stuffed one in my mouth as if it still was and moved through the library to the foyer. I was about to swing up the grand staircase to the second floor when the doorbell rang. It was too late. I couldn't run. I'd already been seen. Father Dooley cupped his hand over his eyes and peered in through the window beside the door.

Contempt curled in Father Dooley's lips. "I wanted to stop by before afternoon Mass," he said, walking past me into the house when I let him in. He placed his cane against the center table as if he was waiting for someone to take it for him with his coat. "I wanted to check in with you," he added.

"I don't think I need it."

"It's okay. Like I said, I thought it was important to check in on you." He studied me. He was trying to find a tone of compassion but not quite locating it. He was patient, and he let the silence hang between us. "I thought I could offer some advice," he finally added. "If any was needed."

"What's there to talk about?" I asked.

Father Dooley looked at me. "That happens, doesn't it, when someone hurts us? We say things to get back at them that we don't really mean. That is why I'm here," he said. "To look after everyone in the parish. We all need a little looking after once in a while. We can't forget that." Father Dooley rarely smiled, but he managed to pull one off. It was ugly and spoiled with insincerity.

"I don't want your help. I want to be left alone."

"But I think you and I still have some things to discuss. Some loose ends."

I couldn't understand what else Father Dooley wanted from me. Couldn't he understand that I hadn't said anything to Mother? Couldn't he understand that I didn't want to talk about it, or even think about it, anymore? Couldn't Father Dooley and I go about our lives and detach, like Old Donovan—just cut loose and not look back? I admired Old Donovan for a moment, his ability to create his own reality and force it upon the rest of the world. He didn't have time to quibble about details. He invented his own truth and stuck to it. There was something like a gunslinger's sense of justice about it, or a religious zealot's: All consequences be damned; they were meaningless when set against the importance of the cause.

Although I couldn't stand Old Donovan, his sensibility

inspired me. I could not go to Most Precious Blood. Imagining myself walking through the rectory door carried me into thoughts I kept trying to purge from my mind. I was not Father Greg. I was not. I wasn't James. I wasn't just another boy in the basement. I wasn't anybody. Father Greg didn't happen, and neither had my time at Most Precious Blood. Nothing happened. The story was being erased. I could erase it further. It could disappear, and what made it easier was that I knew Father Dooley wanted it to disappear too.

"Okay," I said. I gestured to the back hallway, ushering him toward Old Donovan's study. "Let's go sit down."

Father Dooley hesitated, but I insisted. I led him into the study, and I walked straight to the swivel-point leather chair behind his desk. I sat down and gestured to Father Dooley to take a seat in one of the straight-back chairs on the other side.

"I'd rather stand."

"Fine," I said, leaning back in the chair. He was quiet for a moment, and I waited.

When I said nothing, he spoke up quietly. "Look, I wanted to talk to you, Aidan," he said, finally sitting down. I toyed with the small silver-framed calendar on Old Donovan's desk. Father Dooley cleared his throat. "The church, our parish even, has contributed greatly to our society." He stopped again. "Aidan, look at me, please. I need you to understand this. Father Greg is a complicated man. I saw him yesterday evening. He was sick. He is sick.

He'll get better, but maybe somewhere else. You'll never see him in town again."

It didn't seem real. I couldn't picture our town before Father Greg was in it. He was connected to everybody. There was something sad in thinking about the void he would leave behind, but I was angry, too. Angry about all the space he'd taken up. I grabbed a heavy ballpoint pen from its stand and looked up at Father Dooley, tapping the base of the pen on the thick, maroon desk pad.

"He has done a lot for this community," Father Dooley continued. "You know what kind of money he helped raise for the schools, as well. We can't let some of his personal problems overshadow the rest of his career. Just think about what a terrible story can do to a good person. If we do that, we might also ruin what else he worked on. Imagine all the schools, the families there, the kids. We don't want to ruin them, too, do we?" Father Dooley stopped himself and tapped his cane on the ground. "There's a history to our church, a standing in this community. There's the Holy Church itself. It rose out of persecution and became what it is today. Are you listening to me? I'm saying we should forgive and move on."

"Move on," I repeated.

"This isn't about reparations, Aidan. It can't be about that. Sometimes we must sacrifice our personal needs for the greater good. It's religion, Aidan, and it is bigger than you or me or Father Greg. It will survive, and the Church will be here long after you or I or anybody else is gone. It will continue to grow."

"Without me," I said. "I'm not going back there. I'm done, and I'm not going back."

Father Dooley swallowed. "I think it would be important for us to think about forgiveness, too. We must. You'll be better in the long run."

"I'll be better?" I squeezed the pen in my fist and spoke slowly. "Father Dooley, I don't know what you're talking about. We were talking about work, remember? The files are marked. The computer files are easily recognizable." My voice cracked. "I'm only talking about work. There's nothing else to talk about. I'm leaving. That's it. That's the end of it."

"I am trying to speak clearly with you." He looked fragile, too thin for the clothes that hung on him. "We are talking about important things here."

"No, we aren't." I realized I was digging the pen down into the desk pad, and the pad was beginning to shred. I tried to calm myself with a set of Mother's slow, steady breaths. "I'm telling you there's nothing else for us to talk about. I'm done there. Okay?"

Father Dooley leaned closer. He was about to speak, but I cut him off.

"And I never, ever want to see Father Greg again."

Father Dooley eyed me coldly and shook his head. He sighed through his nose. "I suppose I should be going," he said. He looked very uneasy, gripping and regripping the silver handle of his cane. "It's hard for me to trust you completely, Aidan," he said. "I'm still concerned about you, you know."

"You don't have to say that," I said. "I don't need your concern."

Father Dooley stood, bracing himself on the chair. He fiddled with the buttons on his coat, but his hands shook and he couldn't get the first one through the corresponding hole. "I'd also like to say I'm sorry. I wish you could see it from where I am standing. I have to think of everybody— the larger community."

"I wish you would think about leaving too," I said. "Do everyone the favor."

Father Dooley moved closer to the door. He smoothed out his coat and lifted up his voice. "I can show myself out," he said.

I remained in the chair behind the desk as I watched him leave. A long plane of afternoon light stretched across the Persian rug to the giant globe-bar between the armchairs. The angle of light lit up the South Pacific and the Antarctic Circle. I stared at it for a long time, trying to summon some of the Old Donovan I knew. This was who I wanted to be. What had happened between Father Greg and me? Nothing. If nobody knew about it, then it never happened. It didn't exist. It couldn't.

CHAPTER 10

I was on autopilot. Each laugh I crafted, each nod of affirmation as someone else spoke, helped mold and make the *me* I wanted everyone to see. And they saw that Aidan, the one with the growing confidence. I rolled my shoulders as I sat in class or stood in the hall; I straightened my back. I noticed people looking up to meet my eyes for once, as if I had a purpose. On Friday, a teacher even slapped me on the back, just to say "Happy New Year." I flashed back a fierce smile—the indefatigable Donovan party mask. It seemed so much easier to wear now. Everything was just *wonderful*. "Oh, yeah," I said. "You too, man."

At the end of the day, Josie and I snuck a few notes back and forth during end-of-the-day announcements. I told her I noticed she was wearing the same skirt, blouse, and sweater she wore to the Christmas party, and she explained that she and Sophie were going to a Broadway show that evening with their mothers, for their annual January Girls' Night Out. It was her *young lady* outfit. I told her she made all clothes look like the dream the designer first imagined— it didn't matter what she wore, she made it look its best. She was still blushing when we walked down the front steps of CDA together and she and Sophie got into the car waiting for them along the curb. I had meant what I said, but it felt better to know how to say it too.

Everybody was going out that night. Mother was attending a party over in Rye, and as one of their Christmas gifts to each other, Mark's parents had bought themselves tickets to the opera. They were staying in a hotel in the city for the night and not coming home until the next day, so although Mark was grounded and not supposed to leave the house, he insisted we hang out anyway. He said he needed it, and when I gave him one of Mother's lines, "We can't let the world have fun without us," he laughed and agreed. I was grateful not to spend the night alone. I felt like I was gaining momentum, and I didn't want anything to slow me down.

Although I could have started our party midafternoon, Mark had to go home first and then wait for his mother to leave. He couldn't use a car, either, because he was afraid his father would check the mileage when he got back. We decided to meet halfway between our houses at the playground of Coolidge Elementary, and because I had nothing else to do, I went ahead of him and tucked myself into one of the concrete climbing blocks. It was already dark by the time

I got there, and I looked up through the square hole in the roof of the block to the sky. The streetlamps in the nearby parking lot cast a faint gray-orange haze over the playground, but I could still see a few dim stars burning in the picture frame above me. Their light was weak, and I almost thought I could see them flicker, as if they shifted ever so slightly through faded shades of blue or violet. As I continued to stare, a few more stars blinked to life between the other stars. It was depressing to think about the distance between them and me, because I knew it was likely that at least one of the stars I saw that night was already dead and that all that was left of it was its light in my eye. I lit one of Mother's cigarettes and, between drags, held it toward the sky, trying to fix my own orange dot into the vast emptiness above me.

I was taking my last drag when Mark poked his head through the hole. I couldn't see his face at first, but I knew it was him. "Hey," he said. "What are you doing? Trying to send smoke signals or something?"

"Ha, yeah," I said. "Is anybody watching for them?"

"Nope," he said. "Only me."

He crawled through the hole and dropped down beside me. He laughed loudly, and the echo in the concrete cube doubled the volume. I told him to keep it down, in case anybody did walk by, and I passed him a plastic soda bottle I'd filled with Old Donovan's rum. He took it and shook his head. "What the hell. I'm stoned already, man." He took a gulp and wiped his mouth. "Holy shit," he said. I took a swig from my own bottle. It tasted like I'd sucked on the wrong end of a lit cigarette.

"This is supposed to be the good stuff," I said. "I guess it's an acquired taste."

"Like everything in this dumbass world," Mark said. He looked away and laughed to himself. We were both quiet for a minute. "Why not?" he eventually said, as if we'd been carrying on the conversation.

His eyes were bloodshot, but he packed his bowl anyway. We smoked it together, and I lit another cigarette to camouflage the smell. We were cramped too close together, and I stood up through the hole to finish my cigarette. "Hey. You're blocking my view, man," he said, tugging on my pant leg.

"You're on edge, tonight," I said. "Let's relax." I sank back into the block and let one leg dangle out the open back side of the cube.

"Yeah," he said. "Sorry. I've just been thinking a lot lately." What I'd come to recognize in hanging out with Mark was that when a person was stoned, he didn't finish his thoughts. He verbalized about half of them, maybe, and it was up to me to fill in the missing links in his logic. "It doesn't matter what perspective I look at things from, though. I still end up at the same damn place."

"What are you talking about?"

Mark looked back at me and just shook his head.

"Come on, it can't be that bad. You survived after I left your house on New Year's. I did too. We're here now."

"Yeah," Mark said.

"Sorry they found us like that. I barely remember falling asleep."

"No, man. It's all fucked. It's not your fault." We were quiet again, and I listened to a car pass by along the street beside the school. I knew whoever drove it couldn't see through the line of trees to the playground, but it made me a little nervous anyway. Mark didn't seem to notice. He was in his own head now. "I'm supposed to be someone, remember?" he said when he came out of it.

"Yeah."

"Somebody perfect."

"Oh, I know. Aren't we all?"

"Well, my folks think you're pretty far from perfect."

"They're not the first."

"But a *bad influence*. Like, I'm not supposed to hang out with you because you're going to fuck up my future."

"That is fucked."

"Nothing makes sense to me anymore," he said. "Plus, they don't even know the half of it." He drifted back into silence for a moment. We drank more from the bottles, and then he continued. "People say they believe in certain things, but then they do all kinds of other things—things that contradict what they say." He pulled out his one-hitter, filled it, sparked it, and kept the lit bat in his hand. "If they catch me doing anything like I did on New Year's—like driving around drunk—they are seriously going to kill me. Fuck it—if I get caught doing anything, really, they are going to kill me." He sucked in a hit. He offered it to me, and I turned it down. He sucked in another and continued. "We were talking about that shoe bomber in class today," he said. "And I was thinking. Know why the jihadists are going to win in the end? They believe in something. Seriously. They seriously believe in something. We don't, and we're fucked because of that."

"I don't believe that." I tucked my knees up to my chest.

"Yeah, right," Mark said, mocking me. He drank more from his bottle. "My dad wrote a check to the capital campaign at Most Precious Blood. A ten-thousand-dollar check. He said he had to match your dad, even if he thinks you're a crazy person. You know my dad thinks your dad shits gold bricks. Anyway, he sent them all that money, and I don't even remember the last time he stepped into a church. What does that mean?"

"Nothing," I said. "Come on, man, just forget it."

He shook his head. He took another hit, and I waved away his offer for another. He finished it and put it away. He rubbed his eyes and pulled out a bottle of Visine. It had some effect, but not enough.

"I mean, I haven't been to church in a long time, and I'm not going back. My dad doesn't go either, but he wants to believe we're a part of the community. Like it's a necessary badge or something. Part of *this* club: check! Part of *that* club: check! Part of a religious organization: check!" Mark stood up through the hole in the cube and looked around into the darkness of the playground and the baseball diamond beyond. "I feel like I've spent my whole life trying to please other people, trying to become who they want me to be, but it's not like I have any other ideas. It's not like they're stopping me from being the someone I want to be. There is no someone I want to be—isn't that weird?"

"No," I said.

"I've always assumed other people have better ideas, that they do know what is best for me. It never occurred to me that they're all just like me—they're all pretending too. We're all completely on our own." He bent down to me suddenly and grabbed my shoulders. He looked at my black eye, and for a moment I thought he was going to bend forward and kiss it. My stomach dropped, and I stood with a familiar motionlessness. "Dude," he said. "Loneliness sucks." He shook his head and stood up again. He wiped his nose.

Being cramped in the cube now made me uneasy. I kicked my legs out the back side and jumped down into the sand. "Come on," I said to Mark. "Let's not hang out here. We're too loud. Someone's going to hear us eventually. We'll get caught."

"Fuck," Mark said. "I don't know. Maybe it's time I got caught—that I really got caught. Maybe that's what I need."

"Don't be crazy!" I said.

"Fine," he said. He was looking at the school. He cupped his hand over his eye like a visor to block out the glare from one of the parking lot lights. "I know a place we can go where no one will hear us."

He swung out of the cube and marched through the playground into the stand of trees beside the school. The building was shaped like a smooth and blunted scallop shell, with the back being the narrower end and the front of the school fanning out as it faced the street. The front of the school also had more floors than the back, so the roof gradually sloped downward toward the back of the building. A metal fire-escape staircase zigzagged up the side of the building near the back, beyond the playground and the lights from the parking lot. Mark led me to the foot of the stairs and quickly up them to the emergency door at the back of the school.

"Hey, man," I said. "If we try to go in, it will set off an alarm."

"We're not going in," he said. "We're going up." The window beside the emergency door was covered in metal grating. Mark looked to the roof. "Think you can do this?"

"Come on," I said. "You can't be serious."

Mark smiled. It was the first time he had seemed fully relaxed all day. "Yes," he said. "I know I can do it. But I've seen you swim. Think you can haul yourself up there?" He didn't wait for my reply. He grabbed hold of the grate and started climbing. He scrambled up to the edge of the roof, and when he got there, he hesitated, but only briefly. He held on to the lip of the roof, pulled himself up, and rolled forward, out of sight. I followed, but more nervously. The climb was even harder than I realized it would be, and when I thought about how high I was off the ground, I didn't look down. As I pulled myself up, my arms shook, and the grate rattled. I could hear the breeze moving the tree branches ten or fifteen feet behind me. I clung on as tightly as I could and continued slowly. When I finally got to the top and looked over the stone lip, Mark was sitting nearby. "Need a hand?" he asked. He planted his feet behind the lip, grabbed me underneath one of my shoulders, and dragged me over onto the rooftop.

What I hadn't been able to notice from the ground was that the roof was terraced. It ran as a flat expanse from where we were to a low wall, on top of which was another flat expanse leading to another low wall. From that wall, the roof sloped sharply upward to a peak at the front of the building. We sat against the first low wall, drinking from our bottles as I caught my breath. Mark didn't usually drink at all, but he slugged down the rum faster than me. He smiled, but there seemed to be some kind of anger still lingering beneath his smile. He finished his rum and threw the bottle across the roof.

"Careful. This is from the office of J. P. Donovan himself. Last time I chugged his stuff, I hosed down Sophie," I said. I laughed, but he didn't.

"Ha," he said flatly. "Remember that? That was a good time, until my mother came in with her frigging CIA crack-down."

"Look," I said. I grabbed his shoulder. "We're here now.

Let's forget them. We're free. This is how we're supposed to feel. Free!" I gestured out toward the roof in front of us. The lights for the parking lot were below and did not provide much light. In fact, from the roof, we could see more stars, and the dark sky opened up above us. We spun around, lay down with our heads at the base of the wall, and felt our perspective change.

"Whoa," Mark said. "Trippy."

He began to laugh, and I did too, glad that he was happy. We shared the rum in my bottle and smoked a little more from the one-hitter. After a while, we were stupid with laughter. I kept pointing up at the stars, and when I did, Mark would point too and then poke me with his other hand. I couldn't stop laughing.

Mark stood up. "Let's get really free." He started taking off his clothes. I stopped laughing when he was down to his boxer shorts and socks and was staring at me with a straight face. "You too, idiot."

I hesitated but then followed, glad Mark hadn't taken his underwear off. When I was down to my own underwear and socks, I felt the cold biting up at my feet, and I swigged more of the rum to try to warm up. Mark grabbed the bottle from me and finished it off. He wound up and threw it over the edge of the roof. I heard the plastic cap hit the metal of the fire escape. "Woo-hoo!" he yelled. "Fuck them all!" We jumped around like lunatics and shook our fists in the air, dancing around our pile of clothes.

"I think we can go higher," he said. "Watch this." He got a running start, sped toward the wall, and with a leap, scaled it to the next level. "Come on," he said, leaning over it.

I followed him up, and then again, as we did the same at the next wall. We scaled the sharply sloping roof by crawling up it on our bellies. When we got to the edge, we looked over it to the street below. Another car passed, but it didn't slow down. "Fuck them all!" Mark shouted again. The world seemed to flip out from underneath me. My sense of balance was out of control, and although I wasn't moving, I had the sensation that I was slipping forward, up and over the edge of the roof. I shuffled back down the slope and rolled onto my back. I felt a little better, but again, with the dome of the sky all around me, I felt like I was tipping forward, pitching toward the stars. "Holy shit," I said.

"I know," Mark said. "I feel like I'm flying."

I arched my head and looked back at him. He was still up at the edge, but now he was on his knees, with his arms stretched out on either side of him. I shivered. "Come on," I said. "Let's get our clothes back on. I can't do this anymore."

"No," he said. When I looked back at him again, he was perched even closer to the edge of the roof. "No."

"Mark."

"No. Fuck them. They can kiss this Senator Kowolski's ass." He pulled down his boxers and mooned me. He tried to turn himself around on his knees so he could moon the street below, and his feet rose up over the lip of the roof and wiggled in the air above the front of the school. He laughed and tucked his head forward into his chest, but I couldn't tell if he was crying too.

"Hey, man," I said.

"How do you do it? How do you stay sane?" he asked softly. He remained perched at the peak of the roof.

"You're the one who always looks together." His hands stayed firmly planted in front of him and although he pitched forward, down the slope of the roof toward me, his feet still dipped out over the edge behind him as if his socks were drifting off into the neighborhood. "Hey," I said. "Come down from there, man."

"Fuck that. I look together? I'm a mess, man. You know that. You know that better than anyone."

"Dude! You're wasted. Seriously."

He picked up his head and looked at me. "Are you saying you care about me?" His voice tilted upward at the end, and I couldn't tell if he was mimicking or mocking Josie from New Year's or if there was something genuine in his question.

"Come on, man."

Mark stretched one leg out farther behind him until his knee was out over the lip. Nearly naked and thrust over the point of the roof, he looked like a berserker figurehead of some Viking ship careening into the darkness ahead of him. And with a sad madness in his eyes, he asked, "Would you help me, really, if I needed it?"

"Jesus, man." I flipped over and began crawling toward him. "Have you lost it?"

"You know it." He lifted his hands from the roof and began to lean back. His leg sank farther into the air. He grinned, then his body waivered, he pitched to the side, and he cried out.

"Mark!"

He slipped and lost his balance and his whole leg sank over the edge. He buckled and hit the ledge of the roof, but I was able to grab his wrist as he tipped backward. He didn't fall once I had him in my hand. His body trembled as we threw our arms over each other's shoulders, and we slid forward down the roof. Mark didn't resist. I stopped us at the edge of the wall and leaned back against the slope of the roof.

"What the hell is wrong with you?" I asked.

Mark was silent, and after a moment his eyes were red and wet. He had corrected himself, and now he sat beside me with his head down between his knees. He leaned against me, and the breeze across my skin chilled me. "Come on," I said. "We need our clothes." We climbed down the first wall, and as we walked across the second terrace of the roof, we could see back over the entire playground and the parking lot below us. To the left, along the road that led to the school, I saw a pair of headlights flash and come around the corner. I hustled Mark toward the edge, but before we could get there the car pulled into the parking lot.

I dropped to my stomach and yanked Mark down with me. "Stay flat," I said.

I snaked us forward to the next wall and looked over its lip to the level below and to the ground. The car came to a stop near the playground and flipped on its high beams. It was the police. A cop stepped out from the driver's side and waved a flashlight toward the jungle gym, then the swing sets and the concrete climbing blocks. He left the flashlight pointed at the blocks for a while. Our clothes were one level down, but I was too afraid if we climbed over the wall, we would become visible. Flattened, and behind the lip, we remained in the shadows. I was freezing but too scared to move. Mark stayed beside me but didn't look over the edge with me. He lay on his back and, with tears on his cheeks, stared up at the sky.

The cop walked toward the playground and kept his flashlight on the concrete blocks. Finally, after what seemed like forever, he walked back to his car, got in, and switched off his high beams. He remained in the car for a while, idling, until he finally pulled the car around and drove away. When his headlights disappeared behind the corner, I got up on my knees and tapped Mark. "Let's go," I said.

We jumped back down to the next level and silently put on our clothes. Mark looked depressed. I stamped my feet and rubbed my arms, trying to get warm. I couldn't shake the cold. "Let's get out of here," I said.

Mark hesitated. He stepped closer and put his arms

around me. I didn't move at first, but then I felt the squeeze and knew it was more than a hug. I wiggled, and he held me a little tighter.

"Come on," I said to him. He didn't say anything back, and I pushed out of his embrace. "Please," I said. "I won't do that."

Mark stepped back. "You can just do that, huh? Turn on and off? Whenever the hell you want?"

"What?"

"I can't really do that," Mark said. "Be totally free."

"Yeah, you can."

"Really? Fuck you."

"Look, man, it's okay. It's fine. You just can't ask me to do that. I'm sorry."

"Yeah, right." He crossed his arms and stared at me for a moment.

"Look, we're just friends," I said. "We can be friends. This is great."

Mark looked away. When he looked back, his eyes were red rimmed and wild. They darted everywhere. He couldn't look at me. "Please," he begged. "What the hell do you think would have happened if we just got caught up here?"

"But we didn't." I took a step forward and put a hand on his shoulder. "Come on, let's get out of here."

"You don't get it," Mark said, shaking my hand off.

"What are you talking about, man?"

He paced around in front of me and held his arms tight around himself. "I can't take it anymore. I'm losing it. How do you do it?"

"Just try to collect yourself. I don't understand you."

"Drop the act, man."

"What are you getting so pissed about?"

"What about being my friend? Think we can strip down all the bullshit and finally get real? I was talking earlier about not going back to Most Precious Blood ever. I was talking about that, man. And you just ignored it. Come on."

I didn't say anything for a few seconds, hoping that if I stayed quiet, he would begin to calm down and regain enough composure to come up with a plan. I was terrified into silence. I still believed there was some kind of plan—something we could do to spin this and never have to get back to this conversation. But Mark looked at me, and I wanted to cry.

"Please," he said. "I'm trying to tell you." He walked over and stood close to me. "I'm losing my mind, man," he said. "Don't you see it? Don't you think we both know the same thing?"

I put my hand on his shoulder and kept him at a distance. "Be quiet. Just shut up already," I said. "Just stop talking. Please don't say any more."

Mark pulled back. "Why are you saying that? I'm going crazy. I can't be quiet anymore. It's everywhere." I reached for him again, but he stepped away. "What the fuck? Can't you hear me? I'm fucking dying from the quiet, man. My parents want to call in a psychologist. They want to know if I'm 'salvageable.' If they can fix me up before I become completely worthless."

"Don't say that," I said, and tried to say more, but he kept going.

"They already think I'm worthless. What will everyone else think? I can't go to school. I can't go anywhere. I'm so fucked." He looked up into the sky and sighed. "I don't even understand. It just started. I was in eighth grade. Father Greg told me it was love. But what hurts, what I fucking know, is that it wasn't right with Father Greg. What I feel right now, and what I also *know* right now, is that I like guys. He didn't love me. I thought he did, but it wasn't love. But I could love another guy. I know that, too." He looked up at me. "Come on, man. You know what I'm talking about. Right? You must."

I didn't respond even though he kept asking me. He moved closer to me. "Come on, man. Please talk to me."

"Stop talking," I said. "You don't know what you are saying."

"Yes, I do. That's what's making me so fucking nuts. There's no one else to talk about this with. Except you. You know. I know I wasn't the only one. You worked there."

"Stop talking about Father Greg. Just forget him. Nothing happened with him."

"Yes, it did. I need to talk to someone. We don't have to be alone." He stepped toward me for a hug, and I gave it to him. "You were there too. And, for real? Doesn't this mean something to you? You're not alone?" He tightened his grip around me. "You understand, man. We don't have to be alone. We can talk about this." His hands slid up and down my back, and he pulled me closer. "A kiss means something."

"Stop." I pushed him away.

"Come on, man. We're the only two people who can talk to each other about all this."

"No. Fucking stop talking. Don't say another word about Father Greg. Nothing fucking happened there."

Mark shook his fists. "Fuck! Don't make me sound any crazier. I'm not crazy. Everybody else is." He came closer to me. "I saw him at your Christmas party. I avoided him. But I saw him look at you across the room. I'm not crazy, man. I saw it. I know it had to have happened with you, too. I know it."

I pushed him, and he stumbled backward. "There's no fucking way. That's not what happened. Don't ever say that again. Don't say anything about it again. It never happened with me. Not with a single fucking person. Don't you get it?"

Mark looked up at me. "I want to talk about Father Greg, okay? I thought you'd been with Father Greg. Come on. What are you always talking about? Take your face off, man. Talk to me. I need someone to talk to. I'm not alone."

"What's the matter with you?" I said. "Don't you hear me? I don't know what you're talking about." I stood over him. "Why are you telling me this?"

Mark began to cry. "I can't be alone."

"Maybe you are," I said. I trembled and tried to get ahold of myself. "That's not the Father Greg I know. I don't ever want to talk about him again."

"Dude, please. Please help me," Mark sobbed. "I need help. It happened. I feel so fucking alone. I can't keep it inside anymore. It's fucking burning me, man. It's killing me. Please. I need help, dude. Please."

"Look. I'm not like you. Okay? I'm not! I don't know, maybe you were looking for it. Maybe that's it. Maybe that's what you are trying to say. But I'm not you, okay?" I could barely get it out of my mouth, but I repeated myself. "Stop talking about it. Bury it. Bury it so deep, you can't even think about it. That's all anybody does." I hauled Mark up to his feet. "Don't ever mention Father Greg to me again. Don't fuck it all up for yourself, and don't fuck it up for every-body else. Don't ever talk about any of it again. Promise me you'll never tell anyone else."

Mark shook his head. "Can you even hear yourself? Who are you?"

"Don't give me that. Take your life back."

Mark stared at me, and then he looked away. He walked to the edge by the metal grate, down to the fire escape, and swung his legs over the ledge. He paused and looked back at me. "This is my life," he said. Then he dropped down out of view, leaving me on the roof, staring into the darkness without him.

CHAPTER 11

I slept in very late, and the next afternoon I found Mother in the kitchen, drinking a cup of tea and looking over papers scattered across the butcher block.

"I was at the bank half the day yesterday," she began, as if we were already in conversation with each other.

"Hell-lo."

"Yes, hi, but get this: Your father has actually agreed to help. We're still sorting out the contractual details, but this seals it. I'm moving forward." Her legs were crossed, and she bounced her foot. "I've already spoken with Cindy. I thought she was pressed for money, but she's giving me a deal on space in her building. I don't know. Her family is going through a hard time."

I forced myself to stand still. "Why?"

"It's James. Do you know James? He went to Country Day—well, until this week. She's pulled him out of Country

Day and put him in Bullington. Doesn't that say it all? It's like your house has been marked: 'Hi, town, my kid's got problems.' She thinks it's all her fault, too. I feel just awful for her. I don't know why she's beating herself up. Poor James is an emotional wreck. Whenever he isn't in school, he's at the gallery with Cindy. But I'm not going to pry. Honestly, can you imagine?"

Mother continued, and she was too excited talking about her new storefront and the furniture she needed to notice that I was remaining silent. I only half listened. I was fixed on James, and when Mother said she had to go back out, I acted so quickly, I nearly surprised myself. I asked her if I could join her and, giving her one of her own City Center smiles, asked if we could see her new space, too. She hugged me. I continued, and it didn't even sound like me. It was someone else speaking. "You're really making things happen," I said to her. "I want to see it all." She was thrilled, and it was so easy to lie to her—it actually felt good.

When we got there, we stood out front and peered through the windows. It was a raw space, and Mother did not yet have the keys. We stood on the sidewalk and, in her big sunglasses and cool lavender scarf, she looked like a 1950s movie star directing her own movie as she pointed to the area where she would sit and make plans with clients, where she would store some of her design portfolios, and which part of the space she planned to turn into a gallery of parties. "This is the idea," she continued. "People can pick and chose elements and themes. Is it a party we're creating in a raw space? Is it in your home? Do you want the elegance to show overtly, or subtly, as if you yourself threw the whole thing together? It's all a show, isn't it? It's part of the client's identity, and she should feel free to explore."

"Or to invent completely," I said.

"Exactly."

Cindy's gallery was next door—the whole building was hers—and Mother led the way there next. It had been the plan all along to stop by Cindy's, but now that I was actually there, my chest tightened and I couldn't hold still. The storefront was a wall of windows, and through them the bright glare from two enormous hypercolored paintings flashed out onto the sidewalk. Mother pointed at one in particular, but it was too hard for me to focus.

"This show is fantastic," Mother said. "It just reels you in from the street."

The reception desk was scattered with leaflets and catalogs, and Mother introduced me to the young assistant who looked as sleek and modern as the exposed I-beams in the vaulted showroom. The gallery had been built to look like a renovated warehouse, although there had never been a warehouse on this street, but that didn't seem to bother the small crowd that shifted around the freestanding walls in the deep space. The assistant looked up at Mother over her thick, black glasses and repeated my name as if it was something foreign and hard to pronounce.

While we waited for Cindy, it was impossible for me to move without second-guessing my gestures. I was so afraid, I nearly thought my teeth would tumble out of my mouth if I smiled. I stopped moving altogether and stood in front of a print, not really looking at it but wondering, instead, for the hundredth time, if James had told his mother. When I was finally calm enough to let my own voice back into my head, to slow down and control myself, to not let my own breath knock me over, I knew I still didn't want to say anything to Mother. For some reason, telling Mother made me feel as though I was opening the door and letting Father Greg right back into my house, and once he was back, I thought the whole world would know, and the thought of everyone knowing what had happened somehow seemed worse than having been trapped in the act in the first place. If no one knew, it didn't really happen, right? And that was my story: Nothing had ever happened.

I didn't know how long I stared at the print before Mother came up to me. "What are you doing? Why are you acting like a crazy person? Out here? In public?"

"What?" I must have looked slightly deranged.

"What's the matter with you?" Mother asked. I wasn't sure if I had seen her look that pissed since I'd gotten home from Elena's. "Cindy's on the phone. She'll be with us in a minute." Mother looked around and flashed one of her winning, "public" smiles. There must have only been a couple of people milling nearby, and Mother and I had spoken so quietly, I doubt they could have heard anything, but I could feel that old frustration behind Mother's bright facade.

I stared ahead at the print of a man's face. The canvas was broken up into a symmetrical grid, creating the appearance of both a three-dimensional depiction of a young man with a wry half grin and a flat surface broken into patterns of multicolored cubes. I wanted to leap into one of those cubes, hide in the color red or blue, and let the rest of me disappear.

Mother touched my shoulder, and I turned to see Cindy poking her head around the corner from the back of the gallery, waving at us. I smiled back automatically and felt that familiar pose creeping over me. I really wanted to cry, but I wouldn't if the corners of my mouth were shoved way up into my cheeks. There it was again: Mother and her indomitable survival of the cheeriest.

Cindy and Mother embraced and told each other how wonderful they looked. Unlike her assistant, Cindy wasn't wearing any black at all. I assumed she was the type who would never wear black—especially because she owned an art gallery. She seemed pleased to see us, but she looked tired, too, and the makeup caked under her eyes couldn't hide the puffy bags.

"Sorry to keep you waiting. I was speaking with Walter," Cindy said.

"Since when did he start calling to check in with you during the day?" Mother asked.

"We're just trying to connect a little more these days," Cindy said. She seemed a little relieved. "It's so great you brought Aidan along," she said as we kept pace with her brisk strides toward the back of the gallery. "James is here too. You've never met James, have you?" she asked me. "He's downstairs playing video games. You should join him while we talk shop up here."

I tried hard to control myself and mirror Mother's attitude. Stick to the plan, I kept telling myself. Just talk to him. In the back of the gallery there was a narrow set of stairs heading down to the storage rooms below. I could see a row of framed paintings tucked side by side on a rack at the foot of the stairs. Cindy leaned over the railing. "Honey?" she called. There was no answer, but we could make out the electric gunfire and high-pitched squeals of agony from the video game. Cindy tried to smile, but she gripped the railing tightly. "Honey?" she called. "Honey, where are you?"

Cindy ran down the first couple of steps. "James!" she yelled. I thought some of the guests out in the gallery must have heard her. She rubbed her forehead and spoke more softly. "Sorry," she said to us. "I'm just so frazzled these days. I'm sorry. I'm okay."

"Of course, dear," Mother said.

"James!" Cindy said again.

The game noises suddenly stopped, and we could hear James yelling back from the depths of the room below. "I'm here, Mom. I'm here. I was just finishing a level. I'm here," he said, coming around the corner. He stood by the painting rack at the foot of the stairs with his hands rolled up in the tails of a green-and-black flannel shirt. He was a wiry kid, wearing black, skinny jeans, and his curls hung over his face. It was terrible to hear him speak. He sounded wiser than he should, and a hard lump tightened in my throat as I thought about how this little runt had been the reason Father Greg had started to ignore me. Even knowing everything I knew, and knowing how twisted Father Greg's affections had been, I still could not *not* hate James.

He blinked and looked up at all three of us. "Hey," he said when Cindy re-introduced us, and from his unchanged expression—the way his lips remained still and sad—I knew right away he did not want to see me.

Cindy urged James to invite me to join him and play his video game. "We have so much to discuss up here," Cindy said to me. "We might take a little while."

"I can't wait," Mother said.

"Are you kidding?" Cindy said as she composed herself. "We're going to be neighbors. And I have some ideas that might help both of us."

"I'm playing *After the Plague*," James said. "You can play too, I guess." His voice was soft, but it scared me anyway. It had the weight of the whispers.

"That game, really?" Cindy said.

"Come on," James whined.

"Okay. Okay," Cindy said, cutting him off. "I'm not crit-icizing. I was just asking." She turned to Mother nervously and walked back up the stairs. "These kids today . . ." She trailed off for a moment, until they'd moved away from the stairs. "You just have to worry about them more, or for them. I don't know."

There was a moment of silence, and I knew that was my cue to leave them alone. I told Cindy I'd go down and join James. "Sounds like some exciting stuff is going on around here," I said. Cindy beamed, and I knew it had been the right thing to say, like the old script had been handed to me, and I'd picked right up where I'd left off somewhere back at the Christmas party.

I made a U-turn at the foot of the basement stairs and walked past the painting racks and file cabinets. James had already gotten back to his game. There was a row of dim track lighting running down what had become a corridor between the storage units. Two more rows of track lighting had been turned off, and they stretched in different direc-tions across the ceiling. The screams and gun blasts from James's video game came from behind some of the file cab-inets. I rounded the corner and found a small office area James had cleared away and set up with a projector and screen. The characters in the game were as large as he was. He controlled a man in a red leather jacket who wielded a semiautomatic gun and fired away at an armada of zom-bies that groaned their way forward until James blew their heads off. Blood spurted across the screen endlessly, and I found myself feeling a little queasy.

"Excuse me," I said softly, but James jumped anyway. "Sorry, sorry. I just thought I'd come down."

The colors from the screen played over his pale face as he looked at me. He shrugged into himself, collapsing inward, and he took a step back. A zombie hurled an ax at his player, and then another stabbed the leather-jacketed character with a pitchfork. There was another chop, screams, and then James's player fell down in a bloody heap. The zombie hoard moved in and feasted on the corpse. The screen glazed over in a film of red.

A small area rug was spread across the floor between us, and neither of us crossed it. "There's soda in the fridge," James finally said, pointing to a small brown door beneath the desk.

The air was cool in the storage basement, and a mug of tea or coffee would have been more appropriate, but I grabbed a can from the minifridge anyway. I leaned against the desk and realized how much taller I was than James. He looked at the screen and shook his head.

"Well, I guess since you killed me, I could start over. Want to play two-player? I have another controller." James pressed some buttons and flipped through a series of screens until there were two profile head shots floating on the screen in front of a gray background.

"The second player is a girl, huh?" I asked. The digital

warrior wore a leather jacket like her male counterpart, but hers was black. "I'll play. What do I do?"

James dug around in a desk drawer and pulled out the other controller. As he plugged it in, he explained its basic functions, how to kick and punch, how to shoot, how to throw a grenade, and where to look for more once the game started because they were few and far between. He took it all very seriously, and he held the new remote close to his chest as he recited the directions. He seemed proud of himself.

"Thanks" I said after a minute. "But it's just a game. I'm sure I'll get the hang of it."

"Yeah," James said. "But you have to play it right if you're going to play." He stood there in the glow from the projector and the screen, looking like a solemn officiant, and I wondered if this is what I looked like to other kids when I responded to the teachers' questions, one after another—automatic and lifeless. When I reached for the controller, he stepped back and handed it to me at a full arm's length, nearly dropping it into my hand.

"You can just stand back over there," he said, pointing to the other side of the rug.

I followed his orders, and the game began. Although we were both a team against the zombies, James killed most of them while I shot erratically across the screen. If I had cared about the game at all, I would have been glad we weren't playing against each other. He would have slaughtered me, and I could tell he wouldn't have gotten bored doing it over and over. In fact, because he knew the game so well, I assumed he'd already played it through and beaten it before. He was just going through the motions. Enter zombie; destroy it; pick up ammunition; load; fire; fire; fire. I could understand the comfort it brought, the succinct execution of tasks, one after another indefinitely, that kept him busy enough to not have to think about something else.

Across the rug, James stood stiffly; only his fingers bounced quickly across the controller. "Hey," I said to him, "I heard you switched schools."

"My mom wanted to move me somewhere else."

"No kidding, where?"

"I don't know. Just someplace else, I guess. Hey, watch out!" James yelled. I let my player wander too close to a zombie, who bit into my player's shoulder. "Do a roundhouse!" James shouted. "Do a roundhouse!"

I fumbled over the buttons and managed to spin my character and boot the zombie away. Then I blew its head off because I was at close range. Its headless body wavered in place. "Yeah," James whispered. He used the corpse to block an oncoming attack and annihilated the group of oncoming zombies with a grenade. His character pushed forward and marched us deeper into the game.

"She didn't like CDA? It's a good school."

"I don't know."

"What's the matter with it?"

"My mom just thinks I should go somewhere else. I don't know."

Our characters jogged into the middle of a town square with an old stone well in the center. What looked like regular villagers were actually zombies carelessly stumbling through pedestrian motions: yanking on the well chain, although there wasn't a bucket; picking over apples at a fruit cart that was turned over and crawling with maggots. The zombies turned toward us when James hit one of them from behind. James fired into the windows of some buildings, too, and zombies tumbled out of them.

"I heard you're going to Bullington, now. Is that right?" I asked.

"Come on," he said. "This is a hard part."

"Seriously. Why would she make you go there?"

"I don't know. Are you going to play the game?"

"I think you do," I said. James glanced at me briefly, then turned back to the game and tried to concentrate even more. "And you're no longer an altar boy at Most Precious Blood, are you?" I tried to keep my voice from trembling. "You're not even going there anymore, are you?" James shook his head. "I used to work there too," I said. "I'm never going back." James shifted his feet on the carpet and fired at another zombie. I couldn't feel the buttons beneath my thumbs. I found myself standing right next to him. "James," I said quietly.

James stepped back and pointed to the controller I had

dropped on the floor on the other side of the rug. "P-Please," he stammered. "I want to play the game."

"Did you tell your mother?" I asked.

James shook his head at me. "I don't know."

"You did." I was shrill, and I couldn't stop it.

"I just want to play the game," James whimpered. One of the characters in the video game screamed. "I don't want to talk. I can't. I can't."

I ripped the controller out of his hand and grabbed his arm. "I need to know about this," I said. James tried to pull his arm away, but he couldn't get out of my grip. I hunched over him, found his collar in my other hand, and pulled him closer. "You can tell me," I said. "What did you say? Did anyone talk to Father Dooley? Don't you get it?" I yelled. In the game, a mob of zombies screamed and squealed, and our two characters shrieked as the monsters surrounded them, stabbing and clawing. With his free arm, James punched me, but it was weak and useless. He tried to kick me.

"You won't tell anybody?"

"No," he said.

I grabbed his hair and forced him to look up at me. "Promise me you won't tell anybody."

He kept his eyes closed. "No. I won't tell anything. I won't," he pleaded. "No, no." I held on as my stomach bottomed out. Sweat poured down around my neck. I could feel his chest through the cotton, against my knuckles. I knew so surely that I could pull James down to his knees. I could do anything I wanted to him, and that sudden knowledge made me want to vomit.

"No," he cried again. I let go of him. I blocked the exit and still held him by the arm, so he leaned over and bit my hand. He was free in an instant. He dashed under the desk and tucked himself into a ball beside the minifridge. I wanted to hit him: I wanted to hold him.

The zombies gorged themselves on our dead avatars, gore splattering across the screen in ugly, too-realistic droplets. James remained under the table as if sheltering himself from the spray of blood. "Please," I heard myself whining. "I didn't hurt you. Please. I didn't mean to." I nearly choked it out as I listened to myself. "No, no. I'm not like him, James. I'm not him. I'm not."

"I won't talk about it!" James yelled. He sniffled and wiped his cheeks.

I leaned down against the file cabinet and sat on the floor. The projector flashed above me. A film of red covered the images on the screen again, and the game's theme music drummed alongside the grotesque munching sounds. James continued to whimper, and soon I was sobbing too. Dust floated through the bright cone of light above me, and I thought of the grit pressing into my knees on the church basement floor, Father Greg's hand yanking my hair, the smell of dank sweat, the sips of scotch, the burn, a finger with a jagged nail pressed against my lip, the rough moustache scratching at my neck, along my jaw, my ribs squeezed within his massive grip, the cold air prickling the skin on my chest, the edge of the workbench digging, carving a line deep into my back, but how I wouldn't scream, no I wouldn't dare fucking scream, not once, not anything more than the hush it took to survive it, and the breaths that came with the long soreness until finally it was gone, and I told myself, *I've done it, I've survived, and if this is what it takes, and this is all it takes, then I can take it all again and I will.*

I was sick. I found my Coke, swigged it to try to settle my stomach, but I felt worse, and I struggled to keep it down. I apologized to James as soon as I could manage it. He watched me from beneath the desk for a long time, until he finally calmed down. "I won't bother you again," I said. He nodded. Neither of us moved for a while, and I began to worry about our mothers upstairs. "Will they come down?" I asked.

"She'll shout first," James said. "She scared me once. Now she shouts down first."

"That's good," I said. I wanted to give him something to prove that I would not bother him again, some kind of token that meant more than anything I could say to him. In a myth, I might be able to find a cup that would bring blood back into his cheeks, or a cloak that would protect him, but in the real world there was nothing but trust, and I could understand why he wouldn't give that to me.

When I got up, James stayed under the desk. I steadied myself and chugged the rest of the soda. James hesitated.

"Let's go," I told him. I picked up the controllers and tossed one to him. "I'll be the girl again."

James pulled himself forward to see the screen from a better angle, but he still remained seated on the floor by the desk. We played through the level again, and I concentrated, tried to play more seriously, tried to work with James's character so he wouldn't have to cover for me. We got to the village center again, more quickly this time. I shot at the upstairs windows as soon as we approached the well, and pitched a grenade into it, and the whole thing exploded, bricks flying everywhere.

"Awesome," James said quietly. "They would have started crawling out later."

"I'm learning," I said. "But I would suck if you hadn't explained it." James smiled. "You're really good at this game," I said.

"I am," James said. "I know."

Cindy called down to us later, and we walked over to the stairs. In front of our mothers, I thanked James for letting me play the game with him, and he waved good-bye to me. As I got up the stairs, Mother glowed. She put her hand on my shoulder and told Cindy she'd be back on Tuesday. I started out into the gallery, and then Mother went back over to Cindy and gave her a hug. "It's exciting, isn't it?" she said. "Thank you."

"Let's stop saying thank you to each other and just start doing it," Cindy said.

They kissed good-bye, and Mother squeezed her hand and then strode toward me in the doorway.

"It was a pleasure to see your gallery," I said. I almost bowed for all the formality. On the way out, we passed the print of the man's face I had been staring at earlier. When I'd been looking at it before, staring at one cube at a time, the big picture hadn't been as clear as it was when we were leaving. It was a multilayered mask, and what was left of the flesh was nearly gone, present only as the representation of a face that everyone would recognize, not the real face behind it. Who but a sucker, a dumb shit like me or James, ever revealed that soft, trembling stuff beneath?

Mother had an air of knowing superiority about her as we walked back to our car. The sun had set while we'd been at the gallery, and Mother seemed excited by the night sky and the orange glow from the faux gaslights along the sidewalk. She looked both ways down the block and clapped her gloved hands together. I watched my breath billow and disappear.

"It's still early enough to get a seat at Oyster Bridge," she said. "You're hungry, right?" she continued when we were in the car. "Let's get some dinner. Let's go out and celebrate. This is the new us. We're getting back involved."

"Oh, yeah," I said. "We are."

"Aren't you excited? You take after me more than you think. We'll be the vanguard. We'll be the talk of the town."

I could just see her twirling a furious diagonal down the

stage, flexing her hips, and setting her legs for the leap. *Get up there.* I knew it must take more than training to get your body up into the air. Your mind has to push you up too; you must have to see yourself rising, and not from your own body's vantage point but as if your mind's eye leaves you and watches you from afar, and a distant voice says, *Up, up, up, get up there*, and you let it take you away.

It was the power of willing yourself to do something, and I supposed it took the same kind of power to lie to yourself, to redirect memories and push yourself into a different life story. Old Who? Father Nevermind. It was just Mother and me soldiering on, making our way up into that brightness we all want to find.

After dinner, we were home again, blasting some old eighties music, and Mother asked if I'd ever learned to make a martini. She'd had a few at the restaurant, and I supposed it wasn't hard, but Mother said it wasn't about the know-how, it was about the finesse, and we would work on that. I thought about the finesse it took to make it look like I gave a flying fuck. A drink is a drink is a drink, and they all achieve the same end, the same thing that had happened so many nights in our house and that I knew was going to happen again that night. Mother told me to watch while she fixed her next one.

I made one, following her instructions, and once we both had our drinks I slurped mine slowly, but Mother gulped hers down. She walked away from me and leaned back on the piano. She had the drunkard's swagger. "I really am going to do it on my own again. We are," she added when she looked at me.

I didn't need another pep talk from Mother. She smiled, though, and I knew I couldn't get away from this unless I moved on to some other topic she'd prefer. "It'll be easy. You're not old and gray yet. I mean, you still look younger than most of the mothers I see around CDA."

Mother giggled. "Well, aren't you kind. You sure know how to say the right thing," she said. "Who raised you?" She laughed uneasily. She moved away from the piano and sat down on the arm of Old Donovan's recliner. I stayed quiet and sipped at my drink, leaning against the mantel.

"I'm not as young as I used to be," Mother continued. "Men don't look at me like they once did. It's something I once had, and now it's gone, just like that. A man looks at you and you know what he thinks."

Mother was lost in her own reverie, and she stared into the empty fireplace as she spoke. I didn't think it had anything to do with gender. It had to do with being watched, eyes glancing up and down your body, taking it apart, or taking it in piece by piece. Anyone could suffer that kind of moment, could feel the weight of it, could know it, or even want it. It felt good to be wanted sometimes. I didn't need the gravity of time to teach me that. There were many ways to want someone and to be wanted; there was a spectrum of desire between two people and not all of it had to do with the body.

Mother was trying to give me advice. She thought she knew loss, and assumed I still didn't, or couldn't understand it to the extent she did. How can you trust a person like that, a person who claims a monopoly on victimhood?

She had me fix her another martini. "Look at me," she said. "Nobody can say I look sad. I don't look sad. I'm going to make it." She became quiet as she sank down into Old Donovan's chair and the massive padding swelled around her thin frame. Maybe she could smell him, smell his old-man smell, that musty mix of dead skin and arrogance. Soon her head lolled to one side or the other, giving her the effect of a doll thrown aside after the game was over, and eventually, she stumbled upstairs to bed.

I cleaned up for a while and then followed her. From behind the closed doors of the master bedroom, I could hear the moaning of her cello suites drifting through the darkness. She listened to it to remember back to when it had been a partner in her life, the times when the music had swelled in the theaters. I knocked on her door. She didn't respond, but I entered anyway. Faint moonlight reached across the room. The long mirror set into the door to the washroom reflected a shadowy image of the bed, and I didn't see Mother until her foot moved across the bedspread. She had not climbed under the covers. Instead, she had pulled the edge of the comforter off the floor and rolled it over her so that it hung around her shoulders like a cape. Her thin, stockinged legs were exposed and tucked up against her chest. She hadn't even kicked off her heels.

I walked over, took off her shoes, and slumped her into a movable position. In her dead-limbed daze, I was able to get a shoulder underneath hers and lift her as I pulled the sheets down farther. I got her under the covers and tried to look away, even though she didn't seem to care, because as I moved her down the bed, her skirt bunched and rose up her thigh. I swung her legs up and tucked them under the sheets and blankets as quickly as I could, but I still saw her underwear. Her eyes were unfocused. I probably could have slapped her and she wouldn't have flinched.

I stole one of her cigarettes from her bedside table and smoked it as I sat with my back to her. Maybe she would come back to life, if only to yell at me. It was a woman's cigarette, one of those long, skinny ones, but it didn't really matter what kind of cigarette I smoked. I could have slipped on high heels for God's sake: I still would have felt like the man of the house.

I knocked my ashes into the tray on the bedside table. Beside it was a tall glass of water and a small plastic bottle of Mother's sleeping pills. I thought about taking one. I probably needed to be knocked out and dropped into a long, dreamless, protective cloud of sleep. There were only two pills left, however. I turned around and pulled back part of the sheets until I found her hand. I squeezed it, and to my relief she squeezed back. She had a weak grip, but there was life left in it. I was cold, or so I told myself, so I climbed under the covers too.

Old Donovan wasn't dead, but he'd still left her feeling like a widow, curling up each night with the weight of absence lying beside her, and I wondered if, in her comatose state, she thought I was him, or wanted to believe I was him, filling that space beside her. I guess I wanted to be him in some way, or someone like him—someone who had the luxury of feeling needed.

I was on my way, I decided. It felt like my own deck was finally clear. I never had to say a word about any of what had happened to me. I could move forward, telling a new story, a better story—one that I could craft completely on my own.

CHAPTER 12

The problem is that you don't always get to write your own story. You get written into some stories, and if you ask why, there isn't an answer. You don't have any control, because the forces at work are too large to confront, and sometimes too large even to understand. When Old Donovan had encouraged me to read the paper every morning and become involved, I had thought of myself as an armchair general watching and opining about the war from afar. I didn't think I would become a participant. Old Donovan must have been used to finding himself as a character—one whose actions or remarks or at least associations were captured in the text of an article. All that time reading the news, it never occurred to me that I would one day find myself a part of it too.

On Monday morning I flipped open the *Times* while I ate my cereal. The flakes went soggy as I stared at the headlines and let the details of the article blur into a fuzzy black-and-white haze. A pit widened within me, and I sank deep into it, beyond shouting range, beyond light. The Boston archdiocese was in trouble. The *Globe* had broken the story the day before. Initially, one priest had been accused of innumerable abuses, then there was another, and within no time the entire archdiocese was embroiled in a scandal, a widespread institutional cover-up, an epidemic of abuse. *Abuse.* I had a hard time reading the word. It seemed like a misnomer, inaccurate.

There are times when we all want to tell ourselves, *Look at that misfortune over there; thank God that isn't happening here, to us, to me.* You can ignore the bombs and the violence across the ocean until buildings are crumbling in your own country; you can dismiss the gossip about the neighbors across town as melodramatic, until those fists and the screams you'd heard about come barreling into your own home. Then what do you do?

The scandal wasn't only in Boston. There was a larger investigation now, and others had already started to speak out. The pages nearly turned themselves, against my will, and I glanced through the articles timidly, forgetting most of the information after my eyes had left the line and moved on, slipping over the words until I got to the bottom of the article and there was a mention of priests in Rhode Island and Connecticut who had also been accused. Another article later in the paper explained it in further detail, and fear stung me up and down my body.

The article didn't mention Most Precious Blood or Father Greg—they were all other churches and priests—but as I read, the specter of Most Precious Blood and Father Greg burned like an afterimage on the story. Father Greg's laughter boomed up and out of the ink stamp of other names in the article. "A gregarious neighbor," the article said, "a prominent society figure." It was the language the newspapers used to talk about murderers: "the friendly man next door."

I wondered if I should skip school. Missing more days would encourage Mr. Weinstein's wrath, but even worse, it would rouse suspicion. Everyone knew that I had worked at Most Precious Blood. I wanted to run back over to Josie's and shave the ice off the tree and see if I couldn't bring back that image of our bodies pressed together, restore it like an old fresco buried in the vaults of some forgotten city and, by bringing that moment to life again, create a permanent reminder that I, too, was just a normal high school kid who didn't need to be sent to Bullington, who didn't need to be cross-examined and strung up in the newspaper headlines and turned into a circus-freak-show act, a beast with a human face prowling a cage, onlookers beyond the bars asking, *How did he become that thing, how did he let it happen to himself?*

And they wouldn't leave me alone. I've walked through too many grocery-store lines and looked at all the tabloids featuring pictures of mill workers recently crippled, of celebrities maimed by cosmetic surgery, or children abducted. Everyone wants to gossip about those stories, but nobody wanted to be a part of them. There was something monstrous about all the people involved in those stories—the perpetrators, the families, and the victims themselves—everyone seemed portrayed with fearsome qualities: Nobody wanted to be involved with those kinds of people, and I didn't either.

When I got to CDA, I knew I couldn't avoid the story. From outside I could see into the lobby, where small clusters of mothers and nannies chattered softly and eyed each of the students carefully as we passed by. "Awful, just awful," I heard one mother say as I passed through the doorway. As intangible and immaterial fear might be, it still creates tangible effects. It might as well have a taste and a smell. Father Greg's stale cigarette breath and the nose-burning stink of scotch followed me into the school.

As I walked toward Mrs. Perrich's desk, Hazel, the mother of a sixth grader I had mentored the year before, saw me. She tapped a friend of hers on her shoulder, and they pulled away from their circle of mothers to look at me. "Oh," Hazel said, pushing a smile into her face that had all the signs of pity I knew so well. She stepped away from her friend and put a hand on my shoulder. "Oh, dear," she said to me, and then she patted me on the shoulder again. "Look at you. What happened? Are you okay?"

"Of course," I said, and then I realized she was talking about my eye. "An accident. On New Year's," I said.

She shook her head gently. "It's just that people can worry. They can think the worst. You know. The churches," she said finally. "That scandal. Awful."

"It's so hard to believe," the other mother said. I didn't answer; I stared down at her boots. They rose to her calf and were trimmed at the top with a ring of pale fur—I'd seen girls in my own grade wear the same boots. "You just never see these things coming," she continued. "Not to this extent."

Two other mothers now focused their attention on me. Mrs. Perrich was on the phone, but she looked up at me over her glasses as well. "You work at Most Precious Blood, don't you?" one of them asked me.

Hazel couldn't keep her hand off me for too long. She rubbed the side of my arm. "It has to be so hard. I mean, you do work there, right?"

"Danny was in confirmation classes there," another mother in the group said. "How many kids go through confirmation class in our community?"

"I know," the fourth one said. Then she addressed me. "What grade are you in?"

"Aidan's a sophomore," Hazel answered quickly.

"Oh, dear," the fourth mother said. "You work there? Is there any discussion, I mean, are they talking about it?"

"Teal!" Hazel snapped. "Aidan, it's none of our business." The other mothers had already drawn back a little, not rallying around Hazel, but shifting back toward Teal, who stood with her arms folded in front of her.

I didn't know any of those mothers, really—I didn't even know most of their names—and yet they knew I had worked at Most Precious Blood. "I don't believe anything has happened at Most Precious Blood," I said. "If nothing's happened at Most Precious Blood, why does anyone need to talk about it?" My voice grew louder as I continued. I could feel the sweat pouring down my back and curling down my forehead. I clenched my fists and jammed them into my pockets so I wouldn't wipe at my face.

"Dear," Hazel said. "Now, dear. It's okay. We're not accusing anyone of anything."

"No," I said too loudly. "I'm not either."

"Well," the mother in the furry boots said, "I still think the Parents Association should address this in some way. We need to get people talking about this, and I think it's pretty obvious that the kids need some kind of conversation about it too."

"Absolutely," Teal said. "Dr. Ridge should call an all-school assembly."

"Maybe something in a smaller format," the other mother said. "This is all pretty sensitive."

"Exactly," Hazel said.

"Actually," the mother in the furry boots said, "that's exactly what Father Greg should do. That's his responsibility, not only to his parish but to the whole community."

"Father Greg didn't even give Mass on Sunday," Hazel said. "Father Dooley did."

"Father Dooley did?" Teal asked. "Did he say anything about all this?"

"Please, Teal!" Hazel said.

Hazel tried to put her arm around me, but I backed away. "I just don't know what you are talking about," I said. None of it made sense to me. None of them had been there. Why were they the ones talking about it? Some of them weren't even Catholic.

I gestured to the clock in the lobby and broke away from the group of mothers. While the parents were clamoring for assemblies and discussion groups, the students were exactly the opposite. There was more of a hush, and whispers about the students who were associated with Most Precious Blood. I tried to avoid these conversations on my way to class, since there were also plenty of students who knew that I had worked at Most Precious Blood that past summer and fall.

Nick and Dustin found me in the hall too. Dustin stared right at me but muttered to his buddy over his shoulder. Everywhere I looked, I thought I heard someone saying my name, but when I turned, no one addressed me directly.

Mr. Weinstein made us do an in-class writing assignment, but I spent the period staring at a blank page, too afraid of the memories that had taken over my mind. Mr. Weinstein sat back in his chair with his hands behind his head in the same way Father Greg used to as he orated in his office, and it reminded me of a conversation I had had with Father Greg early in my work with the campaign. He had been showing me pictures he planned to use in some of the case materials. Children raised their hands eagerly in a classroom. Two students hovered by a computer screen, and one pointed at the screen with a look of newfound recognition on her face. There were more.

"You know why I like bringing kids like you into this project?" Father Greg had said. "Because you are just like the kids on the other end, and I think it's important for kids to be helping one another." He had flipped to a picture with three Latinas in white lab coats and goggles. "Helping others helps ourselves," Father Greg had continued, and had said this again many times during our work on the campaign. It had been all too easy to believe that the rewards would come back to me, too. Father Greg had promised and reminded me that it was God's way. *I was hungry and you fed me, thirsty and you gave me drink; I was a stranger and you received me into your homes.*

At that time, I had believed him because I wanted to, but staring down at the blank page in Mr. Weinstein's class, I thought about how a belief really begins. It doesn't hit you like a lightning bolt, smack you off your horse, and fill you with visions of a world tinted with more vibrant colors. Instead, it begins with a desire to see something in that certain light, or to see the world in a certain way. The *desire* paves the way. It makes you believe the clouds are parting—and parting specifically for you. You need them to, because their doing so, just for you, gives you some incentive, some inspiration to keep going. I believed in Father Greg. He knew that was what I wanted, and he told me to believe in it.

Mr. Weinstein asked for the essays we'd written, and I handed forward my blank page. Josie looked back over her shoulder at me. *What happened?* she mouthed.

"Nothing," I said.

Mr. Weinstein asked me to be quiet and then began his class. I drifted back into my own mind. Had Father Greg been offering me compassion? Wasn't that what I was told was paramount in the teachings of Jesus—compassion— and that to act compassionately is our ticket to heaven? But is that really compassion—to extend oneself to others with the assumption that that act will be rewarded? Isn't the greater leap of faith the act of compassion in the face of nothingness? But who would do that? Who wouldn't act solely in ways that are best for him or her when the veil has been thrown off and words like *love* and *virtue* are left naked in their hypocrisy? Words that Father Greg had used so often now looked corrupted and dangerous. And what about when someone else used them? Why couldn't I hold them like the threat of the executioners' ax over someone's head until he did what I wanted him to?

I left Mr. Weinstein's class in a daze. I moved down the

hall from one class to the next and saw people glancing in my direction, but they looked away as soon as I looked back at them. It's not like anybody pointed, but after hearing Teal suggest that people were already talking about Most Precious Blood, I spent the day terrified that people had somehow found out, as if an article somewhere talked specifically about me, an article hungry to expose the freaks and monsters in our midst, an article pointing at me that said, "Don't let him in, he'll bring it all with him, it's contagious"—not understanding anything—and that someone had read that article and told others about it and me, and that all those people had made a phone tree with the entire upper school community at CDA, and finally, some kind of announcement was going to be made over the loudspeakers, I was going to get sent to the office, and then everyone would feel free to point and gawk at that weird, fucked-up creature making his final march down the hall to Mrs. Ackerson's guidance office, where I'd be told point-blank that kids like me belonged in the care of the experts at Bullington and I'd be given a special dispensation for transferring right then, right there, without even the chance to eat lunch. They would arrange for a car.

It was impossible to speak to Josie or Sophie. I didn't want them asking me any questions. I just wanted to be back at Josie's pool house, swapping smoke in a circle, lost in an easy numbness, but that seemed so long ago now, and I was too worried about Mark. I didn't see him at school, and by third period I was sure he was absent. It was a small relief. Mark and I hadn't spoken to each other since I'd seen him on the roof of Coolidge, and I couldn't be sure what he'd do next. Wasn't this what he'd been talking about—everybody finding out?

I excused myself from chemistry class and went down to the middle-school-floor bathroom so none of the kids would bug me or tell anyone. I vomited. After I'd cleaned myself up, I felt a little better, but I waited for the class to come to an end before I went back upstairs to get my books and bag. I skipped lunch and sat in a stall in the third-floor restroom, trying to get ahold of myself. Sweat dripped down my neck and soaked my collar. I loosened the knot of my tie and splashed cold water into my face, splashing and splashing, hosing thick, curly bunches of hair until I could slick it all back like a gangster. I scowled at myself and had the urge to punch that reflection. Instead, I snapped the metal clip off one of my pens and scratched the mirror. I stood back to look at myself in the reflection and saw white gashes slashed across my forehead and cheeks, and one cut down through the yellow bruise around my eye.

When the bell rang, I dabbed my hair with paper towels and walked to class. I felt better. *I can do this,* I kept telling myself. Nobody will ever know.

I called for the car service to pick me up after school, and I snuck out before the end-of-the-day announcements. I played the snob and completely ignored the driver from the backseat. With all the snow nearly melted, the town was stained the filmy pallor of tobacco teeth. Once the cold passed and the spring thawed the slats in the shutters, the ice melted from the cracks in the streets, and the soil softened and the rich dirt could be raked up to the surface, the landscape companies, house painters, and asphalt trucks would fan out around town. And with surgical precision they would restore succulence and vibrancy to the gardens and plush life to the rolling lawns, the roads would be filled and smoothed, the weather-stripped houses would get the fine brushstrokes that would make them look as fresh as the flowers that lined their driveways, and all signs of decay would disappear. Why couldn't they come for me, too?

Because I got home much earlier than usual on a school day, I was surprised to hear the radio in the kitchen and Mother's voice. I could smell the cigarettes from the foyer as I took off my coat. "Aidan!" Mother yelled as I walked into the library. "Aidan, come in here." She sat at the table in the breakfast nook, a smoldering ashtray beside her, and she stood abruptly when I entered the kitchen. She was still in her morning workout clothes, and wisps of hair had sprung free from her ponytail. She clasped her hands together, then released them and beckoned me with one, and clasped them again. "Oh. Come here. Please."

I hesitated.

"The stories about the churches," she continued. She didn't cross the room, but her legs twitched slightly, like they were ready to run over. I sat down by the butcher block. The distance felt safer. I had reined in all the control I could muster—it was caged within me—but if she crossed the room and put her arms around me, I wasn't sure I could hold on to it anymore.

Mother sat down too. "Believe me," she said. "I worried as soon as I saw it. With you and Most Precious Blood."

"People were talking about it in school, too," I said slowly. I corrected my posture and sat up straight. Mother's eyes couldn't meet mine. It was easier for me to stay focused on her, I realized. I was used to lying to her—and knowing I was and not fooling myself otherwise. "But nothing happened at Most Precious Blood. Not while I've been there."

"Are you sure?" she asked. "I got a call. You remember Hazel? Well. There are some rumors."

"Rumors," I repeated, still looking at Mother. The fear in her eyes gave her everyday beauty a kind of attractive innocence, something you just wanted to protect and preserve— she was someone who pleaded for help with her eyes and was used to getting it, so you felt even more compelled to deliver it. "They're insinuations," I continued. I spoke as slowly as I could to make it look like I was calm. "It's rude. It's invasive. They didn't work there. I did."

"Oh, Aidan," Mother said. "Please," she begged. "Are you sure? This is serious."

"So am I. Nothing happened."

"It's in the papers everywhere. It's an epidemic. It's a

mass cover-up. There will be a class-action lawsuit—or there should be, somehow."

"Well, I didn't see it," I reiterated. "I'm sick of this."

"Whoever is guilty should be prosecuted like any other civilian," Mother continued. "Not just the abuses—what about those who abet the crime? The bastards." Mother stood up, crossed the room, and put her arms around me. I stuck my head in her chest so I wouldn't have to look up at her. I didn't know how much longer I could keep myself from losing it.

"Everybody keeps asking me about it, like I'm guilty of something. I didn't do anything," I mumbled. "I worked there, and now I don't. There's nothing more for me to say."

Mother held me for a while, and I let her. I didn't say another word. Eventually, she took a deep breath. "I believe you," she said. "I believe you, and we don't have to go on about it anymore. I was just so worried that we were victims too." We were silent again, and Mother squeezed me tightly. I held my breath and let it out slowly. She pulled away but stayed beside me. I could barely hold myself together, and I hoped she didn't notice.

"And, Aidan. I know you already said this, but you are never going in that church again. Neither am I. I wasn't ready, and now? Why should I ever go back there? The whole organization. I just don't understand." Her voice grew softer and quieter; she seemed far away. "It'd be different, though," she said, walking over to the table and lighting another cigarette. "It'd be different if we were the ones who'd suffered this." She lit the cigarette and exhaled, without looking at me. "But we haven't. That's what's important."

"That's right," I said. "Exactly." I didn't feel calmer. A strange numbness buzzed across my skin.

I went up to my room. I pulled my schoolbooks out of my backpack and sat down at my desk, but the geometry problems became a maze I couldn't get through. I knew the theorems, but I couldn't recall them. They were a language that seemed to mock the way I felt inside, as if the lines, one written out below the other, all implied a sense of easiness, a direction that led to a specific end: an answer. I couldn't help but see a pair of narrowing eyes staring up at me through the cylinders on the page. They wanted answers, but what if there weren't any answers, what if there were too many uncertainties, too much muckiness all muddled up in the situation, and there was no way to explain it? That's why the newspaper article was such a lie: The whole story wasn't that easy to explain in a few paragraphs stacked in the inverse pyramid style.

Trying to tackle my homework from the *Norton Anthology* wasn't any easier either. I couldn't remember the sentences, and I found myself rereading and rereading, retaining nothing. I could see Mr. Weinstein holding the book up in class, shaking it above his head when no one answered his question: *The answers are right here! Didn't anyone read the poem?*

They're right there in front of you. You're going to have to learn the material in this book if you think you are ever taking the AP exam!

I threw the anthology across the room at my own bookcase and watched an avalanche of books tumble from the shelves. The cigar box of Old Donovan's trinkets hit the floor and spilled out across the carpet. The snow globe didn't break, but it rolled near the foot of my bed and sent a whirl of flashing flakes reflecting against one of my glossy bedposts. I was up instantly and had the globe in my hand and was hurling it down against the floor before I had any idea what I was doing. The glass exploded. THE MAGIC OF REYKJAVIC the black base of the globe read. Free from the bubble, it was merely a liquid stain in the carpet, and the once-iridescent snow became a gray dusting of nothingness.

I started to pace. Everything in my room looked breakable. The keyboard and the wire music stand could be busted over a bedpost. The photo of two women on the Brooklyn Bridge could be burned at the spark of a match. The old, faded copy of *Frankenstein* that had slid across the floor could be ripped up, shredded, and sent flying out the window like ashes and debris floating down from a great height. My room was no longer safe.

Mother called my name from down the hall and knocked on my door a moment later. She came in without waiting for my response. "What happened? I heard a crash."

"I tried to move my bookshelf without taking everything off."

"What?" She had her hands on her hips.

"I wanted to make more room by the armchair so I could bring up a footrest."

Mother looked exhausted and older. I realized she wasn't wearing any makeup. She sighed. "Are you okay?"

"Yes."

"I'm here for you, Aidan. You can ask me for help." She stood there for another moment, and then her lips finally pushed up into a smile. "I know a thing or two about feeling betrayed."

"I know." I hesitated. "It's just . . . I guess I can't help feeling lied to. All that work I did for them. All that work. There are too many lies. I'm confused." I had to stop myself before I said more. It felt like I was trying to stop myself from vomiting.

"I know, honey," Mother said. "I know. And I'm here for you." She smiled at me. "Okay, look. I thought we could just order a pizza and watch a movie tonight. Do you have homework? Could we do that?"

"I'd like that," I said. "I don't feel like doing anything else."

"Me neither."

I told her I would clean up the mess I'd made first and then join her downstairs to pick out a pizza and a movie. I ended up throwing most of the trinkets Old Donovan had given me from his trips in the trash. What was the point of keeping them?

Later, we curled up in Mother's bed with the box of spinach and olive pizza on the bedside table and watched three episodes of a TV drama, which, in the end, was completely dissatisfying, because all that time we spent watching the show didn't bring us to any resolution. We were left waiting, wanting more, knowing there was more to come, and that we would never know the end of it. But as I got up to go back to my room, Mother grabbed my hand.

"Earlier, I said this and I meant it," she said. "I think it is best to believe you, Aidan, without any hesitation. I have to. I can trust you, right?"

"Yes," I said. "Trust me. Believe me."

CHAPTER 13

If I was going to believe myself, I had to keep going to school without interruption, so on Tuesday I went to every class and sat perfectly poised in my chair as if I was paying attention. Mr. Weinstein didn't call on me once during class, and Mrs. Martelli didn't say anything to me when I didn't pass in my geometry homework. I was getting by, I kept telling myself. It was possible. I could slide through. The suspicions about me, or anybody else affiliated with Most Precious Blood, would ease up and fade away soon, and everyone would fall back in line and resume their daily routines. That was the recommended salve for overcoming a national fear, wasn't it? Get out there and do what you always do. Drive around in your car; go shopping; watch a movie; see a Broadway show. Drop back in and tune back out.

There was something automatic to the way I walked

down the halls between classes too, a stiff march I needed to propel myself forward. I was so oblivious, I nearly bumped into Josie at the end of the day. "Hey," she said. "You've been quiet all day. What, are you playing hard to get suddenly?" I laughed uneasily, and she continued. "Can't we get out of here—just the two of us?"

After end-of-the-day announcements, Josie and I walked over to Blueberry Hill Café. The line wasn't long at the coffee bar, and while I picked up the café au laits and pastries, Josie found a table near the back, where the teenagers always tried to sit, as far away as possible from the front door. It was one of the smaller round tables that could barely fit two wiry iron chairs on either side of it, and Josie positioned herself so she could look out into the café.

Carrying the tray of items over to the table, I sat down facing her.

"Hey," she asked me. "Have you talked to Mark at all?" When I told her I hadn't seen him around, she was taken aback. "Of course you haven't seen him. He's been absent for two days. I tried calling his home during my free period, and there was no answer."

"No, of course," I said. "I just mean I'm not worried. He was grounded all weekend. He probably got sick at home or something." I clenched and flexed my muscles to try to hold still, but jittery nausea swept through me. I didn't want to think about Mark's absence, but I couldn't stop.

"He hasn't been absent in two years," Josie added. I

feigned surprise, but she was adamant. "Everybody is acting like a weirdo right now. If he were here, he'd just pass a bowl and get us laughing about something else, and we'd all forget about it. But he's not here. I mean, I like being here just with you," she added, "but it's weird he hasn't been in school. A lot of things feel weird right now. I mean, the church scandal has everyone feeling flipped inside out."

"Can we not talk about that?"

"It's hard to avoid. Especially with people talking about how something might have happened at Most Precious Blood."

"Please," I said. "That's bullshit. People start rumors because they need drama." I spoke to Josie, but I wasn't looking at her. I was looking over her shoulder in the mirror behind her. Even with my back to everyone, I could still see the whole café in it. It ran most of the length of the back wall and perfectly produced the visual deceit of doubling the size of the café. Blueberry Hill was the kind of place that bustled all day long until the dinner hour. As usual, there was a small brigade of strollers parked around the room, and while the adults were mostly women, there were some men as well, which was a pleasant reminder that to afford a life in our town, not all the men had to work seventy hours a week or find themselves permanently on the road. One of them, in fact, I recognized as a father I saw around CDA, because he was an active member of the Parents Association. He was outfitted in his usual getup, a thick flannel shirt with the top two buttons undone. I'd heard many of the mothers talk about how attractive they found him, but he didn't seem like a flirt to me, at least not when I'd seen him.

When we'd come into the café, he'd been reading the paper at a table by himself with the decimated remnants of a baguette sandwich in front of him. The skin around his eyes was crinkled, and he smiled through a close-cropped ashy beard as he scanned the pages. Only occasionally did he shake his head in a soft and almost patient disbelief. He was the kind of man I imagined I wanted to become. Not a man with an occupation I desired, because I had no idea what he did for a living, but a man whose disposition was a goal worth trying to achieve—a man at peace. But that didn't last. The bell over the front door jingled as Josie and I began talking, and I watched his expression change entirely.

Father Dooley leaned on his cane as he slowly made his way up to the coffee bar. The barista adjusted the bandanna on her head and wiped her hands on her apron as Father Dooley stepped up to the counter. He spoke softly, almost in a whisper, since most of the café was watching him.

"My God," Josie said, leaning in toward our table, "it's so hard to see a priest now and not wonder. It's like they're all guilty."

"They're not," I said softly.

I wanted to look away, close my eyes, or sprint out the back door if I could, but the man with the newspaper folded it down and dropped it onto his little table. He glared at Father Dooley and rubbed his beard. The foot he had crossed up on one leg dropped to the floor. For a moment he sat like an athlete with his hands clasped and hanging loosely between his knees, but then he stood and crossed over to Father Dooley. He said something to the old priest too quietly for us to hear. Father Dooley shook his head and said something back. They exchanged a few more words, and Father Dooley walked around him to the other end of the counter and stared at the hissing espresso machine.

"Hey," the man said, and pointed at Father Dooley, "don't ignore me. I asked you a question."

"Please, Paul," Father Dooley said coolly. "I'm just picking up some coffees."

"You're the superior. You're not without any responsibility here," Paul said.

"Please stop bothering me," Father Dooley said. He glanced around the café quickly. "This really isn't the place to discuss it."

"Don't you dare dismiss me!" Paul shouted. "I've been going to Most Precious Blood for over ten years. I deserve some answers. My kids have gone there."

The woman behind the counter hurried through her tasks and spilled some of the first coffee she put down in front of Father Dooley. She stuffed the cup into a to-go tray and pushed it toward him.

"This is outrageous," Paul continued.

"That's right," a woman near the front of the café echoed. "He's right."

Father Dooley gripped his cane and held it close to his leg. "I'm not the one on trial here. Please, don't treat me like a criminal. There's a better time and place to discuss this. The entire church is addressing this. We have a coordinated response."

"Speak to me like a goddamn human being, Frank!" Paul trembled as he shouted. He steadied himself against the counter. "You think you're above the law. We want answers. Father Greg would be talking to us. Where the hell is he all of a sudden?"

One of the mothers at a table close to Paul stood up and put her hand on his back. "He's absolutely right," she said to Father Dooley. "You . . . you . . . you should be ashamed of yourself." She began to choke up. "Absolutely ashamed. You didn't say anything at Mass. You didn't mention it."

"I'm not a reporter. I don't speculate about things and stir everybody up for no reason, just to create public hysteria!" Father Dooley looked around the room, and when his eyes found mine in the mirror, I froze. He didn't look like he'd wanted to yell back or wave his cane in their faces, but he had. We connected for only a moment, and judging from the way he trembled, I'm sure we felt exactly the same. His glance was a hand reaching out to me, grabbing hold of my shoulder and drawing me toward him. I couldn't break free, and I wondered, suddenly, if he felt the same about me. I probably scared him more than Paul did.

He didn't say anything to me. He turned back to Paul instead. "I'm doing all that I can. I'm trying."

"Well, it sure isn't enough. The hysteria isn't the fault of the news. You're not going to say anything to me, are you? Where the hell is Father Greg? He'd say something. Where is he?"

Father Dooley picked up his tray with the three coffees. "Father Greg is sick right now, so let's not harass him anymore. He's not taking calls. I will, though. At the rectory. Now, we really all should move on to more important discussions and stop this badgering." Father Dooley had always worn a pouting stone face—he was a rule stickler—but as he stood there with the gray cardboard tray wobbling in his hands, he seemed to lose hold of his usual self, and his usual mask began to crumble.

Paul jabbed his finger into Father Dooley's chest, and I thought the old priest would tip over. "You are just as responsible as the rest of the church," Paul said. "You are just as guilty. You can't just reconcile that with your superiors. We deserve some justice too."

Father Dooley nodded in agreement. "I'm sorry," he said, and he turned around to the door. "Please, God," I thought he muttered as he opened the door to the sidewalk.

The woman next to Paul patted him on the shoulder. Paul slammed his hand down on the counter next to the register, and she backed away. "I'm never walking in that church again," he said. "The rest of the world calls that *harboring a goddamn criminal*." The woman next to him led him over to her table, and he pulled over his chair and joined her and her friend. The whole café became a din of chatter.

"Can you believe he came in here?" Josie said again. "He must be the dumbest man alive, or completely oblivious. My dad says it's just plain arrogance," she continued. "Cardinal what's-his-name can't believe it's become such a scandal in the news. They all think it will just blow over." She looked at me, and from the concern that spread over her face I knew my act was failing. "Seriously. What do you think?" she asked me. She waited for me to say something, but I couldn't speak. "I mean, you worked at Most Precious Blood," she persisted. "Really? Nothing?"

"Honestly?" I said softly. "I just want this all to blow over too. Can we please talk about something else?"

"Hey, you're the one always bringing up the news," Josie said. "And this is different. This is even more important. This is about kids."

"Why is that any different?" I asked.

She shook her head. "It just is. It's, like, a double crime. You're not just hurting people now. You're fucking up their whole future. It's like attacking them once and then attacking them over and over for the rest of their lives."

"Attacking them?"

"Look, it's an attack. But this is one we can do something about. What the hell is going on in this world? I'm mean, terrorists are taking over half the world, guys are mailing anthrax to congressmen and senators, Americans are joining

the Taliban. Seriously? And now priests are attacking children? Is the world coming to an end or something?"

"That's insane," I said, raising my voice. "Besides, do
you know how much good the Church has done in the
world too? This doesn't just wipe it all out."

"Oh my God," she said. "You're insane. You're defend-
ing them? Are you, like, a hardcore Catholic all of a
sudden? Circle-the-wagons kind of thing? It's an open-
and-shut case. Those guys are guilty and, seriously, think
of those poor kids. It's not fair. They had to go through
all that, and then it's only because they speak up that we
know any of this."

"Maybe some kids spoke up because they wanted attention," I said. I laughed, even though I didn't have any idea
why. "Like a copycat, jumping onto another news story?"

"That's not funny," Josie said. "You're demented."

"Why are you pushing me like this? Why am I being
interrogated?"

"You?" Josie asked.

She was quiet for a moment as she finished her coffee.
I couldn't think of anything to say because every word
that came to mind sounded like it incriminated me more. I
wanted to cut out my tongue and send it in the mail to Most
Precious Blood with a note that said, *Add it to your goddamn
collection.*

"Maybe we should just go home," Josie said at last. "This
has all been kind of weird."

"Yeah," I said. "It is weird. I mean, you have to believe me. I just feel betrayed, I guess. I worked there. Everything seemed normal and fine to me. And now nothing does." Josie listened to me with her hands folded beneath her chin, and she remained quiet and calm when I paused. "Sorry I was a jerk," I finally added. "I wish it all made more sense. I just want everything to be normal."

She reached across the table and squeezed my hand. "You're not a jerk," she said. "You're definitely not a jerk, of all things."

We left, and Josie still led me down the street and around the corner to a more secluded parking lot behind some of the stores. I felt her lips against mine, felt them press and pull me closer to her. I tried to respond—I wanted to, I thought—but it required effort. She pushed into me, and although I was up against a wall, I seemed to slip away. She pushed into me again. "Please," she said, "hold me." I did as I was told. She pried my mouth open with hers and worked her tongue. I had nothing for her. "What's the matter?" she asked. "Don't you want this?"

I did, but without her enthusiasm, or at least without feeling as excited as she seemed. I nodded along, smiled, and mirrored her expressions. We pressed together, and I reacted as I thought I should, mimicking her moves, rubbing our noses back and forth as we paused between kisses, pacing the kisses with a peck, another peck. I held the back of her head and touched her ear, kissed her and kissed her, using the same pattern: one; two; three; counting steps, marching through my own routine.

She grabbed my wrist and glided my hand up and down the side of her body. When she let go and began rubbing my back, I continued as she'd shown me. The other part of me pulled away, deeper into myself. I suddenly felt like I didn't understand desire and how to recognize it and follow it into a conversation with another person, how to speak with another person through touch, how to listen with my body and respond—I only knew how to be desired and how to obey.

I tried rubbing my hands in different places around her body, but she didn't react like I thought she was supposed to. Nothing inspired me, nothing moved within me. After a while Josie sensed it, or at least became frustrated with me. She redirected my hands a few times. "Touch me here." I obeyed, but not with anything behind it—not desire or fear. I moved my hands faster and squeezed harder, but these weren't my hands anymore. Somewhere deep in the darkest pit of me I could hear Father Greg's voice panting about God and about what was within us and about *love, love, love.* Nothing was within me now. Nothing had ever been there between us— I could say that now. Nothing was there within us.

She felt the emptiness against her, I'm sure, and she looked up at me with dejected eyes. "What's the matter?" she asked. "What do you want? What do you want to do?"

"I don't know. I don't know what to do. I want to know, but I don't."

We were quiet for a moment. "This isn't working," she said softly.

"It should, though," I said.

"Don't you want me?"

"Yes."

She pulled back a little. "Really? It doesn't seem like it." I was quiet and too confused to find an answer or anything else to say. She got closer, grabbed my coat, and pulled me forward playfully. "Don't you think I'm pretty?"

"Of course."

"Don't just say it," she said. "You think I'm pretty?"

"Yes. Yes, I want you." It wasn't a lie. I'd wanted to kiss her on the neck every time she'd moved her hair and exposed the pale slope of her neck in Mr. Weinstein's class. She was the first girl I ever kissed, but I wanted her to be the first person. I wanted to undo all that was behind me and be a real virgin again.

"Mean it," she said.

She unbuttoned her coat, and I put my arms around her. She unzipped my coat and pressed close to me. "I'm here," she said softly. "I'm not going anywhere. Take your time." When I hugged her and moved my hands along her back, I felt the clip of her bra strap, and I wanted to know how to snap it off. She lapped against me in gentle waves, and it released a wash of nerves tingling within me.

We stayed there awhile. I pressed her closer to me, and she moved against me more urgently when she felt my erection against her. I went deliriously light-headed and kissed her harder. I sucked her bottom lip. Both my hands dropped to her ass, and I pulled her tight against me. She giggled and stayed with me for a moment, breathing harder against my neck.

She broke away. "Okay. Okay," she said with a laugh. My insides jumped uncontrollably, and I was shaking on the outside, too. She smiled up at me, but she was a little nervous as well. Her cheeks were flushed. "I, uh, wish I didn't have to go." She composed herself, and then she teased me that we'd have to be more respectable next time. Find someplace quiet. Someplace private. Not an alley downtown. I agreed. Someplace I could sit down, I told her. My legs were giving out on me. "Someplace we can lie down," she said. She kissed me again.

"Why not right now?" I asked.

"Yes." She was still catching her breath. Her nostrils trembled as she breathed. "My mother has a meeting in the city this afternoon. Come over now and I'll sneak you in so Ruby doesn't see you."

We took the same route back to her house we had walked the other day, kissing along the way again, but this time more in a rush. We'd pause, but only for enough time to lick each other's lips briefly, before Josie grabbed my hand and dragged me along. We didn't say much to each other as we came up the street toward her house. When we got there, I wanted to see the film of ice on the elm tree in the small stand of trees at the foot of her driveway. I wanted to see what I looked like beside her, but the ice was gone.

Josie pushed up and down on the balls of her feet as she told me the plan. I followed her instructions, and after she had made it up the hill to her house and closed the front door behind her, I jogged past her neighbor's house and turned right at the end of the block. I jumped the low stone wall, dashed across their backyard to the grove of trees next to Josie's family's property, and crouched at the base of another thick elm tree. Soon Josie opened her back door and walked up to the pool house with her schoolbag slung over her shoulder. She had changed into a pair of bright pink sweatpants and a jacket that cinched tightly around her waist and had a fluffy fur-trimmed hood. I waited for another minute, then ran down to the side door of the pool house.

Josie opened it as soon as I knocked. "Thought you'd gotten lost," she said, and kissed me. She made us hot chocolate at the bar in the main room and spiked it with Kahlúa. We sat on the couch and sipped our drinks.

Soon we weren't talking. Her lips moved to my neck, and I put my mug down so I wouldn't spill it into our laps. We found the urgency again and clung together. She reached behind her and helped me with her bra, and soon after she unbuckled my pants, fished through the opening in my boxers, and pulled me out. Her hand was so small around me, and she moved me up against the flat of her stomach and pressed and pulled. An electricity charged me. And then, out of nowhere, I found myself mumbling to her, telling her she would like this, it would feel good, and the words weren't mine, they erupted from a darkness within me, and I spoke into her ear as I reached into her pants and began to push and pull and knead into her. She scooted her hips back, and I chased after her harder.

She let go of me and tried to push herself back, but she was beneath me. "Ow. Please," she said, but I kept at it. "No."

"No? No. Shhh," I said.

"Stop it."

"No. Shhh."

"Owww. What the fuck? No. Stop it!" Josie hit my shoulder. I leaned back, and she got her knees up between us and bucked me off of her. She pulled up her pants, tucked herself into a ball in the corner of the couch, and stared at me over her knees.

My heart thumped painfully in my chest. I looked at my hands, and they were shaking uncontrollably. My whole body was. It didn't feel like it was mine. And as I pulled up my pants I felt a familiar numbness welling up inside me.

"What the fuck is the matter with you?" Josie said. "You hurt me."

"No," I said.

"What do you mean, no? Yes you did! You hurt me."

"No, I mean, I didn't mean to." My throat tightened, and

I swallowed back the tears. I brought my legs up against my chest too. The huge television was turned off, and our outlines were reflected back at us from the gray screen. "I don't know who I was just then. It wasn't me. I'm sorry."

Josie remained quiet for a while and finally said, "Something is seriously fucked up with you."

"No, there isn't. I want this with you."

"Well, nothing is going to happen between us now."

"I'm sorry. I didn't mean to hurt you. I don't know what I was doing."

"What's the matter with you?" she asked me.

"I don't know," I said, and I looked to the floor. I wanted to say something else, but where the hell would I begin? I leaned toward her, and she must have thought I wanted to kiss her, because she got up suddenly and walked over to the bar. She poured herself soda from the gun. "I'm serious. Something is really wrong." Her voice changed tone. She wasn't asking me. She sipped her drink and waited for me. I wondered what I looked like in her eyes now.

She sipped slowly and waited. "I don't think we should keep doing this," she said finally.

"I don't get it," I said.

"What don't you get?"

"I want it. I want this to work between us. Why isn't it?"

"It's not just about what you want. I have a say in this too. And I say fuck no." She put her glass down and clutched herself as if she were cold. Her face drooped with concern. "There's something you're not telling me," she said. I couldn't pay attention. I sank farther away. I couldn't focus. I felt empty and yet without room to take anything in. "Are you, like, okay?" she asked.

"I don't know. No. I just don't want you to think I don't want you. I do. I want you. I don't know why I'm like this right now."

Josie shook her head. She looked at me with eyes that were sad and scared, but she offered a smile, too. "I'm not talking about that. Listen, I'm not trying to be mean. I'm just asking. Is there anything you need to tell me? Would that help?" With her arms crossed tightly in front of her and head cocked slightly to the side, she looked so brave. I was jealous of her, and something broke within me. I took a step around the couch, toward the bar.

"Just stop with all that!" I yelled. "Why won't everyone stop wondering? Why do I have to talk about anything?"

She backed up against the shelves of bottles. "I'm just trying to figure this all out."

"I'm just fucked up. Okay?" I shouted, gripping the back of one of the bar stools, leaning closer. "Why can't that be it? Why do we have to figure it all out?"

"Please. You're scaring me now. Please don't yell at me." She stayed behind the counter of the bar, but she spoke more forcefully. "Just listen to yourself. Look at yourself. You're being insane."

"I'm not insane," I said.

"Well, you need to leave. You hurt me, and you're scaring the shit out of me right now. This isn't the Aidan I thought I was getting to know. Get out of my house. Now." I looked away from her and continued to lean on the bar stool. I couldn't speak. I held on to the bar. I couldn't find any language. "Go," she said again. "Leave."

She remained behind the bar as I put on my coat and made my way out the back door. On the walk home, I wanted to believe I was as scared as she was, but I couldn't convince myself of that. I was on the point of losing everything I had finally gained. I needed better control of myself. I tried to devise a plan to maintain that control, not lose it like I had with Josie. I wanted my life to be my own, but it wasn't, and it couldn't be, and the whole walk home I thought of Mark on the roof of Coolidge, wondering what he'd seen come over my face as he'd tried to talk to me. Who had he seen?

That night, as I tried to fall asleep, two distinct voices shouted in my head, and I nearly thought there was another person in the room because there were two minds battling each other, one telling me to reach out to Mark and the other barking the same old orders to shut up and stay silent. I scared myself into thinking there was actually someone else in the room, and the urge to turn on the light and double-check was overwhelming. He could have been sitting in the armchair or crouched at the foot of my bed or standing patiently in the closet, waiting for me to open it, when he would say, *Ha! Caught! You little fucker, you can't hide forever.* I switched on the reading lamp and looked around the room quickly. My heart pounded. I got up to walk over to the closet and from the corner of my eye I saw a pale, terrified boy in my window. I cried out. I couldn't see my face in the dim light, but it was only my own reflection, limbs flexed and bent, ready for a fight. I stared at what I guess was myself for a long time, the ghostly impression of my bare chest rising and falling as I tried to catch my breath.

I sat in bed with my legs tucked up against me and my back to the wall, shaking and grunting under my breath. I was too blasted to sleep—I felt like I was hurtling downward without any sense of where I was going to land. Had I asked to become this? I hated myself all over again, because I hadn't meant to be so terrible to Mark. He was my friend. I knew what he wanted. To be heard. For me to see him, the whole him. To know that I understood how he felt. I wanted that too, I realized. Didn't we all want that, and didn't each of us deserve it—two people being with each other honestly?

After everything I had felt for Father Greg, I now had a new reason to hate him. Josie was right. It wasn't only our younger selves he'd twisted and manipulated, he'd also hurt the men we would become: our future as friends and lovers. He wasn't even physically present, but silently and invisibly, mysteriously, Father Greg was there—still demanding a singular devotion to him. What a religion he'd constructed: One that said, *Fear me if you don't believe in me.*

CHAPTER 14

When I woke and got ready for school, I was nervous to the point of nausea. I was unsure how to proceed, but when I looked out the window in the breakfast nook and saw Elena's small car parked in front of the second garage, I felt a sense of hope. I had no idea how long she'd been there, but I realized she'd come back to collect her things. The light from her apartment window shot out into the gray, bleak morning light, and her silhouette paced in and out of view as I walked along the stone path to the garage. The door to the trunk of her car was swung open, and I stood by and waited for her.

She came down the stairs a few moments later with an armload of clothing and a duffel bag. She paused when she saw me and smiled. *"M'ijo."* We hugged awkwardly, and then she gestured to the car. I helped her throw the clothes into the backseat.

I followed Elena up the stairs to her apartment and helped her pack some of her picture frames and books into a box. "How are they?" I asked, holding the one with Candido and Teresa. I looked at the picture. Teresa was laughing in it, but I remembered the rage in her eyes when she saw me last.

"They are happy for me. Tere has stayed home with me every day after school. She's cooking dinner for us all tonight."

"Do you have to look for another job?"

"Soon." She passed me her Bible to put in the box, and I stared at it for a while.

"I'm sorry," I said.

"There is a reason for everything, isn't there?"

She was on the other side of the bed, and I wanted to hug her, but she was keeping her distance from me. She kept glancing out the window toward the house. "Hey," I said softly. "It doesn't matter if we talk now. What is she going to do?"

Elena sighed. "I should be going soon." She was holding back her tears. "This is hard for me. To see you, *m'ijo*. I'm sorry too," she said. "I will miss you." I came around the bed, and she hugged me. She let go, held me at arm's length, and then walked over to her cabinet to pack up the last of her toiletries. "But you do have new things going on, no?"

"I feel like a lot is changing," I said. I pulled the cross down off the wall above her bed. "I almost feel like a different person." She kept her back to me as she quickly packed. "I mean, there are so many things I'd like to talk to you about. And things I maybe should have talked with you about before." My voice trembled. I almost couldn't get it out.

She still didn't turn around. "Well, God will provide," she said. "That is all you need to remember. I will find a new job, and you will grow up, go to a good college, and leave home. Thank God."

When her small box was packed and she finally turned around, she saw me holding the cross and looking at her. "Have you been reading the news at all?" I asked. She ignored me, took the cross from my hands, and dropped it in the box on the bed. She pulled a pair of shoes out from beneath the bed. "Elena, come on. Why aren't you looking at me?"

"*M'ijo*," Elena said finally. She stopped fidgeting. "I do not want to talk about any of that."

"Well, I think I need to."

"No," she said. "Not to me. You need to talk to a priest. Talk to Father Dooley. Remember?"

"Them?"

"I have gone to church every day and prayed." Elena held herself very still and breathed through her nose. "Because God knows best. He knows best, and I keep my faith in him."

I was shaking and sweating. "I don't know what to do," I said. "I need to tell someone. It's about Father Greg."

Elena held up one finger at me. "No, *m'ijo*. No. You need to tell another priest. Do not tell me."

"No. Please, I need you to listen." I walked over to her, but she put her hand up to block me. She grabbed the two boxes off the bed and held them in her arms.

"No. I can't do this. I have been praying—that is all I can do. I have been praying, and I will continue to do that. I didn't think I was going to see you today. I can't do this." She turned and walked toward the door, but I yelled to her.

"What? What are you saying?"

She turned back. "You have to talk to a priest. I struggled, but you have to learn to accept certain things. My priest has told me. There are some bad apples, but they do not ruin the whole barrel." She stepped out the door. "Please. I have to go. I can't do this."

I ran over and grabbed her arm. She yelped. "Did you know?" I asked her. Elena pushed my hand away, but I grabbed her again. "Did you know?"

She stayed silent for a moment. "I washed your clothes. I watched him drive you home. I saw how you looked at him. It wasn't right. But you also stayed, *m'ijo*. You stayed. God has his reasons for all things, and I believe in him. I will always trust in him."

She went quickly down the stairs to the driveway. I followed slowly and stood on the landing at the top of the stairs. Elena threw the boxes into the trunk, and I began to cry. She walked back to the foot of the stairs and stared up at me. "Please, *m'ijo*. Father Dooley will help you. Please go talk to him."

Tears clouded my eyes. I slumped down onto the step and leaned against the railing. "That's what you've always said. 'Go to the church.'"

"No," Elena said loudly. "No. I have struggled, *m'ijo*." She waved her hand above her head. "I'm in pain too. But I believe in the Church. God will provide the way. He will. You have to believe that too, *m'ijo*."

"Fuck." I began sobbing. "Mark."

Elena began to climb the stairs to me, but Mother came out the kitchen door and yelled to us. "What's going on out here?" she asked as she jogged toward us. "Elena? What is going on?" Mother looked up at me crying and shook her head. "My God, this is just enough. Get ahold of yourself, Aidan. Elena's leaving. She's not your mother. She's your nanny, for Christ's sake! Get a grip."

"We have to talk," I said down to her, but I didn't move. I leaned against the railing.

"Aidan Donovan, you get ahold of yourself this minute. I have my first official party tonight, and I have to get going to make sure everything is in order. The world can't slow down because you can't grow up." She turned to Elena. "All right, enough of this. You've made me late enough. Do you have everything?" Elena nodded. "Then it's time to go," Mother continued. "I'm sorry it had to end this way, Elena, but this is just ridiculous."

Elena hesitated and then moved up the stairs to me. She held me, and I cried into her shoulder. "You will be okay," she said. "I am sorry. *Te quiero.* I do. I'm sorry, *m'ijo.*"

Mother yelled up again. Elena pulled away and didn't look back. She passed Mother without saying a word. It wasn't until she backed up, swung the car around, and then sped off down the driveway that I realized I hadn't actually said the words I needed to to her. They were still lodged in me like shards of broken glass in my throat. She hadn't let me tell her. Now she was gone.

Mother chastised me again. "Not now," she said, holding up her hand. "I have to go. We'll discuss all this more tonight." She pulled keys from her purse. "It's only a cocktail party, so I won't be home too late. But what's done is done, Aidan. She's gone. You must move ahead," she said with new command in her voice. "Get going to school."

She marched into the garage. A few moments later, she backed out in Old Donovan's silver Lexus. She didn't beep or roll down her window. She righted the car, and she sped off as quickly as Elena had. I watched her taillights disappear around the corner, and she might as well have been steering toward her own Brussels.

When I got to school, all I could think about was Mark. His locker was near the chemistry lab, and before I went in for class, I found myself staring at it, remembering the way he would hunch toward it. He wasn't there, but I imagined Mark gripping the door of his locker with one amber hand.

He ran his hand through his tight curls, and they all fell back exactly into place. I could hear him humming, calming himself as he often would, but the distance he put between himself and those around him lost its air of confidence. To me, he was now the feral, frightened Mark I'd seen the other night, trying to warm himself on the cold rooftop, looking up at me with a face like a prayer. He was sick with fear. I understood. I knew it well. I needed to tell him.

I looked for him all day, but he was absent, his third day in a row—there was no way for him to escape the consequences now. Josie was absent too, and nothing could ease the pain in my stomach. It felt empty and rotted. Nothing could fill it. The gulps of water at the fountain did nothing to take it away. I didn't feel like I was moving. Rather, the world was moving around me. I couldn't animate or make a decision: The bell rang, so I walked; my teacher said, "Take out your books," so I flipped to the last assignment and poised my hand in the gutter between the pages. I sat there in the lab and waited for something to crush me and turn me back into dust.

Outside, it began to snow. Fat flakes quickly clouded the windows. I sank low on my stool and stared at the chain of little tubes and balls of the model molecules on the lab table in front of me. I was afraid to speak and afraid to make eye contact with anyone in chemistry class. I was afraid of what I'd say now if I saw them, afraid of what I'd make real by finally telling them what I needed to say. In church, stepping into the confessional, what you say is whispered up into the ether, taken like a breath up into the deep lungs of God, or so I was once made to believe, as if what we did with the lives we lived disappeared into the vastness of eternity and our meaning and purpose was to recognize the greater design, revere it and remain anonymous within it. But I could not allow myself to pretend to believe any of that anymore.

Instead, I thought of Most Precious Blood and whichever parish Father Greg worked in before, and the one before that, passing from town to town like a disease, invisible to most of us, but not everyone, walking into party after party hand-first, shaking and backslapping his way from family to family until it was my turn to endure the stink of his whispers and be told to believe it was gospel. He had infected me, and now he was in me, a part of me, forever. He couldn't hurt me any more than he already had. I wanted the chance to tell him no, to say, *I'm not afraid anymore*, to blow his rancid breath right back in his face and watch him and Father Dooley and all of them—all the sick, sociopathic old men who had watched us rot from afar while they let the Father Gregs sweep through our neighborhoods like a plague—feel the pain they'd delivered to us. It wasn't biblical; it wasn't an act of God. It was human; they couldn't hide behind a metaphor forever. Fuck hope and despair. We live in a world of consequence and effect. Look what they had done.

As I left class, I knew people were staring at me. I was ready to rip a locker door off its hinges and smash something with it, and I might have if I hadn't seen Sophie leaning against Mark's locker, hiding her face in her hands. I scared her when I said her name, and at first she stepped back. I thought Josie had probably already told her what I had done, and I expected her to yell or walk away, but instead she grabbed me into a fierce hug and would not let go.

"Do you know what happened to Mark?" she asked. I hesitated, holding her tightly, trying to say it, but I couldn't. "He's in the hospital," she said. "He fell into the river beneath Stonebrook yesterday. He hasn't woken up yet."

"Fell? From the bridge?" I asked, but I didn't ask any more. Neither of us moved, and Sophie cried softly on my shoulder as she explained how her father had told her what he'd learned at the hospital the night before. Mark was in a coma from head trauma and hypothermia. He was lucky to have been found and pulled from the river as quickly as he had been. We continued to hold each other as we heard the bell ring for the next class.

"Does Josie know?" I finally asked.

"No, she hasn't been returning my calls since last night." Sophie stepped out of the hug. "What the hell is going on?" she asked, looking up at me. "I don't understand. Why would he do that? What the hell is the matter? What was wrong? Could I have done something?"

The door to the chemistry lab opened, and Ms. Richards

stepped into the hallway. "Hey," she said. "Sophie. Aidan. What are you doing in the hallway? Get to class."

Sophie shook her head. "I'm glad my dad told me, but I don't think I can do this," she said to me. "I think I'm going to go home. I don't understand. I just don't understand."

"Hey!" Ms. Richards yelled. "Did you not hear me? Do I have to call Dean Berne?"

All I could hear and see was Mark again, on the edge of the roof, shouting, and then later, after, when he said he could never be free. I hadn't realized then from what, or from whom, but as we stood next to his locker I thought about how many times Mark must have stared into it and wondered if he should finally tell someone about what had happened between him and Father Greg.

I hit the lockers with the side of my fist. Ms. Richards yelled again, but I ignored her. "I can't do this anymore!" Sophie looked at me, terrified. "I can't!" I shouted. I left the two of them in the hallway and ran down the flights of stairs to the ground floor, out the door, and into the falling snow.

Father Greg needed to know what I planned to do next. He wouldn't just read about it in the papers. I wanted him to hear it from me. When I got there, the church parking lot was also empty, except for the parish car that was buried beneath a thin coating of snow. The building was completely dark except for two lights in the rectory out back. I trudged up the slope of the driveway, toward the side door to the rectory, carving small trenches in the snow as I walked. The door was locked, and I slammed the underside of my fist against it as hard as I could. I banged harder and harder on the door until I heard the metal bar squeak on the other side and the door pushed open toward me. Father Dooley braced himself against the cold wind that rushed into the rectory, and he gathered the collar of his robe up around his neck. He held his cane in the same hand so it pressed against his chest, pointing at the floor ceremoniously. He leaned heavily on the door while the wind whipped the fine hair on his head.

He was hunched over more than usual, and the wind blew up into his bathrobe, too, ruffling the flannel around his legs. He was dressed beneath the robe, and I had the impression he had just dragged himself out of an armchair, possibly even a nap. "Well, get in here before the wind blows me over," he said.

He slammed the door shut behind me and caught his breath. "I'm surprised to see you here." He leaned on the door as if he waited to open it again soon. Then he composed himself. "The doors are always open to you here," he said more confidently. "I'm glad you know that. It's a welcome surprise is what I mean."

I pressed the leather of my gloves against my lips and blew, cupping and recupping my hands, trying to bring some warmth back into my fingertips. Father Dooley swayed briefly and pitched forward onto his cane, releasing his robe, letting it open, revealing the loose, threadbare sweater beneath it and the woolen pants that billowed around his spindly legs. I paced around the foyer until I finally fixed myself beside the railing to the stairwell that led down to the basement. The weak sunlight was dimmed by the storm, and inside most of the lights were off. Only the lamplight from Father Dooley's office and the Sunday school room at the other end of the rectory diffused into the main hall and just barely lit the foyer and stairwell. I could see the pale gray slab of the landing below, and although beyond the turn of the stairs and the rest was completely dark, it was all too easy to recall Father Greg's forefinger pointing and beckoning me to follow him farther.

"You don't look well," Father Dooley said behind me, breaking the silence. He came around and stood in the doorway to the main hall, the weak light from his office on his back. He looked at the floor, but his voice was soft and concerned, or he presented it that way at least. It had that tentative tone of pity. "Are you okay? Do you want a cup of tea? I made a pot a little while ago. There's plenty left. Let's go inside."

"No." I gripped the railing and didn't move.

"Please. Let's talk. I'm glad you came. It'll be good for us to talk here. Let's go to my office."

"No."

"Help an old man off his legs, Aidan. Come on." He smiled at me but let it drop after a moment. "Let's go back to my office," he continued. "It'll do us both some good."

"No!" I found myself trembling, turning back to the stairwell, unable to make out the familiar fixtures on the wall down into the basement.

Father Dooley breathed heavily behind me. He sighed. "Did you come here for a particular reason, Aidan? I want to help you. I know it's hard for you to believe, but I do."

"I'm not staying," I said, although it was hard to put any force in my words. "Get Father Greg in here. I want him to hear this too. I'm not keeping quiet anymore," I said. "I can't."

"Now, Aidan." I'd heard that tone of voice too many times. "Aidan, please. We should talk about this."

"I'm going to."

"There's no reason to fear," Father Dooley said slowly. "You are okay now. We have to think about the future, Aidan."

"Get Father Greg!" I yelled. "I want to say it to his face."

Father Dooley tried to draw himself up a little. He held his cane with two hands and leaned closer. "Please," he said, almost hushing me. "Let's go back to my office, Aidan."

Every time I heard my name, I heard Father Greg's voice— cold whispers, broken promises, and the long, twisted plot of a lie. I slammed the railing. "There's nothing else left. Get him. I need to tell him what he did. He needs to hear it. He did it."

"Nothing left? Aidan, there's the bigger picture. The tradition. The church. All those schools. The children."

"What about me?"

Father Dooley took a step closer. "Calm down, Aidan. Father Greg is gone. He won't be coming back. He's been transferred. He's in Canada, Aidan. Now, please. Let's calm down. We can talk about this. You're okay, Aidan." He came closer and put his hand on my shoulder.

I buckled. "Canada? You sent him to Canada?"

"He was transferred. Eventually, he'll be back in Africa," Father Dooley said. He smiled. "I told you I would protect you, Aidan. I told you I cared. Now, let's calm down. Think of all that work he has done. All that work that you have done with him. There's so much more, Aidan. Why tear down all that has been good?"

"He needs to hear this. I need to tell him. He's done this. It's his fault. I don't want to hurt anyone else," I cried.

"Aidan, you asked me to make sure you never saw him again. I understood you. You'll just have to talk to me, instead. It's good. I'm here to help you."

His grip was weak, but his voice was calm and level, and the more I heard it, the more it felt like a squeeze around my throat. "Let go," I said.

He did immediately and stepped back. He rubbed his jaw, and his hand shook. "Aidan. There are other ways of thinking about this. Remember St. Francis rebuilding the church? Remember that we are talking about love, divine love? God's love. That's what we're talking about. That is larger than the indiscretions of human beings. That is worth protecting, Aidan. It is larger than us."

He walked toward the main hall, and I shouted at his back. "That's what you are always talking about. All of you. Love?" I looked into the basement and looked back. "Love?" I shouted, and rattled the railing. "I am sick of lying. I won't do it anymore. I don't know how you do it."

Father Dooley turned around in the doorway. "Aidan, don't yell at me. Can't you see the position I'm in? What am I supposed to do? I believe in this church—the Catholic Church, Aidan. It is bigger than you or me or Father Greg. It's universal. I serve the Church, Aidan. I believe in the compassion. I believe in that love. I believe in the Church." He leaned against the door frame and shook his cane at me. There were tears in his eyes. "Believe me," he said. "Please."

I stepped toward him. He gestured for me to quiet down, but I ignored him. "Do you know how many times Father Greg told me that?" I yelled. "Where does the line get drawn? Why do I have to be expendable?"

"That's not the only way to look at it."

"How can you hold it all in? All of it. Don't you just want to scream?"

Father Dooley stood rigid, as if every muscle in his body flexed and he'd lost his ability to move. "There are consequences, Aidan. You have to understand. Please. Think about everyone else involved. Think about all the other people."

"I am!" I hit the door frame beside him. "It's not just me. It *is* other people."

"There's too much in the press. Don't let that confuse things." He reached out to me again, and I batted his hand away. He stepped back.

"I'm not."

"Aidan, don't join the witch hunt," he snapped. "Think about this. You know Father Greg was a good man. Now get ahold of yourself," he said, but then he grew quiet. He receded into the hall, away from me, moving back into the darkness between his office and us. "Now, Aidan," he said. "You're beginning to scare me." He continued to back away. "I'm just an old man, and I don't need to be threatened in this way. Don't make me call the police."

"On me?" I yelled. "What will they say when I tell them?"

"You can't threaten me, Aidan. It isn't right. You're not the first to threaten us. The police know that. I can get a restraining order. They're ready. But, please, let's not do that. I care about you, and you can't ruin everything else just for yourself. Please. Try to see this. Try to think of everybody else."

I pointed toward the basement. "I was there. I know it. He was with James. I was right there. He was with James. I was there!" I slammed the door frame again, and Father Dooley shrank back into the main hall. I followed him. "Everyone else? I am thinking about everyone else. James, me, Mark? Mark Kowolski, you goddamn criminal. Do you know what Mark did? He jumped off the bridge at Stonebrook. Father Greg needs to know that."

Father Dooley turned and moved quickly toward his office. "You need to know that too," I said as I pursued him. "You knew about each of us. You knew what he did to us." I grabbed him by the shirt and forced him back against the wall near his office. "He did this. Do you know what he did to us? He did this." I shook Father Dooley and felt his bony chest bounce off my knuckles. I slammed him repeatedly against the wall, shaking him, crying, and I thought of Father Greg taking James in his arms and pushing him up against the workbench in the basement. Father Greg's breath was a wind in my ears: *Shh. Shh.* Arms useless against a stronger chest. Muffled voices. Clothes rustling. Suffocation. Swallowing something like a roar within me. No: *Shh. Shh.*

Leaning into Father Dooley, I sobbed with my head on his shoulder. "I'm going to say something," I said softly. "I'm going to explain everything."

Father Dooley mumbled. His words were caught in his throat. His arms were not up against mine, and I stepped back when I realized my body pinned him against the wall. His cane fell to the floor, and he staggered forward. I caught him and dragged him over to one of the metal folding chairs nearby. He lifted his hands to his head finally, and a dull moaning echoed softly in the rectory's main hall.

"I'm going to tell everyone everything," I continued. "You did nothing. Say it. Tell me what you did. Tell me, you monster."

"I can't," Father Dooley finally said. "I can't."

Tears blurred my vision. I couldn't remember why I had gone there in the first place, and I couldn't imagine where I might go next. It was as if I had been nowhere before and would go nowhere else again. There was nothing that kept my mind fixed and present other than Father Dooley's broken voice. He was talking again, but the words were incomprehensible to me. I couldn't hear his excuses anymore. His noise became a chant echoing in my mind, a sound that haunted me as it reached for meaning and couldn't deliver it. The gibberish gathered in the room in drifts of nonsense, clinging to me like clumps of snow, a wet fist closing up around me. There was nothing else for me to hear. I left him there, slumped in the chair, mumbling his prayers to himself.

The steady snowfall continued. It had already spread itself over lawns, tree limbs, and the roofs of houses. Beyond the trees, nothing broke through the deadening, washed-out expanse above. I slowly loped across yards and listened to the new snow beneath my feet. Each step made a sound like vigorous scratching, and I repeatedly looked over my shoulder to make sure I wasn't being followed. I didn't wait to catch my breath. I kept moving, watching my own breath drift faintly ahead of me while the snow continued to gather, and as I approached the Stonebrook golf course, I took the long way around the back side of the course, careful to avoid the bridge. I couldn't look at it. I walked by the fourth hole and saw a dark animal cut a lonely path through a nearby, whitewashed bunker. It paused to eye me across the distance before continuing its track.

I let the whole day pass before I finally made my way into Mark's neighborhood, turned onto his street, and looked up at his house. The yard was empty, and the house was completely dark. Blood pulsed in my wrists and at the base of my neck with a rush and thump that was beyond my control. I stood on the street for a while and let the snow stick to my face and bite me as it melted. Finally, I got up the courage to walk up to the front door and ring the bell. No one answered. I rang it again and again, and still no one answered. I walked around the house to the side door to the mudroom, where I had helped Mark on New Year's Eve. I peered inside. Empty shoes and boots made a neat row beneath the bench. I walked around the back of the house to the kitchen. One pale light was lit over the stove. It was the only light on in the house, and a muted blue-white glow spread from the cooking station into the rest of the kitchen. Everything was tidy, spotless, and inhuman.

"Please. I'm sorry," I said into the empty house.

A dog with a slow baritone barked somewhere far away in the patchwork of yards. Its bark carried from one neighborhood to another, becoming fainter. Its voice, as it traveled through the night, would eventually go mute and disappear in the distance, as it seemed everything did, and drift into the nothingness beyond. I hit the side of Mark's house. I kicked at the door. "Please," I said again. "I'm here. I'm here now!"

The snowstorm smudged out any lights in the distance. The Kowolskis' yard was dark, and beyond it was a deeper darkness. It was as if there was no one anywhere, and I thought of that same lonely feeling I had had when Father Greg had first beckoned me down into the darkness of the storage room, and how he must have called Mark down, and James, too, and all the others—an army of boys trudging slowly into the basement, wanting to believe. Over time, how could each boy not have lost distinction? Each of them would become another gray, cold, trembling body to terrorize with words like *love, safety,* and *faith.* I needed to tell someone else. I needed to tell the whole story. Mark deserved to hear it first, but I couldn't wait any longer, and I ran to Josie's neighborhood.

At the foot of her driveway, drifts of snow now swelled up against the tree that had once held the image of us together. I reached toward the snowbank and left a handprint against it. In the morning, it would be a frozen image, a sign of life and recognition, like a cave painting.

Josie's mother and father would be at the same cocktail party with Mother, so I only worried that Ruby would see me approaching the house, but she didn't. I went around to the back of the house and saw Josie sitting at the kitchen table, doing homework. When I knocked gently on the window, I startled her, and at first I thought she was going to scream for Ruby, but she didn't. She composed herself when she recognized me. She pointed toward the back door.

She braced herself when she opened it. She wore the same pair of sweatpants she'd worn when I'd last seen her. Her eyes offered the same concern, too. "I'm sorry," I said to her. "You're right. I need help. I need your help."

I didn't say anything else. I couldn't. I felt my chin tremble, and I turned away and looked to the backyard and up toward the pool house. There were tears in my eyes. Josie stepped into the cold and hugged me. And that was all it took. How is it that a gesture so simple, from one person to another, could suddenly give me a confidence I didn't know I had and free me to say, *I am about to tell you a story that is going to hurt*? What inspires that finally?

Josie brushed the snow off my shoulders and back, and quickly and quietly she snuck me upstairs to her bedroom. Like in my own bedroom, she had an armchair by the window, and she offered it to me while she ran back downstairs to clean up. "Believe me," I'd said to her when I'd seen her last. That's what I'd wanted then, but I couldn't say it anymore. I heard Father Greg saying it. Saying *Love, love, love, believe me, Aidan, believe me, this is love, love, love*. I no longer had it in me. Josie was right, and there was nothing left for me to tell her but the truth.

When she returned, she closed the door and depressed the button in the lock. "I said good night to Ruby," she said. "So my parents won't say hi when they come in. We still have to be quiet, though, in case Ruby walks by for some reason."

"I can do that," I said. "But I have to talk."

She held me, not like a lover but in a way we should all be held at least once in our lives—in a way that lets us know we are not alone. A human absolution.

Being near her gave me strength, and I finally began. I sat next to her on her bed, and I was dizzy and trembling, but steadied by her voice—rocking, holding. She asked questions, but they didn't hurt, they helped buoy what I had to say. She held my hand as I told her everything.

CHAPTER 15

Hours passed. We heard Josie's parents come home, and I knew, although she would be the last to leave, Mother would be home soon too. I called the house and left her a message, telling her I was at Josie's, lest she think that I had run back down to Elena's again. But also it felt important to fill Mother in—I knew very soon I'd be telling her the story I'd told Josie. I tried to imagine how I would tell Old Donovan, too, whether it would be on the phone or across a white-linen tablecloth in a restaurant down in Manhattan when he was next in New York for business. *I was afraid*, I would tell both of them. *And I still am, so listen to me.*

"I don't want to go home," I said to Josie.

"You don't have to," she said. "You can stay right here."

I left a second message for Mother and told her I wouldn't be home but not to call Josie's, because her parents didn't know. I promised to explain. "I'm safe," I added. "I'm okay."

Josie watched me as I left the message. She got up when I finished and hugged me again. She kicked off her slippers, got under her comforter, and called me over. "Get in," she said. When I did, she turned out the light and nestled up to me. We didn't speak, but after a little while, she reached over me and held my hand.

"It's all my fault," I said. "Mark."

"No, it isn't."

I stared into the room until my eyes adjusted to the dark and I could make out the silhouettes of the celebrities in the framed posters on the wall and the outlines of details in her furniture. There was no other noise in the house, and Josie was spooned up behind me with her arm around my rib cage. Her breath warmed my back. Her rhythm slowed and she fell asleep, and eventually, I was calm enough to join her.

When her alarm went off in the morning, we slowly unwound ourselves from each other. I climbed out of bed and tried to press the wrinkles out of my pants. Josie turned on the TV and began her morning rituals. "Don't worry," she said, "nobody bugs me in the morning. We'll get down the stairs and out the front door while everyone is still in the kitchen. This is going to work. We'll be fine."

The clouds had cleared from the night before, and I sat in the armchair with sunlight warming my back. I listened to Josie on the other side of the bathroom door; she hummed in the shower. She had a kind of energy that propelled her, a happiness that was fueled not by joy but by a kind of understanding of connectedness, and her willingness to help, her wellspring of caring, seemed to fuel that connection. I was in awe of it and wondered why I'd seen so little of it before. She opened the door to her bathroom when she'd finished her shower, and the steam rolled out into the bedroom. She was wrapped in a purple towel with another one wrapped in a turban around her head. She smiled at me and continued her routine. She stood on the balls of her feet when she brushed her teeth, and the quick dabs of makeup she applied to her cheeks were perfunctory, just a part of her happy bustle.

I wanted to make her coffee and scrambled eggs. I wanted to cinch up the knot in my tie, kiss her on the brow, and tell her to enjoy her day. When I stepped into the bathroom so she could get dressed, I thought about what it meant to really build a home. I didn't want to think about sex—that could come later. All I wanted now was companionship. That was the real freedom. That was the only safety we could offer each other: what it really meant to love and live without a mask.

It was all I could think about as I stood in the bathroom and did my own quick cleanup, washing my face and neck, rubbing my teeth with a toothpaste-covered finger. While Josie had been in the shower, I'd watched the morning news and listened to the anchors rattle off story after story. There were government investigations into the collapse of Enron; the first lady was running a campaign for teachers and parents to reassure children of their safety; the new terror alert system was being praised by some members of congress; and just the day before, the mayor of New York had begun issuing free tickets to help manage the enormous crowds making the pilgrimage to Ground Zero. I felt like I had survived the night because of Josie's small, brave act of kindness; she deserved a headline too, but that's not the kind of stuff that makes it into the news.

Josie told me to come out, quick. She stood in front of the TV in her CDA uniform, clutching one furry boot to her chest. Mark stared back at us from the TV, and I ran to her immediately. It was his head shot for the yearbook: He looked out at the world with a joyless, skeptical smile, one I'd once read as snobbery but now knew was the only face he could make to hide all the fear behind it. A quick photomontage showed CDA, the pool, a row of swimming medals. He'd been on drugs, the news story told us, and not in his right mind, he'd climbed out over the railings of the bridge by Stonebrook and jumped. A search of his room at home suggested a long history of drug abuse that his parents had not known about. Josie cried into my chest. I held her, and I stared straight into Mark's eyes when they showed his picture again, wishing I could hold him again too. Wishing I had.

The news had switched from national to local while I had been in the bathroom, and Mark's attempt at death was the headlining story. I held Josie as she sobbed. "It's my fault," I said. Josie tried to tell me otherwise, but I repeated myself. "It's my fault," I said again.

"Stop saying that!"

Over her shoulder, the weatherman animated storm clouds along the coast and waved them out over the Atlantic. Mark's story was over. We continued to hold each other.

"They don't have the whole story," I told her. "You know that." The word *abuse* echoed in my mind. The way they used the word, it almost made Mark sound innocent, and the drugs, too, as if he and they were not to blame at all, only the "abuse." They didn't ask why he might have abused the drugs. They let the word linger without any follow-up questions, as if his abuse was an independent choice and that that choice was the aberrative behavior, not the depth and secrecy of all the other things he was weighing in his mind.

"I think I need to see him," I said. "I'm afraid to, but I think I have to."

"I'm coming with you," Josie said. "You don't have to be alone."

I called us a car service and had it wait down by the street. When it arrived, we snuck down the front stairs and out the door just as Josie had promised. We were dressed for school but on our way to the local hospital, hoping he was still there and hadn't been transferred somewhere else yet.

We were lucky. He was still there, on the second floor, but would be transferred later that day to a larger facility up in New Haven. Josie asked the nurse behind the desk if Mark's parents were there. It hadn't even occurred to me, and when the nurse explained that they had not come in yet that day, the sense of relief was overwhelming. I wasn't ready to see them yet. I needed to see him first. Josie linked arms with me, and the nurse offered to show us the way to the room. I was light-headed. The elevator ride up one floor seemed to take an eternity. The bright, white fluorescence in the hallways made me feel exposed and dirty, and when the nurse dropped us off, I was glad the light was dim in Mark's small room.

There was one chair near the bed, but neither Josie nor I took it, and the room felt cramped with all the machines and tubes and drips and wires that were keeping him alive. We huddled close beside his bed, and Josie clutched my arm tightly. Mark was thinner and paler, his cheeks were hollowed and gaunt, and he looked like the ghost of his old self. He'd been propped up in the bed. His eyes were closed, and he might have been napping, except the expression on his face was twisted and mutated by the tubes in his nose and mouth, and if he had been asleep, he could only have been suffering through a storm of nightmares looming behind his eyelids. This was not the Mark I had seen fall asleep on New Year's Eve, the one on whose lips I heard the last breath puff before he drifted out. That night, he'd let his head loll, tilting toward me with a drowsy smile on his face. I could barely look at him now. He was the shell of my friend, not the friend himself, a prisoner trapped in a hell of silence.

Josie felt me pulling away, and she anchored me beside the bed. She let go of me with one hand and reached out to Mark. His hand was out above the sheet and blanket, and she clasped her fingers around his and held him. Through Josie, we were a knot again. She looked at me and then back at Mark. "Mark," she said, "we miss you."

She turned to me again and smiled, and I looked down at Mark. "I'm sorry," I finally got out, and once I said it, the flood followed. I told him everything I'd told Josie the night before, about Father Dooley, Father Greg, James, him, and me. "You're not alone," I kept saying. "I want to tell you, you're not alone. I want to tell everyone that."

Josie held us both as I spoke, and I thought about how people like Old Donovan and Father Greg and teachers and even Mother and Elena had all at one time or another tried to give me advice about who I was supposed to be and what kind of person I was supposed to become, but looking at Josie, I wondered if it didn't all come down to something simpler: *Are you the kind of person who is there for people when they need you, or not? Isn't it in those moments when you have to work harder than you thought you could to reach out to another person, and you do, that you finally find the you who's been hiding behind the mask all that time? Is it there, finally truly naked, and reaching for one another, that we create the chance to hold one another again? And what about the chance to love again? Do we get to create that possibility too?*

I leaned closer to Mark and kissed him on the forehead.

When I stood back up, I realized the nurse who'd led us to the room was standing in the doorway, smiling at us. "I'm sorry," I said.

"No, no, no," she said. "Don't be sorry at all. Do what you need to do." She smiled again and then moved on to another room.

"Mark," I said, turning back to him. "I'll tell everyone."

Josie and I walked downstairs, to the parking lot outside the county hospital, and we decided that I needed to go see Mark's parents first, and then continue from there, marching my slow march from one family to the next until we all shared the truth. Josie reminded me that she would help me, that a march could begin with two people and we would see what it would become.

"I told you," she said, "it's my New Year's resolution." She grinned. "I'm here."

"I'm here too."

We ran down the sidewalk beside the snowy banks of the parking lot, out into the street, through the center of town, behind the golf course, and into the Kowolskis' neighborhood, and it wasn't toward forgiveness that I ran, and it wasn't because Josie forgave me that she ran with me. There was no peace at the end of the road. We kept up the pace all the way across town, and I ran as if in a pack with all my fears around me.

It wasn't until we made it to Mark's house and stood quietly catching our breath that I recognized the cold. The fierce wind that had brought the storm the day before still lingered behind it. Josie hugged me, and that was all there had been that winter, and only briefly: a few warm bodies, strangers I wanted to know better, before they or I were gone.

We proceeded up the walkway to the front steps, and I pressed the doorbell. Barbara's heels nailed the hardwood as she approached. She pushed the curtain aside and stared at me with a face that was terrified and haunted. As she unlocked the door, I reached for Josie's hand and she took it. And that had been Mark once, I realized. Even as we were battered back and forth amid the fearful riot of voices, Mark had reached for my hand once and then again, a natural gesture that alone might have sufficed to brace us as we marched ahead into the furious stammering of tomorrow.

Acknowledgments

First and foremost, there are real children and families who have suffered and who have their own similar stories. It is my hope that this novel honors the courage, dignity, and full humanity of both those who are still searching to find a voice to share their experiences and those who have been brave enough to speak up about the magnitude and devastation of abuse and the system that enabled and protected it.

In the making of this book, I want to thank Rob Weisbach, my friend and superagent, who would not give up. His passion continues to inspire me, and his vision and direction helped shape this story into the novel I'm proud of today. And thank you to my friend David Groff, without whose guidance, support, edits, and nurturing this book would never have found another reader.

I am grateful and proud to be part of the Margaret K. McElderry family. Many thanks to Justin Chanda and the entire Simon & Schuster Children's team, from the copy editors and proofreaders to the jacket and interior designer, to the amazing folks in marketing and sales who make it their business to get people to read—all of whom I admire and am grateful to have worked with on this book—and most especially to my wonderfully fearless editor, Rūta Rimas, whose vision and edits made this a much better book and whose enthusiasm made certain that Aidan's story would find a place in the public conversation.

I also thank Jonathan Rabb, around whose table a few of us sat many years ago and from whose workshop this novel was born. It took another village to raise this child, however, and I am grateful to The City College of New York writing community for being that village. Thanks to the crew who spent too many nights (who am I kidding, are there ever enough?) at Soundz and Dublin House and elsewhere, talking about books, our own and others, and always reminding me why we give a damn and why we write.

Thank you to Fred Reynolds, whose support and mentorship (and invitation to Archer City!) helped me carve out the space to put priorities, writing and otherwise, straight. And my deep thanks to Bill Lippman, Debbie Himmelfarb, and their family for their initial belief in this novel; their support, through the Doris Lippman Prize in Creative Writing, brought this book to the attention of others and asked them to care about it too.

This writer doesn't exist without his two literary mothers, Linsey Abrams and Felicia Bonaparte, who are the intellectual, spiritual, and philosophical nuclei around whom my entire graduate school experience orbited and to whom I will be forever indebted for waking in me a second life in love with literature.

And last, but so very far from least, I thank my family, the Kiely-Shannon-Chaffee clan: Heide and John, to whom I am grateful every day for folding me into their family, and whose special advice, knowledge, and wisdom about books, ideas, and life shaped this book and me in innumerable ways; Joshua, Niall, and Trish, siblings whom I greatly admire for the lives they lead and the footprints they leave that I will follow anywhere, and whose reservoirs of support and encouragement buoyed me through this process; Ted, my brother-at-large, for his infectious enthusiasm—a renewable energy source that can provide for others for a lifetime—and for constantly reminding me why the adventure matters; Grandma Jane, whose spirit, love, faith, vast wisdom, and radiant smile are constant beacons in my life; and especially my mother and father, Maryanne and Tom, who both taught me that defining one's principles, living by them, and using them to learn how to better love another person is what it really means to be a human being. And extra special thanks to my father, the real writer in the family, without whose red pen and indefatigable patience I would never have comprehended the English language.

Jessie, this book, as all things in my life, is because of you and for you, the woman who inspires me every day, from whom I learn every day, and for whom I work every day—here's to loving you, all ways and always.